MURDER ON MENDENHALL GLACIER

A TRAVEL BUG MYSTERY

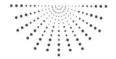

DELEEN WILLS

Life of
Riley
PUBLISHING

COPYRIGHT

Printed by KDP/Amazon

ISBN: 9798422122844

Imprint: Independently published

First Edition April 2022

Second Edition August 2022

If you have any questions or comments, please contact Deleen Wills through Facebook or Instagram at Travel Bug Mysteries or deleenwills@gmail.com.

Cover Design by Jessica Spurrier

Back cover photo by Sue Christopherson, Ireland in 2018

ABOUT THE AUTHOR

Deleen Wills strives to write stories that entertain, enlighten and educate, hopefully encouraging others to realize how easy and enjoyable it is to embrace new friends and gain new insights while exploring our world.

Her passions are writing and globetrotting. She delights in working from her home as a travel coordinator organizing adventures for groups, family and friends. Living with her husband in Oregon after retiring from her work as an administrator in nonprofit education, she volunteers for Habitat for Humanity and Meals on Wheels.

Murder on Mendenhall Glacier, is a cleverly plotted mystery set in Alaska. Join the author who uses her winning combination of humor, memories and a vivid imagination woven together with historical and geographical facts on this adventure cruising to Alaska.

www.amazon.com/author/deleenwills

instagram.com/travelbugmysteries
facebook.com/travelbugmysteries

ACKNOWLEDGMENTS

My deepest appreciation goes out to my family, friends and readers who encourage me to continue writing. They include but are not limited to:

Beth E. Pitcher, for expertly and patiently copyediting.

Jessica Spurrier, graphic designer and photographer. See her work at GreengateImages.com.

Jennifer Leigh Riley, story consultant.

Sue Christopherson, the sister I never had, who encourages and supports me as a true Sisterchick does.

Mark Wills, for his ongoing patience helping with technology issues and sales support.

Robin & MaryAnne, Cousin Woodie, Vinni and the Juneau Police Department.

To my cheerleaders for their continued encouragement: Beth, Carol, Cathy, Chaille, Davette, Dorothy, Heather, Jeannie, Jenn, Jessica, Joanie, Judie, Julie, Kate, Linda, Margie, Michelle, Nancy, Patti, Peggy, Russ, Shawn, my mom and both brothers, and many readers of *Murder on the Metolius, Through Colorful Doors, Because of Colorful Doors* and *Behind Colorful Doors.*

DEDICATION

To all of the women in my family.

In Loving Memory of my dear friend, MaryAnne MacNeill,
whose life touched so many and ended way too soon.
Those left behind are brokenhearted and miss her smile, sharp
wit, love and support. August 2022.

PROLOGUE

ow on their fourth cruise to Alaska, Peter and Anne were splurging on an adventure-of-a-lifetime, using a portion of the 12 hours they'd have in the capital of Alaska—Juneau. The couple had celebrated their 22nd wedding anniversary in March. This was their treat to themselves—an Alaska cruise with 30 family and friends. And today, this pricey expedition.

Several years earlier, they had taken a shuttle to the base of the mighty Mendenhall Glacier. A massive noisy waterfall along with all sizes of ice chunks dump into the silty lake created by the thawing glacier. Walking through lush flowering bushes, Anne pointed out a merganser paddling in the water with four babies close behind.

She faced the glacier and firmly stated, "I wanna be up there." They vowed the next time they came to Juneau they'd get onto the glacier somehow.

That day had arrived.

Their glacier-top stroll was almost over and 30 minutes felt more like five. Anne glanced to her left, envisioning gold miners and their mule trains trekking on their quest for gold over mountains, through snow and over glaciers. Something flat and brown caught her eye. It lay even with the ice.

She freely admitted that she had a tendency to wander off, something her husband didn't appreciate about her at all. He reminded her on more than one occasion that she needed to stay focused on the guides and their safety rules, especially on a glacier.

Instead of directing attention to the intriguing brown thing, and while their guide Tony pointed in the opposite direction, Anne wandered, undeterred, away from the group. As she got closer, she could see the item was the thick sole of the bottom of a shoe or boot, facing down.

Somebody lost a boot? How weird that it wasn't noticed before. Who doesn't need a boot, especially up here? Then came a darker thought: Was the boot attached to somebody? She didn't take a step closer.

Her heart thumped and her skin suffered wave after wave of goosebumps. She reacted like this on some occasions, mostly watching scary movies. Anne hadn't moved an inch. She just glanced once, or twice, or maybe three times, at the upside down boot. Golly, what a difference an hour makes, she thought.

Peter looked left to the vacant air where his wife had just been standing. He did a 180 and saw her almost jumping up and down, flailing her arms. Why was he surprised? She was a magnetic force for discoveries of various types, at least one or two per vacation.

Yes, Anne was a magnet, mostly a good one but not always, Peter thought. She should have worked for the CIA instead of being an administrator at nonprofit educational institutions. Walking toward her he mumbled to himself, "And our vacation has been going so well."

He was getting way ahead of himself. *Way*, way ahead of himself.

Stop. Rewind. Wednesday, Tuesday, Monday, Sunday, Saturday, Friday. Press Start.

CHAPTER ONE

Their wedding anniversary vacation had started six days earlier with a short flight from Portland International Airport touching down outside of Vancouver, British Columbia.

On the flight, Anne read "Who Discovered Alaska?" to Peter from the airline's in-flight monthly magazine called *Alaska Beyond Magazine*:

"When the first white men came to Alaska, they found Eskimos, Alutes, and Indians living there. Alaska was one of the last largest areas of the world to be discovered and explored by the white men. In the early 18th century, the Russians were moving through Siberia to the Pacific Ocean. For the next 200 years, Russian fur traders hunted furbearing animals throughout Alaskan waters. They established many settlements and in some of these places the quaint churches built by Alutes and Indians under the guidance of Russian missionary priests can still be seen.

"Later, sea captains from Spain, France and Great Britain explored the Alaskan coast. It was the Russians, however, who used Alaska as a source of fur, and millions of furbearing animals began to be wiped out. By the end of the 1820s the Russians begin to leave the Alaska coast."

She handed her husband her own made-up list of travel tips and said, "Read this. I sent it to everyone joining us on the cruise." Peter looked down her list of about 24 facts saying, "I hope you're not going to quiz our friends when we get onboard." She whacked him on the left arm not so affectionately.

The eclectic city of Vancouver exhilarated Anne. Acknowledging her slight flair for drama, she really did get a thrill from big city vibes wherever she went. The couple liked the temperate climate, which was great for outdoor activities, if you don't mind rain. They didn't, coming from the Willamette Valley in Oregon.

During their visits, they had only walked through several of the 170 parks in the city. Anne appreciated that nature-loving Canadians squeezed in a park or playground instead of a parking garage or apartment complex.

Having passports stamped at customs and picking up three pieces of luggage, and out the exit they easily spotted long-time friend Robin, in his multi-tone green Volkswagen van. He stood as tall as Peter, about 6 foot, 2 inches, both similar in stature with dark brown hair, one with kindly bright hazel eyes and the other with rather deep-set western bluebird tones.

Robin expertly navigated through residential areas, with homes hidden behind cement and brick walls covered in trailing ivy. When driving through downtown Vancouver,

Robin pointed out some new buildings, before veering toward the west end of the city. After 35 minutes, he pulled into a space right in front of their historic 1890s home, Ashby House Bed & Breakfast, a three-story home painted marine yellow with blue trim.

Anne's heart beat faster seeing Ashby House. For some reason, she felt like she was home when she walked through the oak front door and stepped into Victorian charm. Even Keltie, their fluffy, snowy white West Highland Terrier, remembered the couple.

There was never a dull moment with Keltie around. Looking much like a teddy bear, she had a Type A personality with tons of spunk and always obsessed with her tennis ball. Her perky ears stood up straight. Fur covered her dark eyes like long bangs and except for her nose and lips, these were the only dark colors on her bushy body.

The owners, Robin and MaryAnne, became friends with Peter and Anne when the Canadians established their B&B during the World Expo. Their two toddlers were now teenagers. Peter and Anne had been some of their first guests in the turn-of-the-century home, now remodeled with three upstairs rooms plus a suite on the ground floor for rent, instead of only one room in 1986.

The Oregonians loved this city set on a bay with Grouse Mountain and North Shore Mountains overlooking Vancouver. Then there was the 1,000-acre Stanley Park, where one could meander for hours.

Peter and Robin hauled three suitcases up to the second floor front bedroom, the Whistler Suite. Anne hung up several items of clothing in the antique armoire, only what they would wear for the next three days. Two other pieces of luggage would remain closed until they unpacked in their stateroom on board their floating hotel.

The white lacy curtains covering an open window moved in the light breeze. Lush red and white ivy geraniums cascaded from the window box. Directly out the window stands a Japanese plum and next to it a hawthorn tree that provides shade and privacy. The yard below is small, but brimming with English garden flowers, art, and birdbaths, mixed together in such a way that causes walkers to stop and gawk.

Anne's favorite spot was the front porch, in a rocking chair. She could sit and visit with MaryAnne for hours catching up and watching the world go by. Most pedestrians were students attending University of British Columbia and who moved into homes like Robin and MaryAnne's where owners had remodeled rooms morphing into apartments and making lots of money.

Robin, a craftsman by trade, along with MaryAnne, who had an eye for just the perfect décor, had carefully restored their Victorian home over the years. Their heritage-listed property is conveniently within walking distance to the heart of Vancouver and just a couple of blocks from bustling Robson Street that could lead them anywhere.

Peter looked forward to the daily breakfast that always appeared effortless by the duo, freshly cooked from high quality local ingredients and no request seemed to be too much trouble. One of Anne's favorites was MaryAnne's homemade private-reserve blackberry jam, that was only shared with the most special guests. They'd been privileged to receive a few jars in the past to enjoy at home.

No matter the time of year, the communal breakfast event with all guests sharing the same massive table would supply varied and interesting conversation with people from around the world.

That night the four friends strolled to dinner through neighborhoods and parks arriving at the English Bay Café. Their window table overlooked the bay. The restaurant was known for their Canadian coastal-style cuisine.

Two ordered steak tartare, one had halibut caught that day, and Anne had grilled prawns. This was a perfect way to kick off their two-week vacation. They were looking forward to de-stressing for three days before their 11-day cruise and land tour.

CHAPTER TWO

Peter woke to the smell of coffee wafting from the kitchen one story below. Cleaned up, dressed and downstairs before Anne even thought about getting out of bed, he was already visiting with their longtime friends. The bed and breakfast dynamic duo gathered, blended and mixed ingredients for their infamous waffles.

Anne, knowing she was missing something, quickly made herself presentable and appeared in the doorway, but making sure to stay out of the way. She watched MaryAnne as she cracked eggs one-handed, mixing batter with the other. Robin poured the creamy goodness into the waffle maker. Their sequence of kitchen steps and movements were chore-ographed like a well-orchestrated waltz due to years of experience.

MaryAnne instructed Anne to sit, as the hostess set out a plate of steamy waffles in front of her guests. On a little china saucer was Anne's very own crystal bowl of seedless blackberry jam. MaryAnne smiled with a twinkle in her blue eyes, knowing Anne's fondness for her homemade preserves and pastries.

In the middle of the table sat a silver tray with four containers of other types of jams: currant, strawberry, raspberry, and an orange-ginger marmalade. Anne dipped a clean spoon into the marmalade and murmured that she could eat the entire jar without anything else.

After breakfast cleanup, where Anne and Peter were barely allowed to assist, they discussed the agenda for the day. Vancouver is known for its many diverse neighborhoods, and they unanimously decided they would walk to Chinatown. Changing from slippers into their walking shoes, Anne waited anxiously to see what MaryAnne would wear.

The former theatrical ingénue wore an eclectic variety of items that Anne would never think to put together, but MaryAnne always made any clothing look cool and trendy. Today she wore an ecru hand-woven cape reaching her knees over a lightweight long sleeve grayish-yellow top, paired with calf-length ivory stretch pants. The outfit blended well with her shoulder-length blonde hair now streaked with a few strands of silver. MaryAnne's striking attribute is her intensively azure blue eyes. Anne had blue eyes, too, but nothing remarkable, just everyday blue. She liked to think hers were the same shade of blue poppies in Scotland, but that was in her vivid imagination.

Robin explained that in 1971 Chinatown was designated as a provincial heritage site with shops and restaurants designed in traditional décor. They picked up some piping hot fried wontons and egg rolls then munched their way up and down several streets.

The foursome meandered through Victorian Gastown which is the location where Vancouver began with narrow cobblestone streets that resemble avenues all over Europe. They walked by shops and bistros. Baskets of orange begonias hung from lamppost after lamppost, down the street.

A working steam clock on Water Street nabbed their attention. Looking at the front of the grandfather-style clock standing 16-feet high, Anne could see through the glass at the inner workings with gears turning and some gizmos going up and down. The white clock face has thick black iron hands and Roman numerals instead of numbers. It features five whistles at the top and weighs over two tons. Steam escapes nonstop from the top. Every quarter hour, they heard musical sounds. Anne about jumped two inches startled by the loud steam whistles at the half hour.

Peter watched intently through the window and saw one steel weight—a three-inch ball like those inside ball bearings —transported by steam power to the top of the clock's mechanism and then fall all the way down to engage the gears and chain system. They heard an array of unique sounds: *ching*, sound of metal on metal; *fizz*, sounds of steam.

At 7 p.m. Westminster chimes played, tooting five times with a blast from the top. Anne wondered aloud why only five toots at seven o'clock and got no answers from the Vancouverites who shrugged their shoulders.

On their stroll back through neighborhoods of historic homes, Anne pointed out colorful doors, first a purple, a bright yellow, a blue Dutch door with the top lighter than the bottom, and cherry red. Peter mentioned Anne's new obsession with colorful doors from their trip to Scotland a few years earlier.

Oh, by the way, he added, she had made up a new word— graviosity, a combination of curiosity and gravity. He'd seen her in action several times where she simply HAD to discover what was behind a colorful door.

Anne whispered to MaryAnne that it hadn't taken her long to realize that it was best if she discovered these revelations on her own.

Returning to Ashby House, they devoured dinner that MaryAnne had prepared before they left—pork ribs, potatoes and root vegetables simmered all day.

CHAPTER THREE

One thousand miles north in Juneau, Alaska, at a bar on the outskirts of town, a self-assured willowy blonde sashayed past whiskered, long-haired men wearing too much flannel to ruffian-types with tight tee-shirts and worn jeans. She stopped at a table in the corner where one man grinned like a Cheshire cat. Dozens of sets of male eyes were on her backside as she looked down and said, "Get this through that thick skull, whatever we had, it's over. Never contact me again. Or else." It was about the tenth time in a month she told him the same thing.

He slowly stood, eye to eye, her fierce arctic blue eyes shooting daggers at his assertive ones. It felt like she'd pierced his heart with a laser beam. Many men felt threatened by her height. He wasn't. In fact it was just the opposite for him. He found her irresistible, but she turned him down. Again. Tonight, his blasé, unflappable attitude irked her even more.

She blurted out, "I've told my boyfriend everything about Seattle, and you. I need a new start and it will be here with him. Leave me alone or I'm going to the police," raising her voice to almost shouting. Only part of her diatribe was truthful, but he didn't know that.

"Is that a threat, Missy?" he said condescendingly snickering, as she noticed his usually flinty gray eyes were steely and cold.

How could I have been so wrong? she silently asked herself.

"No, it's a promise."

He watched her confident frame glide out the front door turning for one final glare with fearless glacier eyes staring him down. She wasn't the same pliable girl looking for some excitement and thrills in Seattle.

If she continued to refuse to cooperate with his plans, he'd need to set some kind of an example or maybe a sign to keep her in line. She had been way too valuable to him. He was in trouble. With a capital T. He wasn't taking no for an answer.

CHAPTER FOUR

S livers of morning sunbeams poked through canopies of green trees in the west end of Vancouver as the two friends walked down the hill, taking a water taxi across to Granville Island's Public Market where fresh food and fish direct from the producers and fishermen are sold.

The bay was full of boats. Across from rows of fresh colorful fruits, a man juggled three flamethrowers. A rainbow of green grapes, red currants, yellow kumquats, dark blackberries, red raspberries, and eggplant-colored Bing cherries brightened the tabletops.

MaryAnne and Anne walked by stores under the Granville Bridge. The two wandered in and out of stores selling books and paper goods. One gallery showed hand-carved totems, jade eagles and whales with all sorts of designs in blown glass. Anne added glassblowing to her growing "Retirement To Do" list.

There was no shortage of clothing and accessories, and ceramics and pottery. MaryAnne recognized the Matthew Freed Pottery and they stepped inside. Ashby House had become a regular using much of his pottery for the plates, mugs and serving dishes. Matthew specializes in functional pottery, meant to be used and enjoyed daily. Peter and Anne had been introduced to him at a craft market several years earlier. They'd taken home a set of black stoneware mugs with a cherry red trim atop the softly squared mug.

Peter helped Robin retrieve planks of wood flooring from across town from some future project. Boards stacked on the top of Robin's VW, and some sticking out the windows with Peter in the back seat smooshed against the window, they slowly slalomed through the city streets.

Rendezvousing at home for lunch, the foursome headed to Stanley Park for the afternoon. The park is a showcase of city and ocean views, totems, gardens, forests, beach area and wide open spaces.

They ambled through the spectacular rose garden and other floral displays. Annuals and perennials in colorful beds lined the walkway. Orange marigolds led the parade into yellow and purple. People walked down the pathway under the white wooden arbor that arched over the entire walkway, supporting a combination of vibrant shades of pink climbing roses and exotic white and purple clematis.

The scent reminded Anne of a time in a perfumery in Paris where she watched artisans making perfume and learned about the expertise of this trade. She asked about a perfume made from her favorite flowering bush—Daphne. They had none but many had inquired before her.

MaryAnne knew most of the names of the flowers, but retaining those details wasn't Anne's forte. Nestled between the rose garden and the forest is the Shakespeare Garden, paying homage to the famous William. However it's not really a garden but a collection of trees mentioned in his plays and poems. A grove of black walnut, red oak, atlas cedar and a dozen other trees include fir, beech, Pacific dogwood, and hawthorn. Several trees are affixed with plaques that display appropriate quotes.

A gray cement monument of William stands about five feet high but looks even taller since it is balanced on a pile of flat stones. There are about 45 trees that form the arboretum that accompanies the monument. Peter read the plaque at the base of a huge black walnut tree: "Why, 'tis a cockle or a walnut shell, A knack, a toy, a trick, a baby's cap. The Taming of the Shrew."

For dinner Robin ordered Chinese that was conveniently delivered. MaryAnne served her luscious Nanaimo bars on an oblong ceramic tray. These were Anne's all-time favorite layered delights that MaryAnne caringly made, always ready whenever they arrived. Anne knew how long it took to make the mouthwatering bars. She'd tried it once. Once was enough.

When in Nanaimo on a one-day stop a few years earlier, Anne had done a taste-test stopping at probably a half dozen bakeries, sampling their Nanaimo bars. Nothing came close to MaryAnne's version. After eating the first bar in three bites, Anne picked up the tray looking at it closely. The ceramic glossy tray was made in Anne's colors: teals, blues and aqua. MaryAnne smiled and said it was now Anne's, and a piece she'd gotten from Matthew. They went to bed, full and happy, before it was even dark.

CHAPTER FIVE

As the final shoppers exited the popular jewelry store in Juneau, employees up and down Franklin Street locked up and left work after another brisk day of lucrative sales from cruise ship guests. The familiar farewell blast of the ship's horn signaled the last tourists had departed for the day, or in this case, night.

Vinni, the owner of Celebrity Jewelers, reminded his wife Prerna and salesclerk, Ericka, that in five days Peter and Anne from Oregon would be arriving by ship. It was about the umpteenth time he'd reminded them Ericka thought, obviously excited to see his friends again. She almost felt like she knew the Oregonians after all she'd heard from Vinni's family. Being originally from Washington, Ericka would have something to talk to them about, having the Pacific Northwest in common. Ericka waved goodnight, mentioning she was off to have a late dinner with her boyfriend, Clint.

Vinni knew Anne and Peter would be bringing friends with them; she always did. He had a bottle of special perfume waiting for her. In her email she asked him to have a tray of watches ready for them to look at. He'd have a tray of blue sapphires ready for her, too. He knew she loved sapphires.

CHAPTER SIX

The next morning at Ashby House in Vancouver, while eating a modified version of an English breakfast of eggs, bacon, fried potatoes, grilled tomatoes, sautéed mushrooms and fresh pastries from the Bon Ton French bakery, they visited with a delightful couple from New Zealand who were thoroughly enjoying their first trip to North America. After hearing their personal version of New Zealand's scenery, friendly people, delicious-sounding food and wines, this country moved toward the top of Peter and Anne's list of places to explore.

After breakfast cleanup, the four friends walked down Robson Street to the waterfront. Wandering the water's edge they spotted several yachts including one with a helicopter on the top deck, seaplanes taking off and landing, and boats, canoes and kayakers moving in and out. They could see the eight gleaming white spires from Canada Place blocks away. It reminded Anne of a gigantic sailboat.

The foursome strolled into a diner and sat around the chrome and Formica table. Robin commented that it felt like sitting down for dinner when he was a child. They all agreed, being mostly the same age. The rectangular tabletop was a watermelon color in a crackled-ice pattern. The soft vinyl chairs matched the vibrant melon color. Even though decades old, the set looked like it came out of the store yesterday.

They had been in the diner for less than three minutes and felt they already knew their waitress, Daizee, according to her name tag. "And like the flower," she informed them. While filling their glasses with ice water she told them that the peas were frozen rock hard and the gravy for the open-faced turkey sandwich had so much salt in it, she believed it was from the Great Salt Lake in Utah, where she was originally from. They all opted for salads: Shrimp Louie for three and Chef for the other.

Sitting on the porch that afternoon they sipped iced tea, and after four o'clock, switched to white wine. Rocking back and forth in comfy chairs, they listened to chirping birds, nattering people and creepily smart crows cawing to each other about something. Robin had story after story about the neighborhood's mysterious crows dispelling bad luck. A common superstition is that two crows cawing is believed to mean good luck, harmony and good news. He didn't believe it from his first-hand accounts of these birds, which he declared were smarter than some people he knew.

CHAPTER SEVEN

That afternoon at Celebrity Jewelers in Juneau, Vinni told Ericka she had a telephone call. She crinkled her brow in a questioning look, her incredibly Nordic blue eyes, customarily merry, now quizzical. She had never received a call at her place of employment before. "Really, for me?" she asked.

"The man asked for you," was the reply.

She stepped through the door into the office and picked up the receiver, "Hello????"

"I need to talk to you tonight," demanded the male.

She hissed back in a hushed tone, "Don't you ever call me here again."

"You aren't answering your phone," he said, so she pulled the phone from her pocket and flipped it up, and saw 14 messages from the same number.

"I don't take personal calls at work."

"You better show up the bar tonight. We need to talk."

She replied in a raised voice, "Don't you ever call me again and I will not be meeting you," and not waiting for a reply, dropped the receiver back into the cradle.

If anyone could have seen the rapid change in her eyes from merry and bright to startling and intense, they would have been shocked.

Ericka thought back to the first time she'd met him at a bar in Seattle. She was having a drink with a friend from work. Her coworker Leon from the veterinary clinic introduced her to one of his friends named Tyrone.

He stood five foot ten inches, exactly the same as her, medium build, with thick golden blond wavy hair, pushed off to the right, just slightly covering his ears. His eyes were the color of lakes around Seattle and she imagined herself diving in, deeper and deeper into a pool—of him. If he was happy his eyes were bluish-gray. If he was outraged the blue disappeared. He had good teeth and smile. That mattered to her; she didn't like people who avoided dentistry. His voice was sort of gravely and entrancing. His features reminded her of a young swarthy Robert Redford.

It was obvious that her height didn't intimidate him, as it had many men. As they stood about six inches apart gazing into each other's eyes, Ericka's coworker saw sparks that would ignite a forest fire.

Oh how she wished she'd paid attention to the warning bells, red lights, sirens going off in her head, but she hadn't. Live and learn, she'd heard. She had. Now she was done with him, grateful she wasn't in jail or worse.

The store manager's sensitive brown eyes were as big as saucers when Ericka rounded the corner. It would have been hard to miss that abrupt conversation. Prerna never heard Ericka speak to anyway that way. "You okay dear? No troubles with your boyfriend, I hope?" she inquired motheringly.

Still perturbed and a bit unsettled, Ericka replied, "Oh no, not with Clint, he's absolutely the best. But, thanks for asking. There is a bothersome past friend who won't leave me alone."

"Is he hassling you on a regular basis?"

"More and more," she admitted, when thinking back on the past month of harassment.

"Maybe you should contact the authorities. They could help if you need it."

"Umm, I'll think that over," then she closed the conversation.

The call still slightly unnerved Ericka, but she shrugged it off and greeted a friendly shopper who wanted to look at the new chocolate diamonds everyone was talking about.

CHAPTER EIGHT

Being an unseasonably warm evening in Vancouver, the four friends sauntered about six blocks to a favorite Italian restaurant where the trusted owner prepared any delectable delights he wanted—they called it Chef's Choice.

The Italian extravaganza began with caprese salad made with fresh mozzarella, thinly sliced fresh tomatoes, garden fresh sweet basil drizzled with imported olive oil and a dash of balsamic vinegar. Then came plates of flavorful spaghetti Bolognese delivered family-style.

Piping hot, thin crust Napoli-style margherita pizza was placed in front of each person. Peter and Anne had eaten at a pizzeria in Naples, Italy, which they would remember forever. This tasted identical. The Italians didn't cover their pizza with multiple unidentifiable ingredients. Anne could have stopped there, just eating pizza, but assumed it would be rude.

Italian melodies added ambiance to the brightly painted scenery on the walls. The tall, pencil-thin Italian Cypress formed the backdrop around a villa made of warm golden stone. In the foreground were perfectly manicured rows of vineyards. A narrow dirt road ran down separating two houses. In a field to the left of the estate was a rolling hill of yellow flowers flowing into a body of water. Anne had seen fields of yellow flowers like this and guessed sunflowers. A field of red flowers disappeared over the hill. Anne decided it must be poppies. She wanted to step into the wall and reappear in Italy.

The pièce de résistance was fresh tiramisu for dessert. The layered ladyfinger cookies, soaked in espresso and rum and laced with the creamy texture of zabaglione custard and mascarpone cheese were delish.

Profusely complimenting and thanking Anne's newly dubbed, patron saint of culinary divineness, they waddled back stuffed, taking the way only locals would know. Paths were illuminated with soft lighting from the porches of other historic homes in the West End. Anne loved meandering through gardens, pedestrian paths and tree-lined streets that took them back to their charming Victorian home.

CHAPTER NINE

L ight came streaming in from the picture window facing Juneau's waterfront. "Anything you want to talk about? You seem preoccupied," Clint asked his girlfriend Ericka, still reclining together on the murphy bed.

About 16 blocks north, her apartment was a bit smaller than the guys' place. She had a studio and slept on a pull-down murphy bed which she pushed back into position each morning. She had a dinky kitchen, but she mostly used the microwave and toaster oven anyway. The fridge looked to be the same size as the one in her college dorm room. She had some veggies to make salads, two bottles of wine she got at the liquor store, and other basics. Cans of soup were her main staples along with whatever leftovers she brought home from the bakery. She made enough from both part-time jobs to grab something from the many restaurants along the waterfront.

Nestled safely in the crook of his arm, she avoided looking into his gentle, expressive green eyes. She then shifted around so she could run her fingers through his hair.

"Nope, everything is fine, same old, same old," was her answer, hoping she was telling him the truth.

"Why don't you tell me again about how you fell in love with me at first sight," he teased. She rolled her gorgeous twinkling blue eyes. "Fine, I know you're trying to distract me. I'm really fine.

"Okay, well, one morning a young woman was at Starbucks, the cool original one at 1912 Pike Street. Among three people in front of her stood this guy who looked just like Tom Cruise, only several inches taller. The woman just stared at him. When he got his coffee he turned to leave, and he looked at her with soft green eyes and she boldly said 'Hi.' He smiled.

"Then they serendipitously arrived about the same time the next day. She saw him coming down the street then jumped in line. She'd recognize that dark brown hair and his frame anywhere.

"She asked for a Frappuccino. He said, 'Coffee, black, please.' He hadn't caught on to the coffee lingo, so when asked the size: short, tall, grande, or venti, he just said, '16-ounce, please.'

"Then they both showed up the third day in a row and the Tom Cruise lookalike asked the blonde out for a drink.

"The woman fell in love with him the first time she'd seen him at Starbucks three days earlier. She'd hoped he'd be there same time the following day. She was right. 'Third time's the charm.'"

Ericka fell asleep in his arms.

CHAPTER TEN

Before embarking on any trip, Anne did considerable research. She read articles saved from past magazines and always purchased at least one or two travel books by Rick Steves or some other reliable travel guru to learn everything she could before exploring the new region. It was part of the fun and journey for her, like the October, then November, then December before Christmas. Even like Christmas Eve as a child, now as an adult before a trip, she couldn't sleep.

Oh, and then there were her lists. She had a checklist per trip, customized per adventure. Peter had his own with electronics. Fortunately only one-pagers.

After parting hugs, Robin and MaryAnne dropped their American friends off at the front entrance at Canada Place Pier, to check in for their cruise. Anne's heart skipped a beat or two with anticipation.

As they were snaking their way through the Disneyland-type twisting aisles, sharing small talk and looking for familiar faces, she heard her name called with a British accent. Howard and Pearl had just been dropped off by the airport shuttle, arriving from Oxford, England. Pearl and Anne met when Anne was leading tours of attorneys on educational travel programs while working at a local law school. From then on, the foursome had been best friends, even though 6,000 miles apart, traveling together whenever they could. A nice family of four let the Brits cut in line to be with Peter and Anne as they stepped up to the check-in counter handing over their passports and registration forms. They received their credit card-size room keys and a floor plan of the 12-story ship.

Anne's heart did the familiar flip-flop when the key was placed in her hand after checking in.

She loved: The smell of the salty sea air that reminded her of hundreds of trips to the Oregon coast when she was a child; looking out their veranda seeing different scenery; that for one entire week somebody else cleaned up their room—twice a day; standing on their own private veranda, watching seaplanes throttle noisily by; how their room steward would notice their fun personalities and felt free to decorate their room with surprises like a towel swan, whale or penguin; that no matter where they went, there was the sound of music wafting from somewhere; that she'd get all the exotic fruit, watermelon and bacon she'd want; leaving the veranda door open as they slept.

"What don't you love?" Peter asked her.

Her list: Ungrateful and rude passengers; people who complain about the weather in Alaska and blame their travel agent for not telling them they could be cold; people who complain because the food isn't what they thought it would be; whining it's not like they have at home.

One of her favorite slogans is, *Never a ship sails out of the bay but carries my heart as a stowaway.* She couldn't recall where she'd read this, but it held true for her. The earlier heart flip-flop increased to palpitations now.

But before they would actually board there was always one thing they did—have their picture taken in front of some scenic backdrop. The snowcapped mountains in the background seemed appropriate. The two couples, one British and the other American, separately first, then all four of them, arm in arm.

They overheard a first-time cruiser ask the photographer, "How will I know what pictures are mine?" Anne looked at Peter and shook her head, not even glancing at the staff who would try to explain that one. Peter snickered softly. Anne erupted in giggles.

They were early. They always were because Anne couldn't stand the wait. She'd rather be onboard sitting at the Welcome Buffet waiting for their stateroom to be available than pace elsewhere. They'd had luck on past cruises where the staterooms were ready early. Plus Anne had some official business to do. She would plaster festive "Welcome Aboard" signs on 15 doors of all her friends and family on decks four to nine.

Now past the photo entourage, Anne marched first in line pulling her wheeled carry-on, chock full of one change of clothing, her basket of beauty she jokingly called it—really just makeup products and toiletries. Other necessities included her curling iron, camera battery, medicines, pj's and a few other items she couldn't live without if their luggage didn't show up for a day or two.

She walked confidently up the middle of the gangway through the large open door on the side of the ship. Peter followed close on her heels, towing his own carry-on, some similar items but mostly all their electronics: extra camera batteries, cords, and binoculars. This trip he brought a spotting scope they'd set up on the balcony for scanning the shoreline for wildlife.

Three women and two men dressed in gold-trimmed blue uniforms greeted them warmly. "Welcome Aboard, Mr. and Mrs. Wellsley. It's lovely to have you back." It had taken Anne several cruises to figure out how they knew their names so quickly and when she did, she promised not to reveal cruise line secrets.

Each were presented a warm cloth to moisten their hands. One reached out balancing a tray of tall stem glasses filled with a choice of champagne, a mimosa or orange juice. Anne reached for a mimosa, took a big deep breath, and felt welcomed to her very own floating hotel.

She had been bitten by the travel bug at an early age. It was her parents' fault. A cruise assisted in her healing process, especially one going to Alaska.

Heading for the buffet there was WELCOME ABOARD carved in the biggest watermelon she'd had ever seen. This was just the beginning of what she knew would be a marvelous week with a big group of friends and family.

She enjoyed organizing vacations in her spare time for special people in their lives. It was so much fun traveling with people they knew. Anne wasn't shy, and she thoroughly enjoyed meeting people from around the world, too. Peter knew Anne was happiest when traveling, experiencing new or familiar favorite locations, exploring, meeting new people, some becoming lifelong friends from around the world. They now had friends or acquaintances on all continents

DELEEN WILLS

except Antarctica. He felt confident she'd work that out one day, too.

She had many serendipitous moments meeting a complete stranger who'd then became a forever friend. She thought fondly of her faux Scottish aunties, Margaret and Wilma, who they'd encountered on a Caribbean cruise some years earlier. Anne loved that they exchanged Christmas letters and postcards from each other's world travels.

Walking through the first buffet line of the cruise, Anne felt an overwhelming sense of gratitude. Her previously racing heart had calmed to its normal beat. She knew how blessed they were to be able to travel, quenching her thirst of wanderlust at least temporarily.

Peter stood behind her as she picked up a tray and white plate. Waiting patiently behind a man who couldn't make up his mind, she whispered, "Try it all, it's really okay," as she pointed at food items that were carefully dished onto her plate by attentive staff.

A waiter carried Anne's tray to a table once she'd located somebody with a familiar face. They joined Sherrie, and Joel who was standing to go for a second round. He stood six foot five inches and had lots of space to fill. Anne went for a small plate of fruit, token fruit, because she knew she should. She thoroughly enjoyed the extraordinary colorful fresh fruit display. She selected chunks of watermelon, mango and papaya. Peter would share her choices. She would order grapefruit for some breakfasts as it would come already peeled, cut and sectioned, such a luxury.

She spotted the circular display of desserts with an attention-getting ice sculpture carved into the shape of a three-tier cake. She withstood the temptation—for the time being.

Returning, iced tea had already been delivered. Peter knew what she liked.

After catching up on family and life in general, Sherrie volunteered to check out the dessert options. She returned with a slice of four-layered chocolate and cherry cake; two scoops of sherbet, one raspberry, one lemon; two white chocolate and pecan cookies, and one oval cup of crème brûlée.

Peter shrugged his shoulders as Anne made a beeline toward her favorite dessert, crème brûlée. This cruise line was known in her book, the only book that counted, for their authentic crème brûlée. She came back with two.

"Which one's for me?" Peter asked, already knowing the answer. She disdainfully looked at him. *The audacity*, she said to herself, *that man*.

"What if they don't have it again the entire cruise? Uh, neither one is for you, but while I'm up for an iced tea refill, how many would you like?"

"One is fine, dear," was his reply. Their friends were watching in amusement and while Anne was picking up his dessert and her tea refill, he said, "This happens whenever crème brûlée is involved. She'll have it every night if she can. And key lime pie."

"Wanna do our version of a self-guided tour with us?" Peter asked. Joel picked up a blue piece of paper that Anne recognized as her extensive list of Helpful Hints. Joel sheepishly looked at her when she said, "You were supposed to read this ahead of time." Sherrie poked him and said, "Told you so."

———

Already at the top of the ship, the four strolled from aft to forward, starboard to port. Anne could only remember the port side (left side) by it being four letters. Four letters equaled port or left. Starboard made no sense to her. They would play minigolf on the top deck later in the cruise.

A colorful four-foot tall mosaic dragon stood at the entrance to the solarium. They wandered around the indoor pool with crystal moveable canopy and into the spa, past rooms where one could get a massage or sit in the sauna. The salon provided a shave and a haircut, styling, manicures and pedicures. She signed herself and Pearl up for treatments the next day. It was Pearl's first cruise and Anne wanted to surprise her with a belated birthday gift.

They walked on an eight-foot round mosaic turquoise and white sunburst on the floor. Seeing more and more mosaics, they saw an ocean theme to the tiled art. Anne had taken two mosaic classes creating a couple of unimpressive pieces, a pot and tray. The oval tray was supposed to represent yellow sunflowers from Europe. They looked like globs of dandelions. She was told by a kind soul that dandelions are wildflowers in most countries. She laughed out loud and appreciated the support.

On their self-guided tour they began encountering others from their group. Her parents had arrived with her brother Max and his wife Lola. Her youngest brother Will and wife Michelle, who they called Shelley, would be arriving later due to a criminal case he needed to wrap up before leaving for one week. This would be the first trip away from their three young children who had been farmed out to friends for the week.

Peter's two older sisters, Ashlee and Julee, along with their husbands, Brant and Wyatt, were headed into the welcome buffet. His sisters were named after their father, Lee, and was Peter's middle name.

Most friends were from their hometown area. A portion would be on the entire trip ending in Fairbanks and most would fly home after the cruise from Anchorage. Joel and Sherrie were in a stateroom to their right and Mike and Kathy were on the left. Mike, or Mr. Prankster, was their lovable practical joker. Anne had known them both since childhood. Larry and Suzanne, their longtime "golden retriever friends," were just down the hall.

"Travel friends," Sharon and Phil from Corvallis were next to Mike and Kathy. Her "childhood friend" Peggy, and her husband Rich were about ten rooms forward. Their daughter was sharing a room with his sister. Friends David and Ellen had flown from Indiana to join them. They splurged and were in a suite.

Anne laughed at how she tagged her friends—travel friends, childhood friends, golden retriever friends, Salem friends, British friends, work friends, lifetime friends, Indiana friends, her dad's 10th Mountain Division friends—how many adjectives could she use?

Mike's parents were Anne's second parents and had played a major part of her childhood. They spent a lot of time on camping trips together especially on the Metolius River in Central Oregon. Mike is the eldest son and had been in the military when the younger kids were camping. His mother had coordinated Anne and Peter's wedding 22 years earlier. They were on board, too. Their parents were the best of friends.

As on previous cruises, Peter and Anne vowed to take the stairs instead of the convenient elevators. One for the exercise with the amount of food they would be consuming. Two, because it would usually be faster.

The announcement was made that staterooms were ready. They entered their room on deck nine with floor to ceiling windows and a veranda through the sliding glass door. "Veranda" is the proper term and sounds much classier and suave than deck, balcony, or patio.

"Hallelujah," she exclaimed when their luggage arrived. Timeliness was not the case on all cruises. Anne unpacked the majority of the luggage, informing Peter which built-in drawers his undergarments were in, then which third of the plentiful closet was his.

He unpacked all the important things: technology items, binoculars, one for each, and video camera, storing them away. He reprogrammed the safe and stowed their passports, wallets and credit cards. Peter slid the luggage out of the way under the king bed. The full-length sofa, an oval knee-high sturdy table, a swivel chair and then a padded stool that fit away under the desk was it for furniture.

Shelves were tucked into every corner, nook and cranny, making almost every surface usable and efficient. Night-stands held drawers on each side of the bed. Everything was put away in its place with empty drawers and shelves to be used for souvenirs. They'd both end up opening several drawers for a day or two searching for one thing or another that, at the time of unpacking, made perfect sense where it had been stashed.

Anne taped a list of their family and friends with their stateroom numbers on the mirror above the telephone that also served as their clock and alarm.

Their room steward, Altheah, greeted them with a foreign accent promising to take care of their every need and left her phone number if they wanted anything.

A bouquet of flowers sat on the table with a note from their travel agent and dear friend Jeannie who helped put the adventure together. With the yellow daisies, periwinkle bachelor buttons, dainty miniature pink roses, tall stems of white baby's breath, and ferns for greenery, the fresh arrangement looked like someone walked through Stanley Park illegally snipping anything she wanted. Anne preferred that casual look to the formal look.

Beside the flowers sat a tray of chocolate-covered strawberries with a bottle of bubbly and two tall-stemmed glasses. Peter popped the cork that shot up not quite hitting the ceiling. Both felt a little giddy even without champagne. He poured two glasses as they stood on the veranda looking out at the white-winged Canada Place.

Sliding glass doors opened as their friends experienced what they were—gratitude and excitement all rolled up into outbursts of expressions and impressions. Their ten-minute solitude was broken. All was well with her soul.

Popping corks of sparkling beverages, Sherrie said, "Cheers!"

Anne asked, "What are we cheersing?" an on-the-spot, newly made-up word.

"That's not a word," Sherrie laughed.

Anne replied, "Well, it could be—we're in Canada."

Joel declared, "Cheers to new adventures and good friends."

After repeated tinkling of glasses and toasts, 45 minutes later the first of several impromptu veranda parties were interrupted by an announcement for everyone to put on their bulky orange lifejackets. It was time to report to assigned muster stations for a lifeboat drill.

She spotted John and Rebecca, who traveled with them often, Peter's co-worker Paul and wife Dee, Heather and Tim, all from Salem. Heather had a smile as big as a half moon. Anne's niece Kelly and her husband Darren from Portland and farther down the deck, she saw her other niece Katy and her twin brother Nathan standing not too far from their dad, Anne's brother, Max, and his wife Lola. In their junior year of high school, the twins were the youngest family members of the cruise group. There were 30 family and friends aboard somewhere.

They respectfully listened to what to do in case of an emergency and then the official greeting from their captain.

Many in their group were cruising for the first time, and most had never been to Alaska. They asked Anne for her opinion on shore excursions, protocol and cruise etiquette. She was happy to impart her wisdom from past adventures. One of the most common questions was about dinner dress.

Anne explained: Formal means a dressy outfit for the ladies, and dark suit and tie, dinner jacket or tux for the men. Informal is casual dress or pants and blouse for ladies, jacket and tie, and slacks for men. Casual could be a sporty outfit for women, and for the men a sports shirt and slacks. No jeans, tank tops or shorts in the dining room.

At 5:55 friends and family came pouring out of their staterooms to stand in line at the dining room doors waiting to be seated for the first dinner of the cruise—the official welcome dinner. They laughed as someone leaned against the double doors and said, "Open, Open, Open."

Escorted by a dashing waiter to the guest's preassigned and numbered table was helpful and almost necessary especially for the first night. One could search in vain for hard-to-see numbers as the table floorplan often didn't seem to make sense or follow a logical pattern.

The first dinner on board was always exciting and Anne read every word of the detailed menu. She knew from experience that their foodie enthusiasm would wane toward the end of the cruise. One could only consume so much.

The leather-bound, 20-inch high menu listed appetizer choices: Tomato juice, Guava nectar, Cranberry juice,

Pineapple gondola, Shrimp cocktail, Smoked Norwegian salmon or Chinatown egg rolls. No brainer for Anne, anything shrimp. Peter agreed.

Beverages each night automatically included coffee, hot or iced tea or milk.

Soup selection: Cream of broccoli, Consommé celestine, Chilled watercress. A pass for Anne, and Peter ordered the chilled watercress.

Salad choices: Boston lettuce Bella Vista, crispy Boston lettuce, topped with julienne of beets, scallions and chopped eggs. The "King and I" dressing came highly recommended. Beets and onions, that was all Peter. Hearts of lettuce with carrot curls explained itself and came with a choice of dressings.

The first night out Anne didn't want to be labeled high maintenance, but she asked if she could have a Caesar salad and the answer was, "Of course, madam. If you'd like one each night, please let me know."

The entrée choices weren't easy to select: Crabmeat cannelloni Neptune, pasta tubes filled with Canadian crabmeat, served with a pink Newburg sauce with basil and stir-fried medley of green and yellow squash. Supreme of Boston sole Madagascar, served with mushrooms, green peppercorn sauce, red potatoes and broccoli florets. Stuffed pork loin Scandinavian style, natural jus, served with red cabbage, potato pancake and apple wedges. Roast duckling, complemented with blueberry sauce, served with baby carrots and croquette potatoes. Broiled prime sirloin steak, sauce Bearnaise, served with croquette potatoes, tomato Provençale and broccoli florets. Yum, but she could easily fix this at home.

Peter requested the Boston sole Madagascar and Anne ordered crabmeat cannelloni. Each course was served "Ladies first." After the delicious entrées, an international cheese selection was presented on round silver trays.

Menus were delivered again in case anyone forgot the dessert choices: Black Forest cake, Key Lime pie, Strawberries Romanoff or a selection of ice creams: Butter almond, chocolate, vanilla or lemon sherbet.

There were so many choices of appetizers, salads and soups, entrées, and desserts. What a way to start a trip with several of Anne's favorites: shrimp cocktail, crab, and key lime pie, of which she'd have two. It was tradition. Should they have crème brûlée some night, she'd have two of those also. At least she'd had it for lunch earlier. Nothing else really mattered and unfortunately, many times the desserts looked better than they tasted. Not the case with her favorite two desserts in the world.

After dinner, their waiter presented them with a recipe for the cruise line's famous Black Forest Cake in case one would be having a party for 12.

Anne loved hearing the blast of the ship's horn entering and departing a port. It was also used in case of danger or bad weather. After dinner, they strolled on the top deck as the ship glided easily under the Lion's Gate Bridge, a suspension bridge that crosses the bay as it spans the first narrows of Burrard Inlet and connects the City of Vancouver to the north shore.

The bridge spans almost 6,000 feet with ships' clearance of 200 feet even though, from their vantage point, it looked like the top of the smokestack barely cleared the undercarriage of the expansive bridge. Ships always departed around this time of night because the tides are lowest and large vessels could leave without issue. They stopped to chat with

Mike and Kathy and Phil and Sharon, marveling at the calmness of the beautiful summer evening.

The sky turned shades of an orange glow as the sun began to drop in the summer sky. Lights all around the bay and city flickered on like twinkling fireflies. The sun eventually dropped behind the end of the land as it disappeared into the inky water. Miles back, the golden orange moonrise hung like a beach ball over Vancouver.

They knew from past cruises that each night returning to their stateroom, they would find the bed turned down, a milk chocolate for each on their pillows (Peter usually got both, her being a dark chocolate addict) and the daily newsletter, the *Gazette*, detailing everything to see and do in 30-minute increments for the next day. Anne learned after their first cruise to bring a highlighter so she could put a yellow line through things she or Peter wanted to do.

She reclined ready to read to Peter about the Inside Passage, but he was already fast asleep in about three seconds flat. She'd give Peter a dramatic reading over breakfast.

Just as she was about to fall asleep, familiar leg cramps hit both calves. *Those darn stairs*, she muttered to herself, quickly jumping up, hopping to the bathroom to get a glass of water, drinking two quickly and massaging both legs. It might happen again this trip.

CHAPTER ELEVEN

Getting off work around 9 p.m., Ericka joined Clint for dinner at Juneau's Hangar on the Wharf on Marine Way. Dining late was commonplace since both of their jobs were wrapped around the tourism industry. There could be four or five cruise ships daily at the port city which equated to five to ten thousand people on excursions or wandering the town for shopping.

Sitting at a table overlooking the water, Ericka ordered a Victory at Sea, a coffee and vanilla porter. Clint ordered a Bud and asked for calamari to share before his entrée of halibut and chips and her halibut fish tacos arrived.

They both really liked the history of the building that was printed on the back of the menus. The original hangar was lost due to fire from a welding spark in 1939. Rebuilt in 1940, the interior of historic Merchants Wharf served as an aircraft hangar for many of the floatplane operators that eventually merged to become Alaska Airlines.

Every day the planes would fly in and out of downtown Juneau, using the hangar for washing, fueling, and repairs. The restaurant honored Southeast Alaska aviation history.

Munching on calamari while catching up on their respective day at work, Ericka said, "You know, you never really told me much about growing up. I've told you lots about me and my family. You sort of avoid it all."

"That's because it's nothing notable or interesting. Tony is the one with the interesting heritage," he countered.

"I don't care about Tony nor do I want to hear about him. Tell me about you."

"Okay. Well, my parents are still married. I am the youngest. My older siblings moved out when they turned 18 and went to college, not returning. One brother Owen, just two years older than me came to Alaska. They are all overachievers, like our parents. They all work way too hard and don't really seem to enjoy life. Except maybe Owen, who is the one who got me up here. I don't see him much because he's out on his fishing boat a lot.

"There was pressure being a Sterling. My dad is on the faculty in Ellensburg at Central Washington University. Mom is the first woman attorney in the county and had to prove herself to all the men, actually society as a whole. They are all brainiacs.

"I was repeatedly told I had to fly-right. I didn't want to embarrass my family. Ever. 'Being a Sterling brings along a certain amount of responsibility,' Clint said in a deep, slow, sarcastic voice. I heard it often starting even before I began school at Lincoln Elementary. I grew up living on ritzy Craig's Hill in a colonel two-story home. It even has white pillars on the front porch. Some kids called it the Sterling mansion. I always felt embarrassed by that. My folks are still there, rambling around in a house way too big for just the two of them.

"Most of my friends at Lincoln didn't live anywhere close to us except for one of the three Jennifers in my class. I went through most of my grades with Michaels, Jasons, and Davids, plus Amys, Melissas and Heathers.

"Attending Morgan Junior High, I was popular mostly because anything I tried, I did well. One of the coaches called me a natural athlete. But it wasn't just sports. I excelled in drama and music. I liked playing the tuba and had no problem carrying the awkward thing. I didn't really care for any parts in Shakespearean productions."

Ericka laughed thinking of him as Puck in *A Midsummer Night's Dream.*

"It wasn't a surprise when I got the award for 'Best All Around Student' at the end of the school year. My parents were pretty proud. I didn't want the added pressure or responsibility of the family name and living up to my parents' high standards, nor did I ever ask for it.

"Entering Ellensburg High School, I had about enough of my father's not-so-subtle reminders of continuing to excel for the family name. I felt stuck. I really preferred hanging out with friends eating burgers and fries at Campus U-Totem before an evening of bowling at Rodeo City Lanes," he laughed at the memory. "Everyone wanted me on their teams; guess that coach was right, I was a natural, everything came pretty easy."

Ericka shook her head and commented, "I can't even relate to this, I studied hard and got average grades."

"Often groups of my friends went by this really cool place called Dick and Jane's Spot. It's downtown on the northwest corner of 1st Avenue and Pearl Street, right across from the fire department and police station. I remember as a kid when this couple purchased the rundown house, both artists, started turning the formerly boarded-up decrepit building into their unique home and its junk-filled yard into a tree-shaded garden for art. It was always a topic of conversation and once we held a contest and the winner who found anything new got a milkshake or coke.

"The elderly couple, anyone over 20 seemed old to us kids, collected art that they shared by decorating the yard and exterior of their home for all of us to enjoy. One time I pointed out a new totem. My favorites are still the hundreds of glittery bicycle reflectors made into a fence that lines both sides of the red slab sidewalk leading to the front door. We all thought the heads sculpted from old telephone poles with hammered nails for hair were really cool, too. A Tin Man, just like the one from *The Wizard of Oz*, stands to one side, his chest is open to show the inner piping, gauges and ductwork.

"There was a big generation gap between my Boomer parents and me. We're Gen Xers, you know. In about my junior year, I developed a rebellious streak and just wanted out. But I also knew the only way out was an education.

"At school, volunteering and working, I had an easygoing, fun-loving type of personality so I had lots friends. I walked away from a situation instead of creating any type of confrontation. I wanted to please people, probably some-times to my detriment. Mom thought I had been taken advantage of a few times. Dad said I needed to toughen up. I didn't really think so, but my dad ruled the roost. At home I was unhappy, sarcastic and basically not pleasant to be around.

"My parents, Clarence and Colleen, met at Eastern Washington University. They were Wildcats. I didn't want to go there because they had. I wasn't sure where to go but I didn't want to stay in E-burg.

"Then I was selected valedictorian in my senior year, combined with pretty high SAT scores plus a good amount of volunteer work at the annual rodeo and local humane society, I had the pick of several state universities with a healthy scholarship to boot.

"Because of my hard work, I made it clear that I would select my own college no matter what my parents thought. They were pushing for Whitman, a private college in Walla Walla. The town of around 50,000 people felt too big. Plus scholarship funds didn't go as far at a private college. I didn't want to borrow money from my folks, beholding to my father who'd pull strings whenever it served him.

"I knew I'd get a part-time job somewhere to pay for whatever else was needed. I was never afraid of hard work, but I wanted to party more and relax. This nose to the grindstone thing was for the birds. I'd get into the school of my choice and be happy with passing grades instead of studying almost every waking hour. I thought I wanted a degree in forestry.

"Like I said, my brother Owen had settled in Juneau. It was the first I remember hearing much about that northern state. He is a fisherman which didn't please our parents at all, but they suddenly felt better about their underachieving son when Owen announced he'd purchased his first boat. He was always writing about jobs in Alaska especially in the summertime with shiploads of tourists.

"I just wanted a town bigger than the 13,000 people in E-burg. Washington State University in Pullman had 20,000 more people, yet still felt rural after my first college visit. I'd gone to several football games over the years. At least I'd be out of Podunk E-burg where I lived my entire life.

"When a girl I was dating said she was going to WSU, I decided to follow her. But I was young and entering college so didn't want to be tied down. We remained friends once we broke up.

The Cougs sports team played teams like Portland State, Oregon State, Stanford, Arizona State, and University of Oregon. Why in the world did WSU get stuck playing the largest school in the state—University of Washington? The odds weren't with WSU. I had no interest in going to the University of Washington in Seattle and be a Husky. "Huskies Suck" stickers were on plenty of bumpers on trucks, the same trucks with antlers on the hood and a shotgun in the rack. Had enough?"

"Oh, I suppose, for now anyway. I know you think it's boring, but I sure don't. To my place for dessert?" her gloriously mischievous blue eyes affirmed her invitation. "Absolutely," as he slid the waiter two twenties, and they hastily departed.

CHAPTER TWELVE

Anne feasted on watermelon, sectioned grapefruit, and crispy bacon strips on their veranda while Peter ate a ham and cheese omelet. She read to him the passage from the *Gazette* that he missed the night before. Complaining about sitting outside since they were enshrouded in fog and couldn't see a thing, she reminded him that they always did this on their first morning of any cruise. It was tradition. He zipped his jacket to his neck.

She called it a dramatic reading. He was used to it. "As the glaciers of the last Ice Age retreated from Southeast Alaska and British Columbia, a new land was born. Islands were freed from the ice and the green waters of the North Pacific flowed into the small coves and glacier-carved fjords of the mountain-crowded coast.

"Protected by offshore islands and tempered by the Japan Current, this maze of deep channels, quiet bays and forested islands forms on the world's most interesting and scenic cruise routes—waters cascading from sheer granite cliffs; immense glaciers that release great slabs of ice to crash into the sea; basking seals and migrating whales.

"As you cruise this majestic 1,000-mile inside passage, the ever-changing panorama of natural beauty is much the same that Captain Vancouver viewed two hundred years ago. This channel's eventful past recalls the days of Russian fur traders and gold-hungry prospectors; of ancient and complex Indian cultures that thrived on the rich bounty of the sea."

A way-too-friendly seagull landed on the railing. "Shoo, go away, get lost," Anne demanded. The pesky gull just glared at her, undeterred. It unnerved her slightly. She had heard about the sentimentality of Canadian birders, gulls supposedly being a symbol of freedom and versatility.

Its yellow beak with eerie beady eyes stared her down. This bird had a small chip out of the bottom of its beak, thus reaffirming its aggressiveness to her. One of its friends flew in and Anne immediately thought of the horrific Alfred Hitchcock movie, *The Birds*, that she had watched as a young girl. Truth be known, she was under an afghan blanket peeking through the gaps in the yarn. It was even frightening and spooky as an adult.

She pulled Peter inside to get out of its creepy eyeball gaze just as a third gull took over their private outside space, then continued with her dramatic reading. "Navigation Info: After passing Lion's Gate Bridge it is 108 nautical miles to Seymour Passage, where our arrival time is subject to the slack current time as the current can sometimes be as strong as 13 knots. We will then sail 114 nautical miles before reaching Pine Island."

It was their first full day on board and Sunday, according to the *Gazette*. Anne tended to lose track of days on vacations. The color gray described the morning. Low fog enveloped the decks. About every minute they heard the warning blare of the ship's horn since the enormous vessel was now totally cloaked by fog. Peter promised it would lift. She did trust his instincts on the weather. He'd purchased a snow shovel three months before one of the heaviest snowstorms in Oregon's history several years earlier. He'd had a premonition or maybe just intuition, but he was usually correct on weather issues.

On board, a myriad of things to do were listed in the *Gazette*: Jewelry exhibition, dance classes of all kinds, an art auction, cooking and floral demonstrations, fitness options, spa and massages, bingo, computer classes, ways to lose money in the casino, table tennis, volleyball and basketball, movies in the theater or their room—the choices seemed endless. They purposely avoided the casino; cigarette and cigar smoke and clanging of machines was not their idea of a pleasant time.

A typical first day at sea for Anne might be some type of demonstration or class, just sitting and visiting with friends or family, reading a book, getting a massage or just strolling the top deck getting in her laps. She thought about taking a computer class on Excel spreadsheets. Briefly. Then thought not.

She and Pearl had a spa appointment for their morning's activity. Pearl giggled like a little girl all through her first pedicure and foot massage, mostly because it tickled her feet, while they watched scenery of miles of tall trees and rolling hills as green as emeralds. The ocean alternated from the color of a gray mourning dove to blue as a bluebird, depending on density of fog and depth of water. The sun was playing peekaboo.

Both leaving with identical fuchsia-painted toenails and light pink fingernails, they already felt pampered and spoiled.

Peter and Anne met Mike's parents, Stan and Barbara, for lunch at the Pizzeria, looking over the Italian options. Anne wanted to see if the pizza was as authentic as advertised. They were hooked on thin crispy crust never forgetting their first and best pizza (in their opinion) in the world in Naples. Also, they would compare it to the second best pizza ever that they had several nights earlier in Vancouver. They were snobs when it came to Neapolitan pizza, gelato and dill pickles. Well, Anne was anyway.

Each ordered their own Margherita—tomato, mozzarella cheese, basil and oregano. Their waiter Giorgio wasn't surprised at one pizza per person. It was the Italian way. Fifteen minutes later, out of the wood-burning oven came delicious smelling pizzas. Giorgio skillfully sliced each pizza into six pieces as part of his service and showmanship.

Anne about fell off her chair when she saw the plates the pizza were delivered on. The 14-inch platter was all white with a thin royal blue rim around the edge. The same blue was used on the sketched design of the Rialto Bridge in Venice. A rippled flag attached to the top of the bridge read PIZZERIA.

This extraordinary piece of crockery spoke to Anne, like art and jewelry. Something had to speak to her before she purchased it. She heard it loud and clear, *Take me home with you.*

Anne and Peter had been to Venice the previous summer and loved the city. She *had* to have one of these plates and to make it even more perfect, they were the color scheme of their home kitchen—white with royal blue accents.

Peter had witnessed her in action before when she got her head or heart set on something. Almost reading her mind, well actually because her breathing had changed and eyes were as big as the plates, he calmly said, "Let's ask if we can buy one instead trying to stuff it into your bag."

Giorgio returned to see what else they might like. Anne blurted out the entire Venice, Rialto Bridge story plus matching her kitchen and could she please, please, please, buy one?

Giorgio shook his head left to right and replied in an authentic Italian accent, "No, no, so very sorry Madam, we do not sell the plates to anyone."

Crestfallen, disappointment and heartbreak obviously showing on her face and beginnings of a serious pout, he bent toward her and quietly whispered, "However, you are welcome to take the leftover pizza to your stateroom. Rinse it off and put the plate in your luggage. Don't leave it out because your room attendant will assume it's from room service and return it."

"Really?" Anne asked almost unbelieving, "Just take it?"

"Yours is not the first request, Madam. We have thousands of plates," as he boldly winked at Anne. He became her favorite waiter and she promised to return. Even though the meal was included in the cost of the cruise, some beverages like sodas were not. Peter added a generous tip on the beverage bill for Giorgio.

Two pizza plates were taken to their stateroom, washed and tucked away in Anne's suitcase. She would be sharing the second one with her niece Becky who also loved authentic pizza and everything Italian.

Peter was correct, the fog dissipated and when the ocean revealed itself, it looked like a huge smooth lake with the tip of Vancouver Island in the distance. They stood on the top deck and Anne took a deep, long breath of salty sea air. The smell reminded her of walking in the surf and collecting agates along the central Oregon coast.

That afternoon in the bright warm sunshine, while many children and some adults were in the pool, they attended the first lecture called *First Visitors* in the Showcase Theater.

The historian said, "Scholars believe Asian people first crossed the now submerged land bridge between Siberia and Alaska some 12,000 to 30,000 years ago. By the time European explorers arrived, native Alaskan peoples were divided into four major groups: Inuit (Eskimos), Aleuts, Athabaskans, and Northwest Coastal Indians, who ranged from Southeast Alaska all the way to Northern California.

"The coastal people were hunters and gatherers, as were nomadic tribes of the interior. Chiefs inherited their position and demonstrated their status at "potlatches"—ceremonial festivals. Totem poles stood outside the chiefs' long, plank houses. Totem carvings depicted their ancestry, clan membership and history. Each clan had its special spirits and dances. Almost all animal life was associated with spirits and gods. The ultimate deity was the orca.

"After the salmon and halibut, the most important source of food were several varieties of sea mammals—porpoise, otter, seal and sea lion. On land, the Indians hunted deer, elk, mountain goat, moose and bear. Vegetables were few—seaweed and eelgrass, and many kinds of berries were consumed.

"Because the shorelines were impossibly rugged for foot travel, all movement along the coast was accomplished entirely by water. Canoes epitomized the Indians' skill in working with cedar. Logs were shaped into canoes that ranged from 8-footers to 70-foot ocean-going war canoes.

"Alaska has more than 100,000 glaciers covering approximately 30,000 square miles of land. Glacier ice is formed as snow gradually changes into a granular material called "Firn" which ultimately becomes bubbly glacier air."

A huge round of applause proved to the naturalist that his talk was appreciated. They'd be back to hear him again.

That night they got to dress in their finest cruise attire. It was the first of two formal nights. Peter took the convenient way and ordered a tux with all the trimmings, including black shiny shoes, simply by calling a telephone number and providing specific sizes. He brought his own socks. They even provided a second white shirt, just in case of possible dinner spillage.

Not having that option, Anne brought her own clothing. She and Pearl had both purchased snazzy, spangly sequin jackets on a Caribbean cruise some years earlier. Anne's was multicolored and Pearl's was all white with silver trim. Anne thought hers especially versatile as she would be able to wear any type of solid colorful blouse underneath. She brought a fuchsia sleeveless pullover and a boring but classic black one.

Each woman only wore their cruise attire maybe once a year. And both jackets weighed a ton. Anne almost needed a separate piece of luggage just for her formal night outfits. And then there were the shoes. She finally got smart and brought one pair of black shoes that would go with anything.

If Peter misplaced Anne, he could easily track her down by following the trail of colorful sequins much like Gretel and her brother Hansel following breadcrumbs through the forest.

Anne realized on one of their first cruises that formal night was a fashion show for the middle class. It was entertaining to see what people showed up wearing. Most men were in black and white. Anne always brought a bright blue or red pocket square to tuck into Peter's chest pocket.

One woman got Anne's award for the most outlandish. The floor-length dress started out sea foam at her waist changing to several colors of the water, ending in turquoise touching the floor with a tail trailing about a two-feet behind her. The large sequins looked like scales and reminded her of Daryl Hannah in her famous movie, *Mermaid*.

While the six-piece orchestra played they looked over the menu for International Night. Appetizer choices: Smoked trout. Gamberi al Fra Diavolo or flambéed shrimp in hot & fiery tomato sauce. Pâté (meant liver something). Shrimp for Anne.

Soups: Cream of asparagus. Consommé double diablotin. Chilled gazpacho. Score for both Anne and Peter; they loved chilled gazpacho. Anne had made it once after their first trip to Spain. It tasted better in Spain.

Salads: Both selected hearts of iceberg with bacon and chives, knowing everything's better with bacon.

Entrées: Lobster ravioli thermidor. Pan-seared salmon fillet. Hsiang Su Ya, Roast Duckling. Baked veal loin in croissant crust. Roast prime rib of beef. Peter ordered the prime rib, rare.

Anne loved shrimp of any kind, make, or model. Tonight's highlight for her was the shrimp. She ordered two shrimp appetizers and chilled gazpacho, but skipped the main course. Every bite of shrimp tasted like fireworks going off in her mouth.

Desserts of Mandarin cheesecake, Vacherin glace Romanoff, and Chocolate Frangelico mousse cake were paraded on a tray so one could see their choices. Anne asked for something not on the menu.

Anne enjoyed every bite of crème brûlée with Peter having pistachio ice cream. Their waiter gave each woman the shrimp recipe. Sherrie handed hers to Joel, the culinary experimenter in their family.

Hand-in-hand, Peter and Anne walked around the top deck, still bright at 10:30. Back inside they snuggled in a corner and listened to a harpist play soothing tunes. Anne never missed a harpist when she happened upon one. Petit fours were delivered by the plateful. Joel and Sherrie wandered by and sat to soak in the melodic tones and sweet treats.

Around 11:30 they returned to their respective rooms, standing on their verandas admiring scenery and watching the water for any action. Swift movement and white water caught their attention as dozens of light gray dolphins surfaced, up and down, swimming very quickly, much faster than the ship. Peter grabbed the video camera and had time to get almost five minutes of their aquatic maneuvers.

"How do you know they are dolphins?" Sherrie asked.

Anne said, "Both Pacific white-side dolphins and Dall's porpoises are sighted often. We've seen schools of them on each cruise. Pacific white-sided dolphin occur in large groups of 20 or more. They have a swirl of light gray along their flanks and often leap clear out of the water. Dall's porpoises have a geometric black-white pattern. They don't leap above the surface but create a rooster-tail shaped splash when they swim."

"Yep, dolphins," Joel said, and Peter promised they'd also see plenty of porpoises.

At midnight, Anne and Peter selected what they'd like for breakfast. One of their favorite things is room service for breakfast. It's a lovely way to ease into the day.

Peter was already in bed just about asleep, so Anne didn't bother him with the important information about Ketchikan.

He would recall most of what she'd read but it never hurt to have a refresher course where one would be visiting and exploring.

About 2 a.m., Anne woke to a stirring in their room. Light seeped through the blackout curtains along the sides of the wall. She could see Peter hopping around on one leg. "Are you okay?"

"Darn cramp in my leg. You'd think after so many cruises, we'd know by now to drink more water and eat less salt, and definitely do fewer stairs." He couldn't see her nodding her head sympathetically.

CHAPTER THIRTEEN

In Juneau, Ericka looked at the glaringly white numbers, 2:17, on the clock. She was having a hard time getting to sleep. Her mind reeled with memories from her delinquent days in Seattle and how those shenanigans followed her to Juneau.

She suspected she needed to tell Clint everything. He knew most of it but not all. Would she loose him a second time? She needed to weigh the pros and cons of being completely truthful.

How in the world would she get rid of her Seattle baggage? Tyrone was stalking her. Could she prove it? Her mind veered down a dark path—maybe her nemesis should, could, would be eliminated?

CHAPTER FOURTEEN

Before Peter awoke, she had already peeked out at the arched sign "Welcome to Alaska's First City Ketchikan, the Salmon Capital of the World." The clock hands on the building on Dock Street pointed to 6:15.

Their ship was several stories higher than the golden-colored Tongass Trading Company building with signs boasting footwear, outdoorwear, sporting goods, and curios. Colorfully painted homes dotted the hillside above the trading company. Through some trees she spotted several totems. Across town, a Pepto Bismol pink, eight-story building looked out of place. "Big Pink" as some locals called it, Anne knew as the federal building. She'd read the questionable color was chosen by a local committee. *What were they thinking,* she said to herself.

At five minutes to eight, the rapping on the door indicated breakfast was about to be served. While Peter took another bite of a meat and veggie-filled omelet, Anne recited the history of Ketchikan. They had nine hours to pack as much as possible into their time.

She began reading word for word from the *Gazette* that was set on their bed the night before.

"Ketchikan, near the southernmost tip of the Alaska's panhandle, sits a sleepy little town with a very dramatic title. Squeezed between mountain and sea it is hard to imagine how the town got the Tlingit Indian name, Ketchikan, Thundering Wings of an Eagle.

"Like most communities in southeast Alaska, Ketchikan is surrounded by wilderness and impassable mountains. Without road or rail connections to the rest of North America, everything must come by air or sea."

She interjected, "Remember last time we went on the horse-drawn trolley ride in the pouring rain? The guide told us that there are only 12 miles of roadways. And, they bring in topsoil for gardens because the town is built on rock?" He nodded.

They recalled the unique covered wagon, towed by two sturdy, strong work horses that pulled their group of 20. The horses looked like cousins of Clydesdales. Jerry was the guide and owner of the fledgling business, and Manny was the driver. Jerry did double duty as the pooper-scooper and used the highly sought after fertilizer to offset the cost of owning the horses.

They had ridden by a peachy pink house with salmon-colored trim. A red sign hanging in the middle of the wall had the name WILLS on it. She'd taken a photo for her brother Will.

A golden retriever lay at the steps of a store. His name was Lucky. He was listed on formal documents as the owner of the shop. He also carried deposits to the bank and brought back receipts. He was the richest dog in Ketchikan. The couple were drawn to golden retrievers. Their four-year-old golden was at home with house-and-doggie-sitter, Sharon.

After reminiscing, Anne resumed her dissertation: "History. In 1887 the Tongass Packing Company discovered what natives had known for centuries—the fishing in Ketchikan was excellent. By the 1930s, 11 canneries were processing nearly two million salmon a year. Not surprisingly, by the 1940s the fish population declined and with it sank the economic importance of the fisheries to Ketchikan.

"As with most towns on the west coast of the US and Canada, Ketchikan received a huge boost from one of the many gold rushes that burned through the Northwest in the late 1800s. Major finds in the nearby hills and on Prince of Wales Island brought miners by the boatload. Ketchikan was incorporated as a mining town in 1900, and a customs house was set up to make it Alaska's first port of entry."

Standing on their veranda, warmth penetrated their winter white Oregonian skin. May and June had been on the cool side so far and they hadn't been exposed to much consistent sunshine. Next door neighbors, Mike and Kathy, were already pointing at various sites and reported seeing four bald eagles.

It sort of seemed like Peter and Anne's first time in Ketchikan instead of their fourth. They were looking at a completely different scene. It was the first time they were actually seeing the entire town. On their previous trips it had rained so hard or was socked in with fog that they never saw anything but the water and Main Street. It was a rainforest receiving easily over 140 inches of rain per year with only 16 days of sunshine. It was no wonder they'd never seen it before. It was charming. Now Ketchikan was down to 15 days as they took up one of the sunny days.

There were actually houses up the hill, just one block from Main Street, clogged with shops and restaurants. The first row of houses was a mix of mostly two-story houses on small lots. Most were painted shades of blue and brown with one green. There were some trees and shrubbery but few flowers except in boxes or planters.

A floatplane or seaplane skimmed along the top of the water then lifted its nose, noisily soaring off. Technically there is a difference between the two airplanes, but Peter didn't think Anne would care.

Watching each one take off, one right after another, reminded Anne of graceful flamingos they'd seen in the Caribbean. When one is starting to fly from water, it is peddling its feet fast and at the same time flapping its wings. When wings begin to carry most of the weight of the bird, it looks like the bird is walking or running on top of the water for several seconds. It happens almost the same way when flamingos are landing on water, as they soar down walking on the water, pushing their feet downward and forward. Their speed slows down nearly to zero just before their feet touch the ground. Just like these airplanes, she observed.

One of the couple's favorite things arriving in any port is to go to the top deck and walk the oval loop a few times to see the entire area. And for Peter to get his bearings. Anne had few bearings and it wouldn't matter or help her directionally-challenged compass. Once Peter could see the surroundings he never got lost. Another redeeming quality Anne appreciated.

Standing at the back of their ship, they joined Peggy and Rich as they watched Holland America's *Ryndam* ease its way gingerly against the dock behind their ship. It took about 20 minutes moving inch by inch almost touching the dock before it finally rested in its place for the day. Appearances are deceiving, but all agreed it looked like about one foot between the floating behemoths.

Men on the dock caught thick ropes tossed from the ship's workers. They tied the ropes around posts serving as anchors. Two walkways dropped from the side of the white and navy ship.

From their 12-story vantage point looking down, Ketchikan is a small town that radiates the step-back-in-time feeling. The main street skirts a waterfront built on pilings over the sea. Short side streets and steep, narrow wooden stairways lead to neighborhoods on the rocky hillside, now easy to see as they strolled on the top deck. Floatplanes were lined up along a building where one could purchase a scenic flight or rent kayaks.

Peter said, "Look, there's Sockeye Sam's." He pointed to a new two-story building at the end of the cruise dock.

"What's with that place?" Peggy asked. Peter told them that three years earlier on September 11, their ship bumped the dock on their early morning arrival. He could tell something was not right with odd sounds and extra noisy bow thrusters. Anne enhanced the memory by saying, "I told Peter I'll go see what I can find out. I rode the elevator making a pastry run for a light breakfast. Uniformed staff were talking about an incident. Acting like I was fully aware of the situation, I caringly asked if everyone was okay.

"The reply was no one was injured, and kayakers were fine. Mostly the ship was basically fine. One mumbled about the tons of paperwork ahead of them. Another grumbled that this will put us way behind schedule.

"Then, when getting off the ship, we saw the damage to Sockeye Sam's, the curios and gift shop. The metal flagpole was bent in half; the corner and top of the store were badly damaged with sheets of metal lying on the sidewalk. It was already cordoned off with yellow DO NOT CROSS tape.

"The ship's bow swung in and bumped the second floor of the shop. There was a black scuff mark and small rip or tear on the side of the ship. Of course, I took photos. The captain announced we wouldn't be leaving at the normal time because US Coast Guard were investigating. Good for cruisers, more time in Ketchikan.

"Two days earlier we had been invited to attend a Special Invitation for Cocktails with Captain Antonino Vito. That very evening was the reception. We eaves-dropped on several conversations about the morning fiasco and gleaned that three early morning kayakers were being pushed by the breeze toward the ship. The harbor captain, who was piloting the ship, made a move to avoid the trio bumping the dock. Even though Captain Vito wasn't at the helm, he was ultimately in command of the ship."

Anne wrapped up the saga by saying that when they arrived in Juneau the next day, they were front page news in the local newspaper, *Juneau Empire*, from which she clipped the article and took it home.

Peter concluded by saying, "If we have time, we should stop by the new store."

Before their main event excursion with David and Ellen was due to leave, Peter and Anne got off the ship and walked the wooden footbridge over Creek Street. Peter pointed toward the falls and salmon ladder. Hundreds of shimmery silver-bodied salmon were persistently wiggling their way up the creek. There were so many sharing the narrow creek, Anne wondered aloud if she could walk across water on their backs.

They rode the tram straight up the hill to Cape Fox Lodge taking about three minutes. The view was expansive from the corner of the restaurant where they sat to have a cup of chai—tea hot for him, iced for her. Their ship looked massive even though it was several hundred feet below. Seaplanes, boats, canoes, and kayaks dotted the water around the ships.

Leaving the lodge, someone already had a bonfire burning. The woody aroma of burning logs reminded Anne of her youth and making gooey s'mores around campfires on their camping trips. They easily walked down through the forest canopy. Anne felt a tickle on her hand. Soft lime green new growth on a needly fir brushed her as she went by.

They met up with Indiana friends, David and Ellen, and on the ride from the ship's dock to the excursion dock the friendly driver asked the typical cordial question, "Where are you folks from?" The conversation bounced back and forth between the driver and Anne.

"Salem, Oregon."

"Hmmmmmm, I have cousins who live there. I spent some time with them when I was young and visited Salem several times. They still live there."

"Really? Where did they go to school?"

"Oh, I don't recall, some private school."

"St. Mary's?"

"Nope."

"Salem Academy?"

"That sounds right, they called it SA."

"What's their last name?"

"Rose."

"As in Danny and Jody?"

The stunned guide replied, "Yes, they're my cousins along with a few more kids in the family."

Anne informed him her last name started with an R and she and Danny sat by each other in several classes they had together. She told him she'd seen Danny at several class reunions.

Ellen commented on it being such a small world. Peter added, "This happens all the time to us; she knows everyone or like this, just one degree of separation."

One person was going on the adventuresome excursion just being a good sport. He got seasick easily. The licensed guide would lead in his own zodiac with David piloting theirs. He was deemed captain having years of experience since they had a sailboat at home.

They donned the appropriate rubberized yellow gear for the men, orange for the women, royal blue lifejackets, gloves and boots provided by the company. Meanwhile, the company mascot, a fawn pug, seemed to enjoy watching them squeeze into squeaky clothing.

At the dock, an employee mentioned watching closely for orca as they are common in this area. Just as she finished as if she pushed the "Go" button, off the end of the dock several fins sliced through the water and then a few surfaced. Everyone wondered why several seals had hopped then flopped onto the dock. These were not stupid seals; they'd be lunch if they hadn't moved so quickly.

The orca were in a pack, almost like a migration of Canada geese in a V-formation. Then another group closed in and joined the others. The employee called it a "Super Pod" and they were after a school of salmon.

As the foursome carefully puttered away from the dock, a short distance away a woman was paddling her kayak with her small pooch standing right behind her, paws on the decking, looking forward over her right shoulder. It was picture-worthy.

Following the orca in their black zodiac, they felt like they were part of the super pod. Hearing the sounds of multiple orca spouting water, their language communicating with each other, was better than one of those *National Geographic* television specials. They stayed with the whales for a couple of miles until their guide veered in another direction.

Zodiacs don't come with shock absorbers and there was a chop that caused them to go up, and what goes up, does come down. With a thud. Trying to avoid going completely airborne, David did a couple of turns resulting in cold salty spray that felt chilly but harmless. The bone-jarring, butt-slamming ride through islands and seeing more incredible scenery didn't disappoint. The super pod had long since departed chasing elusive salmon.

After the zodiac experience and returning to the ship, they changed into lightweight clothing then walked a few blocks to Creek Street—famous or infamous, as a former red-light district whose houses, some restored, follow a curving plank road built over Ketchikan Creek. Walking along the wooden planks, Anne felt teleported back over 100 years. During the mining heyday this was home to residents like Frenchie, Dolly and Blind Polly. Several women were dressed in Gold Rush-era attire.

Gift shops line the cool, refreshing creek. A bear reportedly had been seen one day earlier getting his fill of salmon.

"New and Used Books" advertised on the sandwich board on the sidewalk at Hooked on Books, was right up her alley, or creek, in this case. She picked up a topographical map Peter's dad would enjoy.

They went into The Tongass Historical Society Museum with walls and displays of hundreds of exhibits of the Tlingit, Tsimshian and Haida Indian cultures, together with pioneer memorabilia and wildlife displays. A woman dressed in Tlingit clothing sat weaving a basket. They watched another woman sewing slippers and other items from leather, fur, feathers and heavy twine.

Peter picked up a brochure and read, "The bald eagle is found only on the North American continent. Adult eagles generally weigh between 9 and 12 pounds and have a wing-span of seven feet. Females are slightly larger. Immature eagles are mottled brown and white. The distinct white head and tail of the mature bird is developed between four and six years of age.

"Eagles feed mainly on fish, but waterfowl, small mammals, and dead and decaying flesh of dead animals supplement their diet, especially when fish are in short supply. Eagles can fly up to 30 mph and can dive at speeds up to 100 mph. Their keen eyesight allows them to spot fish at distances up to one mile.

"Bald eagles mate for life. Courting behavior begins in early April and often involves spectacular aerial displays of eagles diving and locking talons. Eagles lay from one to three eggs, commonly two, and the eggs usually hatch between late May and early June after a 34-day incubation period. The young usually leave the nest by early September."

Peter and Anne met up for a late lunch on the waterfront with Casey and Cathy. They shared fresh halibut and salmon, and finger-burning, seasoned crisp French fries. Peter and Casey had worked together for many years for the Oregon Department of Transportation Highway Division. The foursome walked behind Salmon Landing to the Discovery Center which had been the historic Spruce Mill. Now it is the location for the Great Alaskan Lumberjack show, really a rowdy competition between loggers representing Canada and the US and their rich logging history.

World champion athletes wearing spiked boots and hard hats compete in 12 athletic events that utilize seven-pound axes, six-foot razor sharp saws, tree climbing gaffs, and souped up chainsaws showing off thrilling displays of strength and agility.

Anne grew up in Albany, Oregon, which hosted an annual Timber Carnival based on Oregon's timber industry. She was used to the real thing with log rolls, axe tosses, men speed-climbing up a tree, tree topping, chainsaw carving, and a variety of chopping, like springboard, underhand and sawing crosscut. So, she skeptically assumed this show would be a waste of money, time and a big disappointment. She was wrong. It transported her back to her childhood, reliving the 4th of July Timber Carnival with several days of thrilling activities.

She read the lumberjack brochure, "In the earlier 1990s Alaska's timber industry was in full bloom. Rugged frontier lumberjacks toiled at work each day in one of North America's most grueling environments to harvest timber for our growing nation. From remote logging camps up and down the coast of southeast Alaska you could hear the pounding of the axe, the singing of the crosscut saw and the cry of *Timber!*

"Hardy lumberjacks would gather once each summer in the small sawmill town of Ketchikan to compete against rival logging camps. The fittest, ruggedest men fought hard to take home the bragging right of becoming the King of the Woods. Today the legends live on."

Anne sat captivated on the edge of the cushioned wooden bench in the covered grandstand the entire 60 minutes immersed in the action rooting for the Canadian team since they were assigned that quadrant of the outdoor arena. These guys were young and buff. In the log rolling competition, the American was the first to fall into the water. Canada won. For the speed climbing competition up the tree, the US won. Cheers encouraged the men as axes flew through the air, men free-fell from trees, and then ran atop spinning logs floating in the water.

After the impressive competition Anne made a beeline to where some of the guys were. Not shy, she blurted out, "Hey, I'm originally from Albany, Oregon. Any of you been to the Timber Carnival?"

Several answered *YES*, they had, and one said he was the world champ in the underhand chop. Another professed his first-place championship ribbon was from the log roll. "My favorite," she told him. The loggers talked of friendly locals who housed them, fed them and showed them around the area. One said he'd been there nine years in a row and still had the Timber Carnival buttons to prove it. Another mentioned the spectacular fireworks display and said he'd never seen anything better. They were as saddened as Anne when, because of lack of funding, the carnival ceased to exist.

On any vacation, Anne and Peter kept an eye out for something special that would remind them of a specific adventure or location they especially appreciated and enjoyed. At the Scanlon Gallery, Peter found a watercolor where the artist used a technique of cutting paper and layering it to create a 3D effect. The ice chunks in the water with a glacier in the distance, along with trees and scenery, would remind them of their special times in Alaska.

Anne discovered a print by Yukie Adams, a local artist, of a blue, red, black and white native Alaskan hummingbird flying toward the heavens with a background of crimson bell flowers. She was also drawn to Richard Shorty's colorful raven, orca and eagle prints.

Anne made some purchases that she'd store away and save for Christmas. She carried the artwork and Peter was loaded with bags of shirts, caps and gloves. Anne feared she might wear the numbers right off her Visa card. Heavily laden with their purchases, the couple buzzed onboard up to their room, dropped off their treasures and were back out in about 15 minutes.

Peter wanted to see the new version of Sockeye Sam's. While Anne looked for souvenirs, she noticed Peter speaking with a man. When they left, he excitedly told her that was the owner. Turned out they were the only ones on the *Regal Princess* that fateful day who had ever come and talked with him.

The store owner told Peter his version of that infamous morning. He received a call from dock authorities telling him his store was basically uninhabitable and if he wanted anything from it, he should come now. They gave him ten minutes before they cordoned it off. Because of the age of the building and with all new standards for building, it was demolished.

They lost income from three seasons. They went back and forth with insurance companies, but Princess Lines covered the replacement plus loss of income. New deep cement pilings and everything else up to standards made it probably the safest building in town. He'd added a second floor for people to use computers for emailing, especially for cruise ship crew from foreign countries.

———

With a few hours to use up before departure, they hitched a ride on a Duck boat with Larry and Suzanne and toured the town before arriving at a bay. The captain drove off the road right into the water, floating between two pillars. At the top of each stood a bald eagle. Another eagle was perched on a Speed 10 sign. This was an eagle hangout only because the salmon were everywhere, easy pickings for the lazy birds.

As they strolled back to the ship, their marvelous day wasn't over yet because after dinner they'd be sailing through fjords.

———

They were in for a real treat—tonight was the Alaska Heritage dinner.

Appetizers: Alaska crab legs, one order each.

No soup for them, nor salads.

Entrées: Pan-seared Alaska salmon fillet.

Desserts: Everyone at their table requested Baked Alaska, a dessert consisting of ice cream and cake topped with browned meringue.

CHAPTER FIFTEEN

After another luscious dinner, as they were changing into jeans before heading to the top deck, Anne took one minute and read, "Sailing the Misty Fjords National Monument, a 2.2 million-acre coastal ecosystem encompassing the east side of Revillagigedo Island and the portion of the mainland between Behm and Portland canals.

"Misty Fjords was designated a national monument in 1978. Within the monument, the deep fjords of Walker Cove and Rudyerd Bay penetrate the wilderness with sheer granite rock walls rising to 3,000. As the name implies, it's a moody and immensely beautiful environment of veiling peaks and waterfalls nourished by 150 inches of rain and snow a year, resulting in deep glacial fjords and waterfalls over 1,000 feet."

On deck, a zephyr touched both of their faces. Wondering if an angel had just brushed by her, Anne looked around but saw nothing. The soft west wind felt light and refreshing. She took a deep breath.

Tim and Heather were reclining in lounge chairs watching for whales to magically appear. "Whale!" both women exclaimed as they spotted the waterspout simultaneously. It was an entire pod of humpbacks.

Tim pointed out a black moving blob on the shoreline. Peter grabbed his binoculars confirming a bear sighting. Heather broke into laughter recalling a childhood memory. She told Anne that she grew up living on about 15 acres of forest in Montana. Sleeping soundly one night, the family woke to noises outside. Their dogs were barking nonstop. Her dad, who Anne had met so could picture the entire scenario in her mind, grabbed his .22, and in his underwear ran outside to find a good size black bear lumbering through their yard.

They lived on an Indian reservation and by law were not able to kill a bear but could scare it. The commotion of the dogs barking sent the bear knocking over garbage cans. The family, hearing a loud bang, assumed the father had shot at the bear.

Instead, the four-legged culprit ran right through the wooden slat fence taking out the top two boards and kept going. Their Shetland pony was fine but a little shaken. Dad reported that he hadn't even shot the gun. He repaired the fence the next day.

Anne had read that Misty Fjords are similar to fjords in Norway. This country was on Anne's list of "Must Visit" because both of her parents had grandmothers who emigrated from Norway as teenagers. She had Norwegian blood and would visit one day.

Entering the fjord they saw massive gray and black granite walls emerging from the depths of the navy blue water stretching toward the sky, blocking the direct sunlight. Several extremely tight areas caused Peter to doubt the mental acuity of the captain taking his humongous vessel through such a narrow passage. A portion of the fjord was blanketed in green forest until halfway morphing into a steep gray wall.

Looping around the top deck, Anne and Peter encountered niece Kelly and husband Darren. The four stood marveling at double waterfalls cascading then disappearing in the firs then gushing out like a gigantic firehose over gray rocks, finally emptying into the ocean. Rain earlier in the week created dozens and dozens of raging torrents that normally weren't there.

Anne stopped taking photos of waterfalls unless spectacular, which to her, most were. But she knew from past experience that seeing something like this in person is much better than as a photo later. She'd also learned to stand and enjoy the moment, soaking it in. Some things just couldn't be captured on film, but she could the retain that snapshot in her mind forever. The orange-streaked sunset peaked through scattered puffy clouds that created shadow creatures on top of the calm water the color of blueberries.

A quick glance at his watch told Darren that it was a few minutes to 12 which meant it was time for the midnight buffet. He hadn't missed one yet and didn't intend to start now no matter how remarkable the scenery. Before heading downstairs, they laughed as he recounted in detail all the food and drink he'd consumed that day.

Anne and Peter did a quick pass through the seafood extravaganza noticing all the fresh shrimp one could ever eat. Crab legs were piled high next to full-size lobster. They were both tempted but didn't even have one bite.

But the fresh bread display was the most remarkable. Breadsticks three-feet long and several different diameters, depending on the type of bread, popped out of baskets made of bread. One breadbasket sat on top of another flipped upside down. It held salted pretzels. Two hearts of swirling knotted bread held two lovebirds inside. Sunflowers were constructed of different breads. Ribbons of thin breadsticks made several shapes, the turtles getting Anne's thumbs up as #1.

Anne and Peter headed to their stateroom and stood on the veranda. The weather was delightful, and they agreed to keep the sliding glass door open all night for fresh air. The sun would not set completely, another thing Anne loved about Alaska, but it did cut into her sleep time.

CHAPTER SIXTEEN

C lint picked up a note left on the kitchen counter in his apartment in Juneau. "Meet me at the Triangle Club by yourself." He recognized Ericka's handwriting.

It was in the oldest part of Juneau and the actual site of the club is seaward of the original shoreline and, like other structures in the 1880s, built on pilings. Ericka liked the warmth of the wood interior.

When she arrived, all the stools along the lengthy wooden bar were filled mostly with men. One woman draped in a flowy white cape sat squeezed like an Oreo cookie.

Joe Junior ran the place after he'd bought it from his dad in the 1960s. It was a family affair with a daughter, Lizann, helping out. She waved as Ericka entered. Ericka nabbed the two-person table in the back corner. Clint arrived and after a bear bug and peck on her cheek, they both ordered a beer and coconut prawns, one of her favorites. Ericka said, "Let's do dinner at my place if that's okay with you."

"Sure, that's great," he replied.

She pensively said, "Clint, I've got something to tell you and I am afraid you're not going to like it. I've been meaning to explain some things to you for quite some time. I just couldn't work up the nerve." Her normally spirited eyes looked apprehensive.

"What's up, Hon, it can't be that bad?" a little nervous himself. He had deep feelings for her and knew he loved her but just hadn't found the right moment to share this revelation.

"Okay, here goes," and she blurted out everything about Seattle, which he silently listened to just as he did the first time she'd told him when she was drunk. At least the stories were the same and she wasn't lying.

"I told Tyrone never to contact me again and I also told him that I told you all about it and him. He hasn't contacted me in three days. Finally, I think he got it."

"You told me all of this a few years ago in Seattle one night when you were very drunk. I didn't know if you were telling me the truth or not, but I chose not to bring it up unless you did. I figured it was all over when you moved here. Now, you need to let me know if you hear from him again, Ericka. This is serious and it has gone on way too long."

She let out a huge sigh of relief, "I promise, I will. Thank you for being so understanding and offering to help. Now, let's go to my place. Cher, Bette, or Madonna?" She knew he really, really, really liked her assortment of famous singers' wigs. She had two of Cher's popular styles. One long, black and straight, and the other long, black with lots of curls.

"Surprise me. But I can't stay late tonight. I have the early shift on the glacier and I'm going up early with Tony. One of the guys called in sick, so I'm taking a double shift. But I'll see you tomorrow night and we'll have more time together. I want to talk to you, but it can wait."

Ericka was already formulating a mid-morning surprise for him.

CHAPTER SEVENTEEN

Wednesday. Well, that's what the carpet on the elevator floor read anyway. She appreciated the daily change because she had a tendency to lose track of days on vacation. It was day four of their cruise.

Zooming up the outside of the ship in a glass elevator, Anne noticed sunbeams ricochet off the flat water creating the impression of sparkly diamonds floating above the sapphire water. One might assume they were cruising on a calm lake instead of the Pacific ocean.

They had neglected to put the breakfast menu request outside their stateroom door before midnight, so while her husband Peter showered, she made a dash to the buffet to bring back their breakfast. Anne piled a plate with bacon and a generous scoop of scrambled eggs for token protein. She juggled a bowl of watermelon and a small plate of four slices of the best breakfast bread ever, a sweet loaf with raisins and other chopped fruit. Using her elbow, she pressed the round glowing deck 9 button on the elevator panel.

Arriving back in their stateroom, Peter was dressed and ready to share what sustenance she provided.

While eating a piece of watermelon, Anne read aloud everything printed in the daily *Gazette*.

"Nestled within the Inside Passage is Alaska's first truly American city. Founded 13 years after the purchase of Alaska, it was Juneau, more importantly its gold, that captured the imagination of the American public. The majority of the US population doubted the wisdom of the purchase. Most considered it a worthless frozen wasteland but in 1880 two drunk pioneers carried home the gold that was to start a series of gold rushes, and established Alaska's worth in America's eyes.

"Today's City — The mountains that cradle Juneau were rich in low-grade gold ore, eventually resulting in the Juneau and Treadwell mines. Although the mines are long since closed, the Gold-Rush flavor of Juneau's early days lingers in such landmarks as the gold-rush style saloons. But even though a modern city has sprung up on the "tailings" of those historic mines, much of the free-and-easy atmosphere remains. Juneau boasts modern hotels and shopping areas, museums, churches and restaurants.

"A few miles by car from the city center—and less by boat —is one of North America's largest wilderness settings—the Tongass National Forest. Thirteen miles northeast of town is Mendenhall Glacier, one of the largest glaciers in Alaska that is accessible by road. Other nearby glaciers including the Taku, Eagle River, Herbert and Lemon Creek. And above them all lies one of the continent's most extensive icefield, the 5,000 square mile Juneau Ice Field."

Anne took a sip of V8 juice and a bite of fruit bread then continued reading—

"History — Juneau Mining provided Juneau's early economic base when in 1880, Richard Harris and Joe Juneau discovered quartz outcroppings streaked with gold. Within 15 days, they had written a code of laws for the newly created Harris Mining District and staked a 160-acre town site along the channel. Many turn of the century buildings still stand on the People's Wharf along historic South Franklin Street.

"By the spring of 1881, Gold Creek was crawling with prospectors. A San Francisco carpenter named Jon Treadwell made a lucky strike near Ready Bullion Creek which was to produce more than 70 million dollars in gold over the next four decades. When gold's tides ebbed, commercial fishing and canneries became Juneau's chief source of revenue. The halibut fleet remains but the canneries have disappeared."

Peter swallowed his last bite just as Anne finished her morning ritual, the *Gazette* reading. Standing on their veranda, she gulped the final bites of her breakfast. The closer they got to the city, more homes with gardens and yards lined the waterfront.

Inching into their place behind another ship, Anne looked up at Mount Juneau at 3,500 feet, squatty in comparison to other mountains. It was partially cloaked in a lacy snowy shawl. The mountain made a picturesque backdrop with the city sheltered at its base. There are plenty more mountains in close proximity but this one is just one and a half miles east of downtown in the Boundary Range.

The mountain receives about 300 percent more rain than downtown Juneau gets, about 91 inches per year on average. Anne thought the 40 inches of rainfall they received a year was plenty. Ready on the port side, seaplanes gently bobbed from the ship's wake with Juneau on the starboard side.

He tapped his watch as a subtle reminder that they needed to head out soon. "Five minutes, maybe six," she promised and disappeared into the compact, yet efficient bathroom.

Four minutes later, she verbally read off her checklist to Peter and he replied to each question.

Camera? Check.
Extra batteries? Check.
Binoculars? Check.
Sunglasses? Check.
Room key? Check.

They walked around the ship's deck and looked down from the 12th floor at the capital city laid out before them. Dozens of stores and restaurants that line the main drag weren't open for business yet. A bald eagle perched on the top of a light pole overlooking the waterfront.

Behind their ship now was a lineup of another cruise ship, three yachts and a fishing trawler.

"Ready for our glacier adventure?" Peter said.

"Let's do this," was her answer as they strolled off the ship to fulfill one of their dreams—walking on a glacier.

Glacier guides rotated their daily responsibilities in determining the safety for tourists. Today was Clint's turn. Following protocol, he walked around checking for any potential or obvious dangers such as new puddles and crevasses. That morning he marked several places with small orange flags which meant *Do Not Approach*. He would do this throughout the day. He had placed four flags today, not bad compared to some warm days.

He and Tony were working the same shift today. This wasn't normal. Tony had the early shift and Clint the later, but they were short a guide today, so Clint had volunteered to come in early and take a double shift.

After his first two tour groups, Clint returned to the camp trailer for a break and to retrieve the pole used for safety purposes. The protocol was always the same—two tours then recheck the vicinity following safety practices.

He was pleasantly surprised when Ericka appeared with his favorite snacks: almonds, bagels and kombucha.

Clint thought he loved Ericka. How would anyone know for sure? They sure felt compatible sharing similar likes in food, drink, books, movies, and outdoor sports. Their indoor activities seemed to please them both, too.

He mentioned at the restaurant the night before that he would take a double shift that day. She made him feel special taking time from her morning job at the bakery to buy a ticket, even though discounted for family and friends of employees, to deliver his favorite munchies.

As she tossed her long black Cher hair, she flirted and winked as she reminded him of dinner that night at her place and waved bye as she rejoined the tour group. He loved her naturally blonde hair, but the long black Cher wig made him slightly crazy especially with her heavenly deep, astonishing arctic eyes. He intended to speak with her that evening about his feelings and their future.

He gobbled down both bagels, two handfuls of almonds from a plastic baggie, and chugged his home-brew kombucha from a mason jar. How thoughtful that she'd stopped by his place and got some of his own instead of store-bought. It reaffirmed his earlier decision to give her the front door key. He needed to let Tony know about the key situation.

Clint put on his lightweight orange jacket and matching hat then grabbed the pole and stepped out of the trailer, leaving a few almonds, a small chunk of super cinnamon bagel in the sack, and the jar with just a drop or two of fluid at the bottom.

He thought it best to check out the areas he previously marked and headed back to one area that concerned him the most.

That's strange, he mumbled to himself, sort of out of breath becoming rapidly exhausted. His right arm and leg trembled causing him to stumble slightly but he caught himself before falling. "Weird," he said out loud. Then his entire body shook like when he got really cold then hot.

As he walked down a slight incline toward the crevasse, his legs ached, then tingled, then stabbing pains like scalding bolts of lightning, then they gave out.

On his knees, he spotted Tony across the glacier. He yelled *HELP! HELP, TONY!!* but the incoming helicopter drowned out his shouts. Clint raised his arm to wave trying to get anyone's attention just as convulsions eliminated any coordination. The piercing spasm caused him to slide closer to the edge of the crevasse.

As he tumbled down headfirst, something caught and stopped him falling into infinity. He could hear his heart beating faster into palpitations. Something was crushing his chest. He couldn't breathe. Feeling his pulse getting weaker and weaker, he fell asleep knowing he loved Ericka.

He would never wake up.

CHAPTER EIGHTEEN

Dock-to-dock transportation was part of the deal. During a 30-minute scenic ride through the Mendenhall Valley, Anne saw fields and lush meadows bursting with purple lupine and tiny white wildflowers growing along streams.

While they sat on the bench seat behind the driver, he struck up a friendly conversation. First typical question: Where were they from? Peter carried on the back-and-forth chit chat while Anne scanned for wildlife, instead seeing mostly Forget-Me-Nots, the Alaska state flower, and indescribably stunning scenery.

Hard to ignore, she overheard some verbal interaction directly behind them. Clearly, a woman wasn't thrilled with her unexpected gift.

Arriving at the heliport, their group of five was escorted into a large waiting room where each was asked to sign a waiver. Anne heard a young female voice ask her companion, "A waiver? Why do we need to sign a waiver? I am not emotionally prepared for this. You should have told me. Is this helicopter tour such a great idea?" She didn't even breathe between words.

Lacking any helpful reassurance, the male dimwittedly replied, "Hey, do you want to grab a snack?" The young woman rolled her eyes and replied, "Are you crazy? A snack? How can you think of food right now?" Anne inwardly laughed especially at the dramatic eye roll and tried not to look their way again.

Each person pulled on bright yellow, slippery rubberized pants then matching long overcoats that reached their knees. They would put on spiked boots over their footwear when they reached the glacier. Anne secretly nicknamed themselves the Yellow Jackets.

The young woman was taking a while to dress into the waterproof getup and Anne couldn't help but overhear the continued dialogue. The woman said the butterflies had turned into rocks in her stomach. Anne simply couldn't overlook or ignore the conversation any longer between the couple sitting beside her on the bench. She felt sorry for the young brunette. The nervous nelly had worked herself up to just about a panic attack. Anne figured she'd soon need a paper bag to breathe in and out to prevent hyperventilating if she didn't get a grip.

Time to butt in, Anne thought. "Excuse me," she started, then reassured the 20-something female that the fear wouldn't last long. Clearly the woman was scared yet the male acted like he wasn't, but who knew. Anne told her a couple of reassuring stories about fearful fliers going up in their hot air balloon. Anne suggested Nervous Nelly take several deep breaths, in and out, in and out, in and out, and Nelly confessed she felt a touch better.

Forms completed and everyone outfitted in glacier gear, they were pointed in the direction of the white and red helicopter, idling on the round helipad. Peter had studied up and reported to Anne that the *Eurocopter* has a single engine and was originally designed and manufactured in France. Its nickname, The Squirrel, is known for its high-altitude performance. This all seemed meaningful to Peter, but all Anne asked about was its safety record, which he reported was excellent. Developed to comply with noise requirements in places such as national parks, together with a low in-cabin noise level where passengers could easily talk during flight, and nice big picture windows, now that's what Anne really cared about.

The idling engine sounded like an airplane landing. The smell of diesel fuel hung in the air until a gentle breeze pushed it away. A man in a navy uniform holding a clipboard walked around the helicopter bending down, touching and jiggling mechanisms, moving objects back and forth, inspecting his aircraft. Anne pointed this out to Nervous Nelly reassuring her that all safety protocols were taken seriously.

After a safety briefing, they climbed aboard the mechanical bird beginning their epic adventure. Peter lucked out getting the prime front passenger seat next to the pilot. Anne sat directly behind Peter with a window view. The fretful fliers sat next to her with Nervous Nelly squeezed in the middle seat. The fifth person in the group sat in the third row by herself. They were instructed how to use the headphones and the switch-type button that could be used to communicate with the pilot.

Once they were situated with seatbelts tightened and headsets on, the pilot started pushing buttons and flipping switches. The idling now sounded like a pulsing *wop wop*, generated by the three blades right above their heads.

A medium-pitch whine started once the rotors reached about half speed. The pitch rose in shrillness the faster the rotors whirled. At full speed the rotors were spinning so fast that Anne couldn't focus on them.

With the gentle liftoff, she didn't even notice until the ground got farther and farther away. Above the heliport she looked at Juneau, with Mendenhall Glacier dipping down through the mountains. They circled over Gastineau Channel so they could get a bird's eye view of the long line of cruise ships on one side and the town of Douglas opposite Juneau.

They left the capital city and water in the rearview mirror. Soaring over the rain forest, lakes, and ice, they could see alpine ridges and mountain peaks. The pilot pointed out Mendenhall Towers—the rock sentinels that extend over 7,000 feet.

This sunny morning, they had perfect visibility for miles in all directions. Climbing above the trees, Juneau became a dot, then disappeared. It looked like they were barely clearing the tallest trees she'd ever seen. She only noticed a difference in the forests of cedar and spruce due to the shades of green. Silty aqua glacial lakes dotted the sprawling views.

Up and over the hilltops that quickly became 8,000 foot mountains, Anne whimsically thought of herself soaring with the bald eagles with their eagle eye perspective. She felt jealous. She wanted the eagle to be her spirit animal. Or maybe a humpback whale.

The pilot told them Mendenhall Glacier is 13 miles long and about 36 square miles, and part of a network of 38 major glaciers. At the speed they were flying, 60 mph, they'd land two miles up-glacier in a short time. It seemed much faster to Anne and they weren't wasting any time whizzing from sea level to glacier level.

Patting Nervous Nelly's gloved hand, "You're doing swell," Anne reassured her. The previously queasy flier got over the butterflies, becoming absorbed in the incredible landscape below. She announced proudly that her fears disappeared like melting snowflakes. They turned in their seats, rotating their heads 360 degrees, not wanting to miss a thing. Too bad their heads didn't spin like an owl.

Sitting in the cushy seats of their flying taxi, they learned about the history from the pilot through the headsets. He said the glacier and surrounding area is all part of the Tongass National Forest which is the largest national forest in the United States standing at over 17 million acres and covering most of southeast Alaska. Surprisingly, about ten million acres of Tongass are actually forested, while the remaining seven million are covered in ice, rock, water and wetlands. Most mountains are over 8,000 feet high. Some even higher.

Anne poked and pointed, making sure Peter wasn't missing a thing below. Her nose was pressed flat against the window and she saw Peter's would have been too except he had a video camera between him and the window. The large windows provided a remarkable view of rock formations, rain forests, waterfalls, ice spires, vibrant blue crevasses, crags, mountains and valleys. They scanned the peaks for wildlife including bears, deer and mountain goats. They didn't see one. Now calm, Nervous Nelly excitedly said that the glacier looked frozen in place.

Flying over rivers of ice, blue emerged and the backseat passenger asked the pilot, "What's with the blue streaks? Snow is white, isn't it?" The pilot explained that glacial ice appears blue because it absorbs all colors of the visible light spectrum except blue, which it transmits. The transmission of this blue wavelength gives glacial ice its blue appearance. The ice can also appear white because some ice is highly fractured with air pockets and indiscriminately scatters the visible light spectrum.

In other words, after it gets pressed into glacier ice it turns into a beautiful cobalt color. Evidently some glaciers can even be red where certain algae have started growing, or grayish brown where dust, gravel and rocks have accumulated.

The flight up revealed miles of blue and white ice that had created the glacier, named after a scientist in 1881. The sapphire sky reflected off the snow. Even wearing sunglasses, Anne's eyes squinted almost shut.

She wasn't silent often but sat spellbound by the remote beauty of frozen rivers of ice backed by rugged, ice-capped mountain peaks, most with snow. It looked like a master painter had dipped her brush into a bucket of white then splashed and sprinkled it willy-nilly.

The glacier reminded Anne of a softly crumpled piece of striped blue and white writing paper used in high school. Yet it transformed before their eyes into huge peaks of ice stretching toward distant mountains.

They saw a torrent of melted water that made a hole into the glacier's side, carving out a huge void. It looked treacherous. Equally intriguing were the sides of the glacier, as it ripped the mountainsides, pulling down boulders, gravel and dirt.

The pilot approached slowly, inching down onto the famous glacier that now appeared not to have a flat place on the entire surface, just many pokey spires of ice with deep blue crevasses and glacial pools, all creating the mighty Mendenhall.

With wheels, or rather helicopter skids, they landed gently on the ice two miles up-glacier. With rotors whirling, Anne couldn't hear the pilot's instructions as they clambered out of the winged taxi, but they understood his hand signals. He pointed to the man waving his arms and holding a small orange flag. They disembarked in the yellow shiny gear, right onto the slick ice.

The helicopter pilot loaded up five now experienced glacier-walkers and flew away. A guide named Tony greeted them and explained that the only sounds they would hear for the next 30 minutes were cracks and pops from constantly moving ice. They were instructed not to step in what might appear to be a small pool of water. It was more likely than not to be the top of a deep hole. He added that safety protocols are taken very seriously and several times throughout the day one of the guides tests ice, puddles and deep crevasses.

Some distance away was a stream of large rocks and boulders about the size of a Volkswagen Bug. On the ice beside the river of rocks looked to be about a 15-foot metal hut, shaped like a travel trailer. It reminded Anne of the one that her family camped in during her childhood. An American flag on a pole was poked into the ice. It was a shelter for the guides to use for a break.

Having slipped on the heavy spikey boots, she nervously announced, "So far so good," with the first several baby steps and just minor slippage. Peter was feeling secure but Anne not so much. She declined a ski pole for extra stability as it could inhibit her picture-taking abilities.

Strangers to each other only one hour earlier, the troop of five carefully ambled with Tony who would show them around the glacier. Anne recalled a favorite song by the sister and brother duo, The Carpenters. Karen had a marvelous, pleasing-to-the-ear, contralto range and she sang, "I'm on the top of the world, looking down on creation…" Anne felt like shouting it out but refrained.

Boots with metal spikes clomped into the solid ice as the previously nervous couple stomped with gusto into hundreds of feet of layers of snow that created Mendenhall Glacier in the Juneau Icefield of southwest Alaska! Anne pinched Peter just making sure they were really, really there —on a glacier.

Guide Tony looked about 16. Anne was slightly reassured when he said that he'd been a guide for two summers on the glacier. He explained that the annual snowfall on the Juneau Icefield exceeds 100 feet. Mild summers cause winter snow accumulation to exceed summer snowmelt at higher elevations. Year after year, snow accumulates, compacting underlying snow layers from previous years into solid ice. Mendenhall Glacier is one of many large glaciers that flow from a 1,500 square mile expanse of rocks, snow and ice known as the Juneau Icefield. As glacial ice continues to build, gravity pulls the ice down the mountainside. The glacier slowly scours the bedrock and grinds down its 13-mile journey to Mendenhall Lake, where Peter and Anne stood years earlier, when they first dreamed of this adventure.

Tony told them that President Harrison appointed Thomas Mendenhall, who served as superintendent of the US Coast and Geodetic Survey from 1889 to 1894. He was a noted scientist and served on the Alaska Boundary Commission that was responsible for surveying the international boundary between Canada and Alaska. In 1892, the glacier was renamed to honor Mendenhall. Anne felt a bit sad when Tony added that it was previously called Auke Glacier, named by naturist John Muir in 1879 after the Aak'w Kwaan of the Tlingit Indians.

Tony directed the group to stay together and to follow him, because the area could be dangerous although it had been checked earlier and would be throughout the day.

Cracks and crevasses were deceiving and hidden. Only an expert eye could see where holes and possible deathtraps were hidden under the fresh blanket of snow. Even though mid-June, it could snow all year round in the icefield. It just needed to be cold enough, which was often. They followed him in a row, like baby yellow goslings after their mamma goose. They walked gingerly yet firmly, watching each step, Anne uneasy about the possibility of falling to her death down a deep crevasse, never to be seen again.

During the trek, they discovered tunnel-like sections of ice, as well as tiny waterfalls that proved the ice is not as firm as it appeared when they flew over earlier. Tony said that the landscape continually changes, and each day brings something new for the glacier.

The group carefully walked on some gravelly ice. On a slight incline, Anne felt skittish. She wasn't a mountain goat after all, and she had a propensity for turning her left ankle. The terrain across the glacier was varied, with some areas flat and easy to walk on while others had daunting slopes or deep crevices.

Seeing it from above was one thing but walking on it was totally something else. It's even more striking when standing on the surface and seeing the chasms you could slip or fall into if you are not careful enough. Peter had his right arm tucked firmly through Anne's left arm, leaving her picture-taking arm free. She had adapted well over the years learning a one-handed technique. He would have harnessed her if he could.

Tony reminded them to step firmly, almost stomping their feet. Standing at the end of a wide crack in the ice, Anne felt like she was looking into a kaleidoscope of her favorite hues: Aqua to turquoise, cobalt to periwinkle then disappearing into deep teal and blackness. It looked like velvety streamers of colors in the blue family.

Meltwater generated a rushing stream of glacial silt. Tony said that every minute of ice melt could fill an Olympic-size swimming pool. He had a walking stick with a sharp pokey thing like a long nail on the end that he used often to test the depth of a puddle.

He told them about the glacier as they explored the surface of the ice. He said, "Glaciers form because snowfall in high mountain ranges exceeds snowmelt. Snowflakes first change to granular snow—round ice grains—but are soon pressed into a mass of ice by the weight of the accumulating layers above. When the ice becomes heavy enough, the entire mass breaks loose at the bottom and begins a slow motion avalanche down the mountain, moving from an inch to as much as several feet in a single day. Fragmented bedrock and boulders are pushed aside and over the years fjords and inlets are created. Softened by the warmer sea air and eroded by seawater, tremendous chunks of the 300-foot high ice cliffs calve or crack and crash into the bay below." He guaranteed that on the cruise the group would see a glacier calving.

He explained, "Blue bergs are dense and old. Greenish-black bergs are from the glacier's bottom. Dark-striped brown bergs carry remains from the joining of tributary glaciers. How high an iceberg floats depends on its size, the ice's density, the water's density, and how much rock and debris the berg has collected. But whatever the conditions, know that the part showing above the water is minuscule compared to what is below, and what you see is just the tip of the iceberg." He concluded that what they were seeing that morning would end up as icebergs going to Mendenhall Lake, and how long that would take would depend on the weather.

Peter looked left to the vacant air where his wife had just been standing. He did a 180 and saw her almost jumping up and down, waving her arms. Why was he surprised? She was a magnetic force for discoveries of various types, at least one or two per vacation.

Some of their serendipitous sightings included seeing Prince Charles and Nelson Mandela in a car in downtown Oxford, England. Nelson waved at her. They were so close to Queen Elizabeth II and Prince Philip at the Empress Hotel in Victoria, British Columbia that Anne could have offered the Queen a cup of tea. Instead, Anne bought a china teacup and saucer with the Queen's face on it. She encountered the Duke of Marlborough's younger brother, another case of a spare to an heir, outside of Blenheim Palace in England.

He remembered several years earlier on a cruise when their ship bumped into a dock in Ketchikan and wiped it out along with Sockeye Sam's store. She had discovered what really happened by striking up an innocent conversation with crew in the elevator when returning to their stateroom with breakfast.

Anne's flailing not only caught the attention of Peter but Tony, too, and three others in their group. Waving her hands wildly in the air, they probably thought she was having a seizure. Tony asked the other three to stay put. He and Peter carefully walked toward Anne.

———

Her memory transported her back almost three decades when she was 14 years old and her family had discovered a body in the headwaters of the Metolius River in Central Oregon, while on their annual camping trip.

She instinctively reached for the gold cross hanging around her neck hidden under layers of clothing. She didn't wear it every day like she had when her parents gave it to her on her 13th birthday. But she brought it along on the trip because she knew they'd appreciate seeing her wear it all these decades later.

Anne felt light-headed. She remembered her advice given to Nervous Nelly—breathe deeply—three times, in and out, in and out, in and out. She did but this time it didn't help.

Déjà vu 29 years later, now Anne wished they never had gone up that glacier. Their expedition turned out to be a lot more than they bargained for. Anne discovered a boot that they could only assume belonged to a person below.

A somber Anne and group returned to their whirling taxi taking their original places. In a complete role reversal, the previous Nervous Nelly patted Anne's gloved hand and told her reassuringly, "You're doing swell." Anne turned and eye-to-eye gave Nelly a grateful little smile.

Their informative pilot flew over the icefield, low so everyone could soak in the grandeur and the awesome power of the glaciers. To Anne, it looked like a soft billowy ribbon of light to dark turquoise hues. Reaching the end of the icefield they flew over the edge of a sheer mountain that abruptly ended. Land was thousands of feet below. Anne made the mistake of looking down. She peeked just enough through her tightly closed eyes to see ocean and Juneau in the distance.

When they landed, a Juneau police officer stood awaiting their arrival. The helicopter pilot pointed at Anne and the officer approached her. He requested she come to the station to make a statement. She agreed they would come at three o'clock as they had another excursion to do.

CHAPTER NINETEEN

On the glacier, Tony recalled that the tourist said she hadn't looked down into the crevasse, only seeing the boot sole and maybe she'd seen some piece of clothing or maybe a hem.

But he did need to look. He couldn't see very far before the blackness enveloped the crack in the glacier. There was somebody attached to the boot. Tony yelled, "Hey, are you okay? Buddy, are you okay?" Stillness was his answer. With only two years' prior experience, he had been made supervisor of the team. He hadn't been trained for this. A twisted ankle, yes. A broken arm, yes. But not this.

With a new group of glacier explorers, Tony professionally explained there was a safety issue that had to be checked out. His five were integrated into Brad and Kent's groups and Tony told the guides to move to another area of the glacier keeping far away from the boot.

All sorts of things darted through his mind: a person, dead or unconscious? Knowing they all had first aid training, should they trying to hoist the person out and deliver CPR? What to do with all the tourists?

Tony knew that the helicopter pilots came with five and returned with a different five, never more or less. Everyone paid by credit card for their ride, so would be easy to track, if necessary. Within five minutes, all pilots reported back that their numbers matched perfectly, five up and five down.

So, if it wasn't a passenger, it had to be one of them. There were normally three tour groups at a time on the glacier. Two other guides would rotate giving each guide time for a coffee, lunch break, and toilet stops, too.

He nervously radioed the small camp trailer and asked who was there. Brandon replied that he was the only one there. Tony radioed the two other guides again. Brad and Kent were accounted for. He asked, "Have you seen Clint?" The answer from all was no but Kent added, "I haven't seen him since he had the snack his girlfriend brought him." The hairs on the back of Tony's neck stood up. "His what?" he almost shouted into the radio? Kent replied, "You know, the tall blonde he dates? Except she had black long hair today. Like Cher."

Tony had a sickening sinking feeling. They needed assistance from the police and fast. *Call the police now!* a voice thundered inside his head. He headed to the trailer to make the emergency call for help.

The boot was near one of those flags. Why did someone go over there? When did someone go over there? Tony kept wondering. If the boot did belong to Clint, this would shock Tony. Why would he wander into an area that he had clearly marked earlier in the morning as potential danger? He knew better. It didn't make any sense. Unless he was just checking to see if there were any changes. He also knew Clint well enough to know he'd never leave his job without telling someone. Clint was the only person unaccounted for.

Time was about up for this batch of tourists. Three helicopters landed this time with empty seats, departing with the final groups of the day. Soon the area would be swarming with law enforcement.

This single event set off a chain reaction like a row of falling dominoes that would change lives forever.

———

Tony's mind wandered as three guides huddled together waiting for police to arrive. He stood away from the nervously jabbering trio who shared all sorts of recollections of that morning.

He thought about Clint, his friend. It couldn't be him down there, but his gut was telling him differently. Tony's mind jumped back several months earlier. As a result of Clint's past in Seattle, Tony was going to bite the bullet and tell Clint who he's seen twice. His old wacko girlfriend, Ericka.

While having dinner and listening to a mix of Elton John, Jewel and Backstreet Boys, the roommates caught up on their day. Drinking a freshly brewed batch of kombucha, Tony told Clint about spotting Ericka, and pointedly added who he still considered a whack job, unhinged and mentally unstable.

Clint had seen her, too, then pleaded for Tony to give her a second chance. "She's fine and doing really good," he convinced Tony. Tony gave in. So she's been over a few times. As Clint escorted her the first time to their apartment, she was hit with an aroma of spicy Italian sausage and cheeses. She said it smelled just like an Italian restaurant in Seattle. Clint told her it's Tony's special lasagna.

"Mmmm," escaped from Ericka's lips, after the first bite.

"Mmmm good or mmmm needs something?" Tony inquired.

"Mmmm delicious."

The three of them ate an entire pan of it in one sitting, and Tony conceded to himself, they had a good time with no alarm bells going off. Tony wasn't blind and could plainly see Clint and Ericka were crazy about each other. This was much more serious than their time in Seattle.

Tony did admit it was fun cooking for someone other than just the two of them. Another time having ravioli, she was equally impressed. She asked Clint if he cooked and he sheepishly admitted, "Ramen noodles and maybe a tuna noodle casserole, if absolutely necessary." His soft, yet mischievous deep green eyes with flecks of brown, sparkled at her. She could care less if he couldn't cook, lost in the kindest eyes she'd ever seen.

On their second glass of vino and Ericka's final bite of the most delicious ravioli she'd ever tasted, Tony asked about her upbringing.

She said, "Well, Clint has heard much of this already, but I am Ericka Rose Engebretson and, contrary to Clint, I am proud of my heritage and last name. My grandparents never thought to shorten it like many immigrants. If someone doesn't pronounce it right, I correct them: en-GAAAH-brrrrret-son."

Both men sat intrigued as Ericka told the story about her grandfather who said he watched Europe falling to Hitler starting in 1938 with Austria. Then in 1939, the remainder of Czechoslovakia. By August 1939 Poland fell. He'd always used the same verbiage, "Repeatedly, allies did nothing to help." In 1940, Denmark, Norway, Belgium, The Netherlands, Luxembourg and France were invaded.

Her grandfather Lars saw the Nazis rolling across the area with not much stopping them. He packed up his wife Hannah and they left by ship fleeing on February 1, 1940, two months before Germany invaded Norway. They left their comfortable family home and took what they could of their private belongings.

They emigrated to Minnesota where other Norwegian families already resided. Lars had been a butcher by trade and easily found a job. Her grandparents spoke little English when they arrived, but Lars insisted that he and Hannah, and any future children, would only speak English, the language of their new homeland.

Many Norwegians joined the American military fighting the Nazis. Lars was seriously wounded by a bullet that shattered his left arm. He wrote with his right hand, so felt as grateful as possible. He was shipped home and after several surgeries, recovered and went through rehabilitation for nine weeks in a hospital around Washington, D.C.

During his recuperation he heard that Norway's Crown Princess Märtha, who also fled Norway, lived in the area with her three children. During a visit to the United States before the war, Märtha and Crown Prince Olav V had established a close relationship with President Roosevelt.

The Crown Princess' father-in-law was King Haakon VII. Crown Prince Olav, who had extensive military training, stood by his father resisting the German occupation of their homeland. When the Norwegian government decided to go into exile, he offered to stay behind with the Norwegian people, but this was declined. He reluctantly followed his father to the United Kingdom, where he and his staff continued to be advisors to the exiled government and his father.

One memorable day that grandpa Lars would talk about his entire life was when the Crown Princess came into the hospital recovery room and stopped, picking up his chart attached at the end of the bed. She greeted him by name asking about his wounded arm. He said it was really nothing compared to others.

She told him he was brave. He was awestruck by her kindness. He only saw her once, but others said she came often and visited other hospitals where Norwegian soldiers were recovering.

After grandpa mended, he returned home again working as a butcher. By the late 1940s, her grandparents were convinced they could not have children. Then ten years after coming to the United States they did. And then two more US citizens would be born. Their first son, Nels, was Ericka's father. He had married Martha Nybro, also of Norwegian heritage, and undoubtedly named after the Crown Princess.

"Cool," was the only remark Tony thought appropriate. Clint had developed an interest in European history because of Ericka's family roots.

Another night the trio shared a drink. "Cheers!" Clint raised his glass of freshly brewed kombucha.

"To what?" Ericka asked.

"New beginnings."

While eating the most delicious cannelloni ever with crispy crusted French bread, Ericka said to Tony, "You asked me the other night about my heritage. Now what about some background of yours?"

"Okay," Tony replied and told her he'd graduated in the middle of his class of 400 in Olympia. He needed to pass to get into a state college but his motivation for good grades was sports. His two older brothers were the smart ones in the family, he said. He had no inkling what he wanted to do. Maybe a coach of something. His favorite sport was lacrosse but there wasn't a big calling for lacrosse coaches. He discovered he preferred computers.

He'd heard over and over how his dad started out selling cars before going to college. He didn't want to sell cars like

MURDER ON MENDENHALL GLACIER

his dad. He really preferred playing computer games. If truth be known, he was geeky. A solitary existence would be just fine for him. When he was younger, his mom called him "introverted," always adding, "He'll grow out of it." His dad said he needed to make more friends. College friends with parents who had influence.

Tony, short for Antony, had Italian roots on his mother's side with his grandparents immigrating from Italy and settling in eastern Washington. His mom was born in Washington, a first-born American citizen. His grandparents had done everything within their power to send their first daughter to college.

After WWII, his grandpa worked two jobs and extra on weekends. His grandmother took in clothing for mending. When people in their Catholic church tasted her ravioli and learned of her skills in making pasta, she found herself selling it by the pan full. "Their daughter Arabella, my mom," according to grandpa, "would never work as hard and be as poor as they were."

"Mom wanted to be a teacher. Her parents were over the moon as she would be the first in the family to graduate college. She was a proud Pellegrini, and pleased to share that it meant, 'A pilgrim.' She would soon be an elementary school teacher. She goes by Belle and met my dad, Winston, in college at WSU. Everyone calls him Winn. She used to tell the story how they had several of the same classes in the teaching department. He wanted to be a principal one day. She'd married a Spencer, with his roots starting in England.

"They were both Cougs. Dad went on for his master's in administration and had been in a variety of roles as principal for years at the high school level."

Tony was a mix of both dark Italian hair and lighter skin from his dad's side of the family. His ocean blue eyes were attention-getting with his dark hair, almost ebony, and lighter complexion. He had gotten height from his dad's family, standing at six-foot, one-inch.

"Boy, oh boy, could Grandma Pellegrini cook. She'd fortunately passed down her skills to mom. I even learned some pasta techniques and specialty meals over the years. To impress a girl, I'd make mom's spaghetti Bolognese until I realized how messy it was to eat. I switched to grandma's famous spicy Italian sausage and four-cheese lasagna. If I really wanted to impress someone, I'd spend hours making homemade ravioli, but it was rare."

"Who are you trying to impress tonight with your scrumptious cannelloni?" Ericka teased Tony.

Tony continued saying that being an elementary teacher wasn't quite what his mother expected, so while he was in junior high, she got her master's degree in counseling. She really liked helping children find their way. Before Tony graduated from high school, his mom had gotten her doctorate and was now Dr. Arabella Pellegrini Spencer. His grandparents bawled like babies at each of their daughter's graduations. "We were darn proud, too. Now she is on the faculty at Pacific Lutheran University in Tacoma."

Tony's British grandparents left England right before WWII and moved to Washington. His grandpa had a cousin in Renton, about 30 miles north of Olympia, who'd moved to the area decades earlier because it was cheaper living in the western part of the United States. Both sets of Tony's grandparents had accents—the Pellegrini's from Italy, the Spencers from England.

Tony was a second-generation Cougar. His brothers, too. They ate some flavor of Cougar Cheese at every family event. They attended the rival football game between the Cougs and University of Washington Huskies every year that it was in Pullman. The Apple Cup was in their crimson blood like the Cougar Gold Cheese was in their clogging arteries.

For many years a bumper sticker on his dad's car read, "Huskies Suck."

Ericka laughed, "So that's where you learned to cook. Thank you, Grandma Pellegrini. Your mom sounds like an amazing woman, really a great role model."

"I guess I never thought of it that way, but mom has achieved a lot."

They all easily laughed together and agreed about the Huskies. Tony sat silently just observing. He hadn't trusted her but didn't really see any reasons not to now. Yes, he did have major issues with her but maybe it was all because of the Seattle craziness.

After Ericka headed home, Tony jokingly told Clint just to let him know if he needed to show up at the justice of the peace for them.

———

All three were Generation Xers, children of Baby Boomers. Their grandfathers served proudly in WWII. Their grandmothers stayed at home raising children and overseeing the entire household as their veteran husbands worked for the other guy.

Their Boomer parents all worked outside their homes except Ericka's mother. They grew up with minimal adult supervision and learned the value of independence and work-life balance. Both young men missed their parents being home, if they'd ever admit it.

CHAPTER TWENTY

Just a tiny speck standing on the glacier, Tony's thoughts bounced from Juneau to Seattle and back. Did he recall Clint had confided in him that he'd almost split with her, again, maybe a week or so earlier? They seemed so in tune and happy last time he'd seen them together at their place eating a cannelloni dinner.

Since that time maybe Clint had his suspicions confirmed that she hadn't been forthcoming about some past illegal activities that she'd supposedly left behind in Seattle. She told Clint one night that she had gotten involved in something she shouldn't have in Seattle and didn't know what to do. The person and incidents were haunting her in Juneau. Now Clint promised to help her. Clint told Tony all about it, but everything now was muddled in Tony's mind. He wished he'd paid more attention to the dramatic saga.

At this moment, Tony really didn't know the current status of their relationship. He assumed they were together because Clint seemed really happy. If she'd brought him a surprise snack, they must be doing fine. Unless she poisoned the food. Tony's head throbbed and his entire body was sweating even though it was about 50 degrees where he stood.

Had Ericka gone from being emotionally unstable to blaming Clint for her issues, turned angry, then vengeful? Did she come up the glacier and kill him? But how? Tony's mind was a jumbled mess.

He shook his head hoping to clear up the mixed up time-lines in his head. He felt like he'd been sucked into one of those pinball machines in the arcade he and Clint stopped at a few times. He was the ball hurtling down the shooter alley toward a frenzied maze of ramps, dropping through the flip-pers, down a black drain, through bumpers and traps, him zigging and zagging at the mercy of sinking and rising surfaces.

While waiting for the police to arrive, Tony stepped into the huddle. Brandon asked him about Clint and his friendship. He told them that they'd been assigned the same dorm room freshman year 1993, at Washington State University in Pull-man. Eighteen-year-olds, Tony Spencer and Clint Sterling were selected by the powers-that-be to be roommates. They guessed it had been because both last names began with the letter S. They were both born in June 1975 two weeks apart.

They were both crimson and gray Cougs and darn proud of it. Most of their clothing included a crimson cougar head somewhere. They had Cougar Cheese with almost every meal, trading off between Cougar Gold, smoky cheddar, dill garlic, hot pepper and Clint's favorite—crimson fire. Except it hurt Clint's stomach so he had to slack off the spicy stuff.

Both Washingtonians, Tony grew up in Olympia, the state capital. Clint harkened from the central part of the state, in the small town of Ellensburg. They were different, like oil and water. It didn't matter, they became best friends. Over the four years in college they'd be roommates first in the dorms, then after graduation sharing an apartment, or in their case, a houseboat.

A city slicker, Tony never called himself that, but Clint did. Clint called himself a country hick, but Clint was far from it. He'd been valedictorian of his senior class of 127. He would study forestry in college with the goal of securing a job in the great outdoors. But as life goes, not all things happen according to one's college degree printed on a piece of paper. The piece of paper proving a college degree was more important to most prospective employers than actual work experience. The young men knew it. Tony told the guys that Clint didn't know his family roots like he did. Honestly, Clint didn't care one bit. If somebody asked him what his surname meant or its origin, he'd say Sterling meant silver.

"Then what?" Kent asked.

Tony said, "After graduation we took the plunge and moved to Seattle. I took a job with Microsoft. Being the first generation to grow up with computers, I think we learned and adapted to new technological programs easily.

"Seeing both of my parents gone nine plus hours a day, I valued a healthy balance between time spent at work and personal time. I had plenty of college friends who tended to have a strong entrepreneurial spirit. I felt loyal to Microsoft and especially liked the hefty paycheck.

"I took to programming like a guppy to water. The company had launched its groundbreaking Windows 95 and proclaimed being the first consumer-friendly version of Windows. I worked on Windows 98, too."

Tony took a breath. "But Clint struggled looking for a job that he felt passionate about, at least drawn to or even somewhat liked. He job-hopped, using the excuse that variety would add to his versatility. His parents didn't agree with their son's occupational philosophy.

"His folks questioned his choice of going to work for a fairly new, privately owned company called Amazon. Clint liked the small family-feel about the company and laughed when he told his folks a bell would ring in the office every time someone made a purchase. Everyone would gather around to see if they knew the customer. His parents weren't amused. They were slightly more impressed when Clint updated them that it only took a few weeks before the bell was ringing so frequently that they had to turn it off.

"Clint heard stories around the lunchroom that in the early days, the servers that the company used required so much power that the owner and his wife couldn't run a hair dryer or a vacuum in the house without blowing a fuse.

"He told his parents the business employed about 2,000 employees. At that point his father did some research and discovered it sold music and video content and branched out internationally acquiring online sellers of books in the United Kingdom and Germany. His father found out that in December 1996 the company's customer base had grown to an impressive 180,000. By October of the following year, this figure had leaped to around one million registered accounts. Revenues had reached about $138 million in 1997, a significant jump from 16 million the year before.

"Clint was excited the company was branching out selling items including video games, consumer electronics, home improvement items, software, games and toys.

"His father assumed Clint was working in technology or maybe as a marketing manager. Clint never corrected the assumption. Only I knew he was really running around pulling items from shelves, dropping them into bins on a conveyor belt that went somewhere else to be boxed and mailed.

"Then Clint heard rumors about an employee who worked so tirelessly over eight months, biking back and forth from work in the very early morning and very late night, that he completely forgot about his car that he'd parked near his apartment. He never had time to read his mail. His car got towed and sold at an auction. He heard from another coworker that when the kitchen category was introduced, knives without protective packaging would come hurtling down conveyor shoots. His friend was almost stabbed with a butcher knife, so he walked out that night.

"Although exciting and fun at first, Clint didn't last long at Amazon. He quit when it became common knowledge that the owner expected employees to work 60-hour weeks, at least. The idea of work-life balance didn't exist and reminded Clint of his parents and how he was raised basically parent-less.

"Clint's parents really didn't understand their easygoing, nonchalant son. He saw his parents as overachievers. He wasn't applying himself, his parent's told him. He was way too pie-in-the-sky, too trusting and gullible in their opinion. Clint would disagree." Tony ended with watery eyes looking down.

"Where'd you live in Seattle?" Kent asked.

Tony laughed when the told the guys about how he and Clint found a nontraditional apartment, well, a houseboat on the tree-lined corner of Lake Union dock under the Aurora Bridge, right before Westlake becomes Fremont. It included a kitchen in a corner of the living room. A big picture window allowed plenty of natural light and the wood stove provided warmth. Facing land on one side and water on the other, the views gave both the impression of a secluded cabin and a waterfront home. The main floor included a bedroom, and upstairs was the second smaller bedroom with a twin bed. Clint took the smaller room as he paid less rent.

It was smaller because the large deck took up the rest of the space.

After rent was paid and food purchased, they pooled their money and bought a used 1990 Isuzu Trooper. One of Tony's coworkers was selling the low-mile, mid-size SUV at a deal. It came with air-conditioning, power windows and a V6 engine. Clint's first impression was that it looked like a sideways soda cracker box on wheels. Tony laughed and agreed it looked blocky, but it would hold lots of their outdoor gear in the back and on top, plus the 4-wheel drive would be perfect for outdoor sports.

After Amazon, Clint worked for a fishing company, not what his parents thought he'd use his degree in forestry for. He dated frequently but no one for very long. In one day that changed. He met Ericka and probably his demise.

Tony confided in the trio that after just two visits with Ericka in Seattle, he had concluded she was bad news for Clint. He noticed too many inconsistencies in her stories and when mentioning it to Clint, he just shrugged his shoulders. He made excuses like she got confused easily and was tired from working two jobs, one in a veterinary clinic and pharmacy, where she mixed herbs, vitamins and other stuff together for prescriptions, like holistic medicine for animals. She worked at a jewelry store, too.

Shaking his head, Tony added that several months later Clint told him that he and Ericka were done. And Clint added, "Don't ask." Messages were adding up on the answering machine, all from a chagrined Ericka who was very sorry and didn't understand why he'd broken it off. Tony heard several messages, enough to confirm his original thoughts about her lack of character.

Clint told Tony she hadn't really lied as far as he could tell, but she certainly hadn't told him the entire truth about her third job. But he wasn't really sure since she talked a blue streak when she'd been drinking too much. He never told Tony what that was, only saying it's safer if he didn't know. That comment sort of creeped Tony out. Tony was sure he'd seen Ericka around their boathouse several times sort of lurking behind bushes. One morning two tires on their Trooper were slashed. Clint didn't report it to the police even though Tony suggested he should.

Tony continued that Clint had a string of low-paying jobs and nothing in his educational degree field. But he made enough to pay his share of the bills which was fine with him, and Tony didn't mind. Clint wanted to find a job that allowed for flexible hours, like freelancing. He adapted well to change and liked an informal environment. He liked to work hard and play hard.

His brother Owen reminded Clint often about a variety of seasonal jobs along the coast of Alaska. One day looking at the Help Wanted ads, Clint spotted an attention-getting advertisement from the State of Alaska promoting tourism and work opportunities with high-paying wages.

Clint convinced Tony they should fly north and check out job opportunities. At first Tony thought it'd be a super place for a vacation with tons of sports, so he agreed. After the two-week vacation, Tony contacted his supervisor at Microsoft explaining the opportunity and they agreed Tony could use all his vacation time plus two months of comp time for working extra hours on the company's last project.

Tony stopped and looked toward the sky, then continued. "We both immediately got jobs as guides on Mendenhall Glacier since both of us are hikers and had experience rock climbing in the Cascade Mountains. That first summer flew by. Clint, having no great job possibilities in Seattle nor a personal reason to return, decided he'd stay. With his new contacts and personality, Clint was sure he'd find some odd jobs during the winter to pay for their small apartment.

"Clint dropped me off at the airport in Juneau and his parting words were, 'E-mail me, I'll miss ya.'"

"I'll be back next summer, maybe for good."

"That's basically how we got here. The next summer I quit my job, packed up mostly personal stuff and moved to Juneau permanently. I felt sure I'd find a good job in technology once the summer tourist season ended.

"We found a small but adequate ground floor unit in a triplex and took the corner place because it had a small yard off the back door and we both wanted a dog. We went to the humane society and picked out a friendly small mutt with shaggy brown fur. The dog made a beeline to Clint and its entire body wiggled when he petted the pup. The "it" was a "he" and his face was full of expression and both of us laughed at the patches of tan fur directly above his black eyes that moved up and down. There was matching tan fur under his nose to his mouth.

"It's a one-bedroom and since I paid most of the rent, I got the bedroom. Clint didn't mind and slept on the pull-out sofa in the living room. The kitchen is fine and large enough for me to cook. The plus about the place are the windows facing the bay." Tony rambled and the guys let him.

"Oh, back to the dog. Even though we both worked on the glacier, I had been assigned to the early shift and Clint the later one, so one of us was around during most hours of the daytime. The shelter didn't know his name, so he was dubbed Oliver, Ollie for short. Wherever we went, Ollie went along with us usually riding in the back unless the passenger seat was vacant.

"Jeez, you guys know more than anyone else now," Tony finished the saga, emotionally exhausted.

He ended their life story, "Then low and behold, who should show up in Juneau? Ericka. Coincidence? Serendipity? Karma?" None of the guides said a thing.

"Finally," Kent muttered, as they heard the distinct and deep *wop wop wop* approaching in the distance.

Ericka had returned to Juneau from the helicopter ride, jumped in her Audi Fox and headed home to change clothes. She pulled off the Cher wig and hopped in the shower. She swished her hair back from both sides of her face air-drying naturally. With her dexterous fingers she used an elastic blue band to gather her hair into a ponytail.

She dumped a package of Top Ramen noodles into a glass bowl and four minutes later sat at her table eating lunch. Kirbie meowed. She opened the only piece of mail, a card with musical notes on the front, from her mom. Then propped it up by the phone.

A smile crept onto her lips as she recalled the priceless look of surprise on Clint's face when she dropped off the snack. She looked forward to him thanking her properly after they both got off work later.

She arrived at Celebrity Jewelers with plenty of time to spare. She prided herself on her timeliness and thought it rude to keep people waiting.

CHAPTER TWENTY-ONE

On Mendenhall Glacier, finally helicopters arrived with Juneau police officers including a detective and the captain who had the overall authority on the case. He was a seasoned veteran of law enforcement and could have retired years ago. He would have if he didn't still enjoy the work. Well, most of the time. The next helicopter landed with retrieval gear plus the search and rescue team.

The investigative team split up. Half worked in the snack trailer and area around it. The others were around the body site.

The captain told Tony he wanted a list of all passengers from the morning flights, ASAP, like yesterday. "Get names, telephone numbers, anything the passenger had provided when paying for the reservation." Tony called the office for the rush task.

Sergeant Fitch and Officers Kruse and McFeeters set up the perimeter. Using a very strong flashlight, it indicated what Tony and the other guides didn't want to hear. A body was wedged tightly down the crevasse. They weren't getting a verbal response when calling out.

"So it's a homicide?" Kruse asked Captain Malloy.

"Unknown."

"I'll get forensics up here," another one said.

Malloy said, "And the medical examiner, too."

"I've already called Dr. Canoy, and he'll be on the next chopper."

Captain Malloy pulled Tony aside who quickly blurted out, "I think that's my best friend and guide, Clint. I hope not but he's the only one unaccounted for. I think his girlfriend killed him." The captain told him to slow down.

Tony told Malloy that on their second season working in Alaska, one morning Tony was sure he saw Clint's old girl-friend, Ericka, walking toward the Red Dog Saloon. It shook him. He remembered what they'd both gone through because of her instability and just plain weirdness. "I couldn't mention it to Clint, until I saw her again a week later. When I saw her for the second time I walked across the street and accused her of following us to Juneau," Tony said.

"She said that wasn't true and that she was there because her cousin owns a bakery and she needed to get out of Seat-tle, so she moved several months ago. I called her a liar and had good reason. She replied, 'I can't help it if you don't believe me.'"

"I warned her to not have any contact with Clint and said that he had a really hard time getting over her. She said, 'I won't. I promise. He never returned my calls in Seattle anyway.'"

Tony told Malloy that Clint said he was the only person who could pin her to a small gang of embezzlers. *IF* she had actually told him the truth one night after drinking too many tequila shots, *IF* being the operative word.

Clint never told her what she'd revealed that drunken night on her sofa. Instead he broke up with her. There was nothing provable or in the press.

"She might take off knowing she killed him." Tony could barely get the words out.

Malloy replied, "Sorry son, but we don't know that he was killed or how he died. It could be an accident. Natural causes. We have to wait to hear from the medical examiner. We're getting way ahead of ourselves."

"Unbelievable," Tony muttered.

The leanest member of the search and rescue unit rappelled down through the wider end of the crevasses and carefully inched his way tying a cable around the body. After taking photos from every possible angle, three men slowly winched the body up. Tony still wasn't totally convinced it was his best friend. It could be somebody else, he tried to rationalize.

Captain Malloy pointed out the medical examiner to Tony. Dr. Canoy had arrived and watched the process carefully. Malloy spoke softly and explained to Tony that as medical examiner he was a licensed physician and a pathologist. Medical examiners investigate deaths due to homicide, suicide, or accidental violence, and deaths of persons unattended by a physician. They also intervene in cases where death occurs amid suspicious circumstances, like this one. "Dr. Canoy will prepare a record for the deceased person, not unlike a medical record other physicians prepare."

"It sounds like a TV program."

"Oh, much more thorough and much longer than a two-hour medical program. This will take days, maybe weeks."

They watched the doctor meticulously document the scene, including any disturbances, position of the deceased, as well as the presence of a container or spilled poison. There were no drug containers, just the sack lunch.

The medical examiner checked off his list. He saw no bullet wounds, puncture wounds or anything else unusual. Bending down to the victim's face, he did smell a scent of almonds. Almonds. He knew it could be a symptom of cyanide poisoning but that would be determined later. Poisoning was a real possibility in his mind. He asked if the ingestion of poison was witnessed by anyone.

"I just saw him eating the snack," Kent replied.

"Anything odd about it or did you notice anything strange after he ate?"

"No, Sir."

Dr. Canoy took notes after observing the access to the food and drink especially if it was a poisoning. It could be the result of an overdose of prescribed medicine. There were many possibilities.

He motioned Captain Malloy over saying something that nobody could hear. Captain Malloy waved Tony to come over. "Son, we need to confirm who this is." Tony's world came to a screeching halt. Reality hit him in the face. "It is Clint," was all he could choke out. The whole process seemed like a B-rated movie. How in the world had his best friend ended up here? Tony assured the medical examiner there would be no drugs or alcohol in his system except for whatever had been delivered by his so-called girlfriend.

The medical examiner noted that the body temperature was under 70 degrees, not totally frozen and fortunately well-preserved. Dr. Canoy estimated Clint had been dead for 70 to 90 minutes. He hadn't frozen to death, Tony heard somebody say.

"Respectfully, you're nuts, Ericka did it," Tony told Malloy.

"Do you know where we might find her?"

"Works at a bakery and jewelry store. Maybe for a vet clinic, too."

Malloy asked Tony, "Do you know if Clint had any enemies? Anyone who'd want him dead?"

"YES! Ericka, her name is Ericka."

"What's her last name?"

"I don't know. Wait, it's long, something European. Maybe Russian or Scandinavian. Norwegian actually. Enga, Enge, Engle something. Englebright, Englebrecht, Englebert…"

"Like the singer?"

"What?" Tony said incredulously. "What singer? I don't know."

"Do you know what jewelry store?"

"It's a name of a cruise line, like Princess Jewelers, or Caribbean, no, it's Celebrity Jewelers. Oh, and a bakery. Ericka's cousin opened the bakery one year ago. She'd been after her to come work for her. And maybe a vet clinic. She mixes medical potions for animals or at least she did in Seattle. No, she didn't push him, she poisoned him. I know she did."

Tony rambled on that a month or two earlier, while fixing dinner, he tentatively mentioned to Clint that he'd seen Ericka.

Clint just shrugged his shoulders, "Yep, you're right. We bumped into each other at the grocery store. We're seeing each other. She's got a couple of part-time jobs."

He told the entire story as Tony sat dumbfounded. Clint relived their chance meeting weeks earlier. He didn't know she stood two feet quietly in front of him, just waiting, while he picked out steaks at the grocery store.

Clint said surprised, he had backed up flattened against the meat counter. It felt cold, the same feeling he had the last time he'd seen her in the Seattle area.

"What are you doing here, Ericka?" he said snippily.

"I'd just like to talk to you for a few minutes."

He raised a brow.

"Can you spare 15 minutes for a cup of coffee?" making a shooing motion with her hand.

Clint considered leaving before she could get to him again. However, he admitted to himself that he was slightly curious how she had landed in Juneau. "Let's go next door to the café."

Clint leaned back in the wooden chair, crossing his arms over his chest. She did look amazing.

"Well? Start."

"Do you hate me, Clint?"

"I don't hate you, Ericka. You've been the biggest challenge of my life. It took me months to forget about you."

"Knife to the heart," she replied. "I've thought about you everyday, and what I could have done differently."

"It is what it is, Ericka. I did the best I could. But I couldn't deal with your deceit."

"I know and I'm sorry about not telling you about part of my life and circumstances. I am much better now and understand what I did was wrong. I've been in therapy for the past year and learned a lot about myself."

Clint stopped her by saying, "Again, what are you doing here?"

"I needed a change from Seattle and there were several jobs here that I qualified for. You know I worked for the jewelry store chain downtown?"

He didn't agree or disagree. He didn't even acknowledge anything.

"My cousin owns a bakery and she needed help, so I work there in the morning."

She wondered if he remembered what she'd told him about the contraband tanzanite or maybe he thought she was lying about that, too.

"I almost yelled at Clint that night," he told Malloy. "What in the world, man, don't you remember she's unstable? Nuts? A stalker? Remember the tires on the Trooper? Were you even concerned when she just happened to be in many of the same places you'd been? That's part of the reason why we left the first summer and came here to work." Tony blurted out in a run-on sentence.

"Clint told me that she seemed fine and he had decided to forgive and forget. He enjoyed her company more than any other women he'd met in Juneau. I felt shaken to my core. Like a 5.3 earthquake just hit us both, with Clint totally unaware of the danger."

After hearing Tony's dramatic recollections, Malloy called headquarters and told them to locate a young woman named Ericka, who worked at the bakery. Fortunately there were only a few bakeries. Then to check animal clinics and Celebrity Jewelers because she probably worked there part-time, too. Malloy relayed they didn't know if she was involved or not, but they needed to speak to her.

"Hopefully she hasn't left the area," Tony grumbled, wanting to add, *because of your incompetent delay*, but didn't say out that part out loud. Departing Juneau would only be by water or air since there were no connecting roads out.

Malloy turned to Officer McFeeters, handing him a black plastic bag with a smaller brown sack tucked inside. "Fly this down now and get it on the next flight to Anchorage. Get the contents of the lunch bag to the crime lab and tell them we need this ASAP."

"Do you want it to go commercial or private?"

"Call Russ. Ask him to drop everything and take it for us. Even though it's less than a two-hour flight, we need this NOW." A personal friend, Captain Roberts had retired as a Delta airline pilot and currently was flying as needed with a few local companies.

"If he's not out on a flight ask him to be fueled up and ready to roll in one hour. If he's not available, get this on the next commercial flight and McFeeters, you take it. Call the crime lab and let them know you're coming. We need everything tested: almonds, bagels and beverage. Ask them for a 24-hour turnaround, not the usual 48. If you need to, remind them they owe us." The captain rarely pulled strings, but he was calling in favors on this one if needed.

McFeeters nodded, walking toward the idling helicopter. Twenty-three minutes later, he climbed out of the helicopter and into Roberts' twin engine *401 Cessna*. Sitting next to the pilot, McFeeters explained the situation while they were already speeding down the runway.

———

Riding a shuttle bus from the helipad, Peter and Anne were back at the ship waiting with a boatload of friends going together on the next adventure. The couple agreed not to mention the episode to anyone.

Having pale skin, as light as a white wall, Anne would get a sunburn in about 20 minutes. Already sunny and warm, she knew being on water would make it even worse. She pulled out a small tube of sunscreen smearing it on her face, neck, and arms. The oddly pleasing smell reminded her of being slathered head to toe on their many beach trips as a child.

Anne's thoughts detoured momentarily to the glacier incident. She pushed it down. Probably into the same compartment decades ago when they found a body in the headwaters of the Metolius River. She silently reminded herself—live in the moment, live in the moment.

Climbing aboard the catamaran, friends milled around the back, some sitting on cushioned covered benches. Several miles from shore, someone spotted a bald eagle in a tree on Shelter Island. Anne zoomed in and snapped a photo of it. She took another, this time the black speck was surrounded by deep blue water and in the background the shoreline with a deep green cape that had been created by thousands of firs, topped with mountains blanketed in white snow. Sunbeams glittered like diamonds on the smooth water of the massively deep Auke Bay.

Peter had purchased a Sony Cyber-Shot for Anne as a Christmas present one year earlier. She was reluctant going digital, knowing she'd miss printed photos and putting albums together after each trip. He explained she could take all the photos she wanted, not just two or three of something.

Prior to that, she burned through rolls of film like crazy. They were accumulating more and more photo albums even though she tried to limit herself to one roll of 36 a day on past vacations. Photos were Anne's souvenirs of any trip and helped her recall every minute of each day. Peter would be forever grateful for the technologically advanced people who created digital cameras. Anne could take thousands, then delete hundreds later. This was the perfect case where she'd have many of just water, missing the tail of a diving whale.

Anne heard it first—*puff*—their first up-close-and-personal encounter with a humpback in Alaska. It gave itself away by the ten-foot-high spout of water through its blow-hole. Gliding gracefully, the gentle giant treated the humans to a once-in-a-lifetime happening. Peter pointed out that this particular whale had a scar at the base of its two flukes right below the notch.

The pilot said its nickname is Crater and is several years old. He added that some whales have nicknames, but most don't.

A passenger asked how long the tail was from tip to tip. The pilot answered that the flukes measure up to 15 feet and move up and down rather than fishtailing sideways. He added that the black and white markings on the underside are unique to each whale just like a human fingerprint.

With the motor off and everyone perfectly quiet, they heard a high-pitched *chirp*, then another. The captain whispered that the whale was communicating with others.

With one magnificent lunge, the water giant dove, its all black flukes submerging with hundreds of water droplets glistening and reflecting light in zillions of rainbow prisms as it disappeared into the deep cobalt water.

Another whale surfaced and Peter pointed out the white patches at the ends of each fluke. The pilot said she is commonly seen with Crater and her name is Magma. She slapped her flippers startling everyone with the loud smacking sound, like a gunshot. The pilot said sometimes flippers are used to herd prey or as weapons, strong from swimming and sharp with barnacles.

More bald eagles shared Lincoln Island. Sentinel Island houses a white column lighthouse. On Sentinel Island, a huge nest was wedged tightly in a craggy dead treetop. A bald eagle was feeding its eaglet. Smelly, noisy seals gently rocked back and forth on a round red tube that also held a buoy.

The captain heard on the radio where a pod of humpbacks were bubble-net feeding. Making a U-turn, the captain said that these intelligent gentle giants have suffered heavily during people's conquest of the sea. Overall, whale populations have declined to about 25 percent of pre-whaling numbers, and certain prized species, like the bow and hump-back, have been hunted almost to extinction.

Even though humpback whales weigh close to a ton per foot and can grow up to 50-feet long, they are the most acrobatic of whales, heaving their massive bodies out of their underwater world and into ours. They are coastal feeders who prefer shorelines and bays and are frequently seen in Alaska for that reason. They feed heavily while in Alaska, storing enough fat to fuel the long migration to Mexico to raise their newborn calves.

Orca, otherwise known as killer whales, are fast and smart. He didn't care for people calling orca killer whales. Traveling about 30 mph, they hunt in teams, preying on sea lions, seals, and sharks for their meals. The passengers concluded not only was the captain skilled at boating, he was very interesting and well-versed in marine life.

The captain shut off the engine again and there they sat, bobbing slightly in the seemingly bottomless bay. Silent. They were all quiet, waiting. Camera shutters were pushed halfway, ready to snap the perfect picture.

Without any warning, five giants with gaping mouths burst up with gallons of salty seawater cascading out of the side of their mouths. Then straight down they went. One little boy jumped up and down summing up the breathtaking experience.

The captain said that bubble-net feeding is a complicated, highly synchronized effort that shows high biological intelligence. Humpbacks often travel in groups. They bulk up in Alaska, only eating half of the year in the summer, consuming up to 3,000 pounds of fish a day.

One whale usually leads the endeavor, diving deep then rising up to the surface. From deep below, it begins to blow air to create bubbles. It confuses and traps the fish above. Then the rest of the team follows, creating a circle around the prey sort of like a corral. The whales then gather inside the bubble-net and rise to the surface, mouths wide open.

He added that bubble-net feeding is a cooperative feeding method used by groups of humpbacks but not all. This behavior is not instinctive; it is learned and not every population of humpbacks knows how to bubble-net feed. Whales use vocalizations to coordinate and efficiently execute the bubble-net so they all can feed. One typically begins to exhale out of their blowhole at the school of fish to begin the process.

Humpback whales have 14 to 35 throat grooves that run from the top of the chin all the way down to the navel. These grooves allow the mouth to expand. When they swallow, they stream the water out through their baleen, a filter-feeding system inside their mouths, as they ingest the fish. They don't always feed in large groups. On their own, they feed using an equivalent method referred to as lunge feeding. It is similarly executed as the whale dives down beneath a school of fish and rises to the surface with its mouth wide open. Once it reaches the surface it swallows, separates the fish from the saltwater and spits it out.

He said that humpbacks are known as the "songsters of the sea" because of unique, varied sounds they make.

After watching this magnificent feeding display three times, the captain heard on the squawky radio about a whale that had been breaching for hours. He turned the boat and in a few miles they could see a gray giant leaping out of the water, over and over and over again. Basically it was flying out of the water upside down with its back horizontal with the water and its white shiny underside facing up as tons of water flowed off its body.

"Why?" a child asked. The captain responded that there are different theories. It happens when a whale picks up speed and then lifts its body and leaps out of the water. In doing this it shows up to 90 percent of its body above the surface. They could clearly see that. During the breaching the whale landed on its side, another time on its back, creating a tremendous splash much to the audience's delight.

The captain said that it's thought that whales may breach in order to notify others of a desire or as a form of play. During mating season a number of species are known to breach a lot more often than during their feeding season. This simply means that the males could be breaching in an effort to signal a desire to mate. Or they want to show off their physical prowess and youthfulness, which may help them find a partner. Or maybe they're trying to wash barnacles from their skin. Or maybe just to play. He added that once a humpback was seen breaching more than 40 times in a row.

They may also decide to breach in order to watch out for nearby predators and to notify other whales of likely threats. One method for watching is called spy-hopping. It occurs when the whale lifts itself partly above water to get a good look at its surroundings. It is less dramatic and exposes themselves less than breaching.

Breaching could possibly be a territorial action. If a wary whale senses an approaching intrusion or menace, he might attempt to frighten them away from his personal turf by breaching. These menaces may be anything from gatherings of other animals to ships. If a humpback whale hears a noise that is bothersome, he might just breach as a way of seeing exactly what's on the horizon, perhaps another irksome ship.

Again, the radio squawked. There was a pod of orca not far away, between the boat and the shoreline. He cautiously moved closer and again silenced the motor.

The pilot pointed to one that was slapping its tail on the surface. He called it tail lobbing probably warning others of a potential threat. Another surfaced, clearly looking around.

"It's spy-hopping," the pilot said as another orca lifted its upper third just high enough so that the head and eyeballs clear the water.

An adult asked if orca sleep. He replied they don't breathe automatically like humans do. The whole pod dozes together in one big slumber party, breathing in unison while swimming slowly and making shallow dives.

Anne panicked as the blinking battery indicated she'd soon be out of juice. She moved into the covered area and opening her bag, she pulled out the fresh one, loosened the annoying screw and dropped in the new battery, turning her camera back on.

Headed back to the outside area, she saw a bushy mist of water venting about ten feet high. Out of the water surfaced a black and white orca swimming right at her. Astonished, Anne giggled as the curve of the orca's mouth looked like it was smiling at her. Anne stared at the amazing creature for a couple of seconds then she raised her camera and started clicking photos.

The orca's black body shimmered in the sunlight with droplets tumbling from its slightly arched fin. Then the orca disappeared under the water. Then surfaced again making a clicking sound. The glorious creature continued forward, passing the boat. And for the grand finale, a calf surfaced to its mother's left.

It would become a snapshot in Anne's photo album in her mind that she'd never forget. The pilot told them they were truly blessed with this trifecta of whales. It was his first time in over 20 years seeing three magnificent displays all in one outing.

On the glacier, dozens and dozens of photos were taken of the body, the crevasse, snack trailer, and pathway between the two. The crime tape remained though no one would return today.

Glacier guides Tony and Kent were asked to go directly to the station to give their statements. Kent's would be brief; he saw Clint and his girlfriend, and she brought him a bag. Tony's would be much, oh much, much more. Brandon and Brad really had nothing to add but they would go and give statements, too.

Hours later, they all left with Dr. Canoy, Officer Kruse and Captain Malloy escorting Clint in one helicopter.

A Chevy Suburban was awaiting their arrival. The body was placed on a stretcher then rolled into the back of the black vehicle heading to the medical examiner's office.

Toxicological analysis would be carried out first since finding no obvious cause, it was considered a suspicious death. Dr. Canoy suspected poisoning from circumstantial evidence. He'd been surprised more than once and would wait for the tox reports. The kid could have had an untimely cardiac event, but he thought that unlikely.

The medical procedure would begin with external examination of the clothing as well as the body. Blood, urine, and bile would be routinely collected and analyzed.

Downtown, Peter pushed through the old-fashioned red saloon doors at the gold rush-style bar, the Red Dog Saloon, for a late lunch. The sawdust floor matched the era of the songs emanating from the piano player completely dressed in black. They were ushered to a table in the middle of room.

With Howard and Pearl, each couple ordered the restaurant's infamous sandwich called the Cookhouse Burger, weighing in at three pounds. According to the boastful signs it promised to be ten inches across served with two pounds of fresh cut fries from Idaho's finest potatoes. While waiting, the foursome looked around at walls full of paraphernalia—stuff from all over Alaska and the world. A full-size mountain goat is mounted on a wall by a display of hundreds of caps.

The Oregonians recognized a cap, "Mo's Est. 1946, Cooking up the tastiest clam chowder on the Oregon Coast," their favorite coastal restaurant. A black bear climbs a floor-to-ceiling post. People had taped, stapled or pinned business cards to wooden beams and posts that also covered the entrance and most walls. Animal heads line the perimeter. A long wooden bar had one place open revealing metal stools and red vinyl seats. Servers behind the bar wear red and white plaid shirts or vests. Chandeliers are made of wagon wheels. One sign read, "Like Old Times."

Four pairs of eyes widened when their meals arrived. Anne cut their burger into quarters. Each bite was surprisingly juicy, well-seasoned and delicious. They barely put a dent into the mound of hot-out-of-the-frier crispy, salty fries. During a lull in the conversation, Anne decided to share with their English friends what had transpired on the glacier. Speechless, Pearl got tears in her eyes and so did Anne.

Waddling out from the hearty lunch, they agreed to meet up again at 3:30 at Celebrity Jewelers, following the police interview. Peter and Anne needed to make a few jewelry purchases and Howard wanted to get Pearl a belated birthday gift and special remembrance.

CHAPTER TWENTY-TWO

At two minutes to three, Peter opened the door of the police department. Anne squared her shoulders and stepped into the lobby spotting the reception counter. Coming toward them was a man probably in his fifties. Anne wasn't really very good about telling ages anymore. Some people aged well, others didn't. She was 43 and people thought she looked 35. She had good genes—fair complexion, blue eyes, dimples that showed when she smiled which was often, sandy hair highlighted with a few silver threads curving just below her chin.

The man looked slightly familiar. However, she and Peter really didn't know anyone in Juneau except Vinni's family who owned Celebrity Jewelers. And Peter's cousin, Woodie. There stood a six-foot, two-inch-tall man maybe 15 years older than her. From the top of her head to the tips of her toes she had a total body hot flash.

Two hours earlier Captain Clay Malloy had held the manila file folder in his hands and read: Annette Rollins Wellsley, Salem, Oregon. The name of the town caught his attention first because his sister Heather and family lived there. Annette Rollins Wellsley. It wasn't the Wellsley name that rang a bell. "Annette Rollins," he said it out loud a couple of times hoping to jog his memory.

There was no photo or any other information of the woman who had just discovered a body at the two-mile landing zone on Mendenhall Glacier. Within 30 seconds it all flooded back. *Rollins, Rollins, Rollins. Yes! The Albany, Oregon family*, he said to himself. It was probably Anne, who didn't go by Annette back then as a young teenage girl.

He had the element of surprise finally recognizing her name while perusing the file of accumulated paperwork and photos in the case. He would be overseeing this case along with Alaska State Troopers and the US Forest Service. This was an uncommon situation since glaciers are located on state lands so all would have a hand in this case. SAR (Search and Rescue/Recovery) teams as well as volunteers from Juneau Mountain Rescue assisted earlier on the glacier. He sat in his office thinking back and waiting for the unsuspecting Anne to walk through the door. Where had 30 years, actually 29, gone?

They'd met because of a murder that the family had discovered. Then bumped into each other at the Sno Cap in Sisters for lunch one day. He could tell the teenager had a crush on him. She smiled at him the entire time he spoke with her father. Then that was it.

After the grand finale of the attempted arrest with the suspect fleeing, driving at speeds close to 100 mph and his dramatic demise, the infamous case was talked about over the years, but the family faded from his memory. He'd been 29 years old when Anne was 14.

His memories transported him back and he laughed thinking about his past boss, Sheriff Perkins, who broke his own moral code of not getting involved with his deputy's personal lives. He recalled vividly when the sheriff took him aside and backed him up against the wall. He called him about the densest kid he'd ever known. He told him to open his eyes and smell the coffee, instead of roses, and told him to take at good hard look at Twila, the sheriff's favorite niece.

Once Clay did, two weeks later he arrived early before the rest of the team for daily coffee, and boldly walked up and said, "Twila, will you go to dinner with me Friday night?" The coffee mug just about dropped from her hand, he remembered with a chuckle. They were married six months later. He was 30 and she seven years younger.

He would have been happy to live in Central Oregon forever, same with Twy, as he called her. One sunny July day in 1983, an attorney contacted his wife and said some long-lost relative on her mother's side of the family had left a piece of property to her. It was just outside of Juneau, Alaska, the 49th state.

"Why me?" Twila asked. Her great uncle Tom remembered her being a baby boy. It irritated Twila's mother but she ultimately turned it into a joke. Uncle Tom only named Twila in his will. Whatever it amounted to was now hers, all hers.

She asked, "But why not to my mother's brother, Uncle Hamlin, isn't he next of kin?" The attorney shrugged his shoulders as did Uncle Ham when Twila told him the story.

Clay and Twila flew north one summer to check it out and both fell in love with the coastal area even though the property was inland several miles in the Valley. Clay was quite taken with the wildlife. While standing on the property with a rundown house with chipped paint, curled shingles, and crumbled wooden front steps, a moose meandered through and into Twila's woods. It had to be good luck. He had decided long ago he wasn't a hunter for sport and wouldn't kill anything unless it threatened his life or his family's. He could do all the salmon and halibut fishing he ever dreamed of.

But they both had good jobs. Their children, 9 and 11 years old, were rooted with friends and their schools. It wasn't the best timing. He was very close to his elderly parents, who he could barely think about leaving. They relied on him and Twila. Maybe he and Twy would go there one day when they retired. The land just sat and waited.

Things changed in 1987 when Twila's Uncle Ham, actually Sheriff Perkins, decided after 18 years as sheriff, to retire. Clay had been on the force just over 25 years and technically could retire with a full pension.

Then his parents who had visited Arizona several times during the winter decided they wanted to move outside of the Phoenix area, an hour north to Prescott, elevation 5,000 feet. They liked the idea of warmer temperatures and informed their flummoxed son they were putting their house on the market within two weeks. The grandparents would come visit during the Arizona hot summers and Clay, Twila and kids could go see his parents during Christmas and spring breaks.

During summer break, they'd taken their teenagers north to see the area and property. Both were intrigued with the mountains, scenery, and wildlife and there were kids that didn't live too far down the road. Their daughter Summer asked if she could finally have a horse. And maybe a moose.

Twila was a high school guidance counselor and employable wherever she went. He'd retire and work the land. In

1987, they packed up the two kids and moved lock, stock and barrel to Juneau. Their items arrived on a transport ship that docked at the port of Juneau. Since then they'd purchased other parcels around their property and now had nine acres to roam. His daughter had her horse.

They had a golden retriever named Jasper, a yellow lab named Honey, and chocolate lab named Raider. Each one was named for a specific reason: Jasper had been one of his and Twila's favorite camping places in Alberta, Canada. Honey, named by his daughter, was the color of the lab's coat. Raider was the name of his all-time favorite football team. They had always been the Oakland Raiders to him no matter where the team moved.

They'd also acquired four Alaskan Huskies that were being put out for retirement. Twila didn't want to know what that meant. She just knew they should care for them since she and Clay loved dogs. He renamed them after favorite dogs from TV programs when he was a kid: Lassie, Rin Tin Tin, Bullet and Astro. To this day, Clay was enthralled when a bear or moose ambled across their open acreage.

It hadn't taken Clay long to miss law enforcement and when a job opened up in the Juneau Police Department, he applied on a Thursday. They snapped him up so fast he started the following Monday. That was 12 years ago. He'd discovered Alaska was one of the states that didn't have counties but boroughs instead, Louisiana being the other.

Alaska State Troopers handled what city police departments couldn't. The population of the city of Juneau was almost 30,000 when they moved, ten times the number of people living in his hometown of Madras, Oregon.

Anne felt the same as she did when she was one-week shy of turning 14, 29 years earlier. Her mouth dropped into an O shape. It was her Deputy Tall, Dark and Handsome, with dreamy blue eyes, back then a much younger Deputy Malloy. Anne was speechless. Her left hand moved to her heart that she felt was thumping out of her chest and she was shoving back in. She instinctively reached out her right hand, palm up, like greeting an old friend. She tried to say a complete sentence, but instead incoherently uttering, "It's, it's, umm, golly, hmm, really, it's you?"

She cleared her throat. Something stuck and she could barely swallow. She remembered the instant crush on this handsome deputy in his tan uniform that lasted all through her ninth grade in junior high. Well, at least the summer before ninth grade. When school stared after Labor Day a new boyfriend named Mike erased most of her heartache. Her mom knew it was her daughter's first crush and stayed calmly sympathetic, knowing this too would pass. Funny how those memories flooded back so easily. Her memory caused the O to close and a smile crept onto her lips.

Captain Malloy reached out his hand and took Anne's and said, "It's good to see you again, Anne.

She blurted out, "How? When? What are you doing here?" mystified to see him after almost three decades.

Peter stood observing the interaction. He had never seen Anne starstruck like this before. She'd had plenty of opportunities to be tongue-tied with personalities and dignitaries she came in contact with over the years in her profession.

"I have been assigned this case; it seems I get all the unusual ones." He moved to Peter and shook his hand introducing himself.

"I'm Clay Malloy. I met Anne and her family under unfortunate circumstances in 1969. I remember it like yesterday. Anne's family stumbled across a body in the headwaters of the Metolius River and I answered the phone in the Jefferson County Sheriff's Office when her mother called. The case was unusual back then. The ending wasn't what I or the department expected or wanted."

She said, "You know, I've wondered off and on over the years about that case. I recall you were removed from it, something about a relative?" She continued before Malloy could answer, "We read about the dreadful end of the killer in a newspaper sometime later."

She felt very uncomfortable, out of her element, and she didn't like being taken by surprise on anything. Peter seemed to be amused by her discombobulation.

Clay could see she was nervously twisting her hands and when she took a breath, he answered her question. "Yes, one of the boys involved was my younger cousin. And I knew the victim slightly and the other young man. They were all roommates."

"What happened to the other two?"

"My cousin left Sisters and moved to Corvallis then attended Oregon State University graduating with a degree in business administration and minor in finance. He is ten years younger than me and is a bank manager in Albany at First Citizen's Bank. He and his family have been here a few times to visit.

"His roommate Vernon went into the military for two years, then got out. He wasn't much of a student or soldier but really enjoyed painting. So he worked his way up and is a manager of a Miller Paint Store in Salem. The guys were estranged for some years probably because they both felt so guilty and maybe even blamed each other, but they got over it and see each other occasionally."

She noticed the upward curves of the corners of his mouth as he motioned for the visitors to come with him and they walked into his office. She spotted a photo probably of his wife and two children in a silver frame on his desk. At their feet sat three dogs. The stark white walls were decorated with articles, commendations and certificates. It was rather utilitarian and could use a splash of color and updating, in her opinion anyway.

"Coffee?" he asked. "Sure," Peter answered. "No thanks" was her reply.

She watched as Malloy drank his coffee just like her brother Will, in a couple of gulps. Will had said that working in law enforcement makes one eat and drink fast never knowing when they might get a call.

Malloy explained that he was in charge of the case and had started collecting statements. Could she please tell him what she had seen?

"So I was standing on the glacier looking around"—here she swallowed—"I saw something unusual on the ice and walked to it." Those crazy goosebumps again, she kept to herself.

Her voice was just about the same, thought Malloy. He scribbled that the witness approached and saw it was an upside-down boot. She could see something else, maybe the end of a leg of pants but she went no farther and didn't look down the crack. Now that she thought about it again, maybe she saw the pant leg gathered, like with elastic at the base of the boot.

Malloy didn't think they'd need anything more from her but in case, he suggested they exchange emails should further information be required. She asked if he would be able to let them know the findings when it was solved. He thought he could but had no timeline. The only thing they knew for sure was the victim's name. He was a guide on the glacier. It could be accidental, but a coworker didn't think so. Malloy felt confident in telling them that much. They were leaving that night to continue their cruise northbound, but he asked that they not talk about the case.

In a quick shift in conversation Malloy asked about her parents. She animatedly pointed toward the dock and said, "Thank you so much for asking. They are very well and actually onboard, along with my brother Max and his wife. He is in sales and always takes top awards with his company. In fact, we are traveling with about 30 family and friends."

"Celebrating our 22nd wedding anniversary," Peter squeezed in.

She continued not even taking a breath, "And Will followed your footsteps into law enforcement. Well, actually our great grandfather's footsteps. He is First Sergeant with the Linn County Sheriff's Office."

Malloy, having been in Jefferson County for decades before moving to Juneau asked if he'd been hired by Sheriff Ken Goin? "Yes, as a reserve deputy. Then in 1987 he became a full-time deputy under Sheriff Art Martinak. Will had moved up the ranks and then-sheriff Dave Burright promoted him to First Sergeant."

Malloy asked if Will had aspirations of being sheriff one day. Anne shrugged her shoulders and remarked, "He hasn't projected that far but I'd say most definitely; he's perfectly suited for it."

"Didn't I read about your father in the newspaper involved with state election laws?"

"Good memory. And yes you did. He was elected Linn County Clerk and discovered over the years there was a more secure, cost-effective, less time-consuming way to hold elections using vote-by-mail.

"He'd done a lot of research of other counties in other states and became convinced it would be perfect for his county. He had some voters in rural precincts who didn't vote. Most farmers couldn't leave their property and drive 30 miles to vote in person, so they didn't. When he tried it in Linn County he laughed when there was 100 percent voter participation where there had been none. But he did make it clear there were only 17 registered voters in that particular precinct.

"Linn County became the guinea pig and for years through trial and error, it was finally successful. It certainly didn't happen overnight. More and more clerks wanted his help to start this in their counties. Even though he retired about ten years ago he is very involved with the Oregon Legislature and there is a push right now to pass it statewide. All indications are that it will pass in November. He and mom spend winters in Arizona." She beamed with pride speaking about her dad.

"It was better for me and other officers, too. Many times we couldn't leave our jobs during work hours to go vote," he concluded.

"What has your life been like, Anne?" he asked. Anne reduced almost three decades into about 90 seconds flat. "School, college, met Peter through mutual friends, got married, work and travel. I have wanderlust; it's a disease really. And I'm addicted to colorful doors. I just want to explore and see exciting places, meet new people, try authentic food and enjoy as many cultural experiences as possible."

If her husband hadn't been so secure, he might have been a little jealous at this serendipitous reunion. Instead he enjoyed watching it.

She asked what some of the differences were between working in Oregon and now the southeast coast of Alaska. He thought about it for a moment and said, "When I arrived in '87 officers were directed to use all reasonable means available to deter bears from the course of activity that led them into contact and conflict with humans. Officers were directed to cite people responsible for poorly contained garbage when it was the reason a bear was in the area.

"A plan was announced to trap Juneau's notorious "blue bear," a little seen variation of the coastal black bear often referred to as a "glacier bear." The young bruin and his family had moved into Juneau territory and were raiding garbage cans in a neighborhood. Although garbage bears were normally destroyed, the zoo in Anchorage expressed an interested in displaying the rare one to visitors.

"Black and brown bears mix in Alaska and along the coastline. Brown bears are normally high above the tree line browsing in the berry fields. Black bears are plentiful around Juneau. You'll see them in creeks when the salmon are running and at Mendenhall Glacier. Black bears can be brown and brown bears range in color from black through cinnamon. However, black bears are smaller while brown bears have prominent ears, a hump between their shoulders and longer claws, not that you'd get close enough to see."

He added that his work wasn't always about bothersome bears. Budgets had been slashed increasing workloads, cuts in services, and due to cutbacks some offenses weren't being prosecuted.

One humorous case occurred when some officers were following a trail of Cheetos from a stolen car to the residence of a man they later dubbed the "Cheeto Bandito." The guy was arrested for stealing the car from a neighborhood, driving it to a liquor store in the Mendenhall Valley and using it as a battering ram to enter the building. He took more than $2,000 in wine, candy and cigarettes.

Officers responded to a loud party call at the house and spotted a bag of Cheetos. They seized a pair of shoes that matched footprints taken from the burglary scene. Both Peter and Anne were in stitches. Clay concluded the saga by adding the bandit was sentenced to two years in prison.

Juneau had their share of assaults, murders, domestic abuse, mining accidents, swimming deaths, boating accidents, a few bank robberies, arsons to investigate, sightseeing planes and helicopter crashes, even though those were rare. There had been lawsuits, hiring, firings, and retirements.

But honestly, he noted, many had to do with bears. One time a young black bear attempted to enter the Foodland Supermarket. Anne always laughed easily and was cracking up again.

Another incident that got a chuckle from the visitors was about almost $500,000 in unpaid citations and warrants. The police department announced it would begin to publish the names of the perps in the *Juneau Empire*. Payments came rolling in.

One call was from a resident at 11:30 p.m. one night. He said an intoxicated man near a dock was outside his vehicle trying to dance. Police found a sober man trying to teach his fiancée how to dance before their wedding.

He concluded by saying that if he didn't enjoy his job so much and feel like he was really making a difference and a contribution, he'd pull the plug.

Anne, still partially stunned by divine intervention or coincidence, noticed now-captain Tall, Dark and Handsome looked basically the same except his walnut hair had ribbons of white that made him look quite debonair, somewhat older and wiser. Why did men look distinguished with salt and pepper hair and women were told to wash that gray right out of your hair?

As she looked closer, there were some crow's feet around his eyes. Good, she thought, he wasn't perfect after all. He'd aged like the rest of them. Their conversation winding down, Malloy told Anne to give her parents and brothers his regards. She ended by saying that they planned to cruise to Alaska often. He said, "You have my email."

Even at 43-years-old, Anne felt like a teenager and couldn't wait to tell her mother and see the expression on her face. Not about the episode on the glacier but Deputy Tall, Dark and Handsome.

CHAPTER TWENTY-THREE

A t 3:30, still somewhat flabbergasted Anne and easygoing Peter breezed into their favorite fine jewelry store, Celebrity Jewelers, on south Franklin Street. In the entranceway stood a rotating glass display just like the revolving dessert case spinning around at their favorite dessert place at home called Konditorei. Instead there was a selection of watches by different manufacturers.

Already inside, Pearl yanked Anne aside and asked how the meeting went at the police station. Anne looked at Pearl and answered, "Later." The short answer made Pearl a little nervous.

A tall, attractive young woman smiled and greeted them. Her name tag read Ericka. Anne mentioned they were there to see Vinni, who waved but was stuck behind a counter making a sale.

Anne had emailed Vinni that they were coming and what they would be looking for this trip just like she'd done prior to other arrivals. On one visit, her heart's desire had been pink sapphires. Vinni was ready for them and pulled out trays of earrings and pennants. It was her fortieth birthday present from Peter several years earlier.

Ericka mentioned she knew they were coming because Vinni and his wife Prerna were looking forward to seeing them. Vinni had told Ericka a bit about their combined history. Ericka mentioned she worked for him the past several months since she moved here from Seattle. She added that she worked mornings at her cousin's bakery then she worked here on the afternoon shift until closing, or when the cruise ships departed.

With the sale completed, Vinni made a beeline for Anne and Peter. They hadn't seen each other for three years, so all received customary big hugs. Prerna and their young children came out to say hello. Originally from India, they lived in Juneau full time and the three children were doing very well in school.

Anne and Peter both bought new watches, receiving the rock-bottom family pricing, plus something else Anne would wear later on the cruise. She had sent lots of friends on Alaska cruises with strict instructions when buying jewelry only to go to Vinni.

A commotion outside caught Anne's attention along with everyone else in the store. Two Ford Crown Vic's parked hurriedly at the sidewalk. She watched as two police officers walked in, surveyed the crowd and approached Ericka. One instructed her to come with them.

"What? Why?" she asked.

Officer Kruse said, "Please come with us, ma'am."

"Why?" she demanded again.

"Ma'am, it's best you don't cause a scene."

"I'm not causing a scene, I just want to know what's going on."

Vinni and family and customers stood wide-eyed watching the scene unfold in front of them as Ericka looked anxiously over her shoulder.

Vinni approached the officers and said, "Ericka is our employee. Is there anything I can do to help?"

"We just need to speak with her at the station."

The first police officer opened the vehicle's back door and Ericka slid onto a cold vinyl seat. When she bravely asked again what was going on, the reply was, "We're almost at the station, ma'am."

"Poor girl," Anne said. "I really like her. I hope it's not serious."

Vinni said, "It certainly seems like it could be."

No one noticed a man sitting in car down the street watching as Ericka was taken from the store and loaded into the police car. He knew this would wake her up and she'd see only he could protect her. He laughed so hard at her expression of utter confusion and almost panic that he put his head on the top of the steering wheel.

He remembered what a rush she got and that she hadn't minded taking a small gem or two when opening a box of tanzanite at the big chain jewelry store in Seattle. They'd never miss it, he assured her. That got her started in the thrill of the game.

Then she wanted out and just up and left him and Seattle. She couldn't do that to him. He'd lucked out when Leon found a piece of mail that the post office mistakenly left with a forwarded address of Juneau.

He figured she'd get a job at a jewelry store because that's what she knew. But she refused to steal from them. It's a mom and pop store and she liked them, she said. She was finished with him she repeatedly told him. Well, this was totally unacceptable to Tyrone.

At the station Ericka entered a room with stark walls and cement floor. White and gray, so depressing she thought. She heard a man reading something about her rights, and that she could get an attorney. The rest was lost on her, but she said yes when he asked if she understood, then signed a piece of paper. The black metal chair felt like it burned her hand. The seat was hard with no padding. It was the interrogation room and the first time she'd been in one.

Two men entered and introduced themselves, Captain Clayton Malloy and Detective Wallace Perry. When Jill asked her later about their looks, Ericka honestly couldn't recall one thing about either of them.

The detective said, "Tell us your whereabouts starting when you left home this morning."

"Okay, but why am I here?"

"Just answer our questions."

"I wanted to surprise my boyfriend, Clint, with a treat today, so my cousin Jill, who owns the bakery, gave me three hours off. I drove my car to Clint's to get a jar of kombucha, his favorite beverage since he and his roommate Tony had just made a new batch. I picked up a full mason jar and slipped it in a backpack. Then I drove directly to the bakery."

"Do you have a key to his apartment?"

" Yes, Clint gave me one a few weeks ago," as she pulled it out of her purse attached to a red Audi key fob.

"Does anyone else know you have a key?"

"I don't know. You'd have to ask his roommate Tony. He's a guide on the glacier with Clint."

Malloy wrote a note then slipped it to Officer Kruse.

"Confirm with Tony that Ericka has a key to the apartment."
The returned reply was, "No way does she have a key,"
according to Tony.

"How did you pick up the jar?"

"What do you mean?"

"From the top, middle, bottom?"

She curled her hand around the center of an invisible jar,
"I picked it up like this."

"Did you leave the jar unattended?"

"No, I didn't." As she thought about it, "Well, actually, I
guess I did. I parked down from the bakery in front of
Northern Lights Bookstore and ran in to get three bagels. I
never lock the doors. I went to the bagel case and saw there
was only one left of the cinnamon raisin and caught the
attention of the Billie Joe to grab it, plus two super cinnamon. She fills in when my cousin Jill or I can't work. Clint
loves cinnamon. Cinnamon toast, cinnamon bread, cookies,
just about anything cinnamon. Cinnamon in his homemade
kombucha, though, is his favorite." She rambled then stopped
talking.

"So someone had easy access to your unlocked car?"

"Yes, I guess that's true."

"Did you see anyone around your car?"

"No, just a bunch of tourists walking down the sidewalk."

"Then what?"

"Then I drove to the helicopter company and I purchased
a ticket for a ride to see my boyfriend Clint. He's a guide, like
I said. Relatives and friends receive discount prices on helicopter rides when family works for the company as pilots,
guides, whatever," she went on. "I surprised Clint with a
snack for a mid-morning break because he was doing a
double shift today."

"Did you wear a disguise?"

Embarrassed, she sort of chuckled, "No, not a disguise.

But he likes surprises, so I wore my long black Cher wig that I have along with several other styles. How do you know about my wig?"

Ignoring her question, detective Perry resumed his line of questioning. "Did you speak with him?"

"Of course."

"How did he seem?"

"He appreciated that I came and said he was looking forward to our date tonight. I dropped off the sack of bagels and almonds and the jar of kombucha for him in the trailer they use for breaks. Then I went back and joined the group for the rest of the glacier walk. Then rode down, went home and changed clothes then went to Celebrity Jewelers about a half hour early," she said without taking a breath.

"Why are you asking me all these questions about Clint?"

"We're the ones asking the questions, ma'am; we don't answer to you. When did you connect with Clint again after arriving in Juneau?"

Malloy thought Perry was unnecessarily abrupt because he'd already come to the conclusion Ericka really didn't know a thing about Clint's untimely demise. Even though Tony was convinced, Malloy wasn't unless she was a pathological liar and he was missing something.

"I was walking in downtown Juneau one morning when I saw Tony. I wondered what the heck was he doing in Juneau. Did that mean Clint was close by? Clint had disappeared off the map but never out of my mind."

The detective repeated most of the same questions just asking in a different way. She was consistent with her answers.

She still didn't know why she was there. "What has happened? Is something wrong with Clint?"

Their dialogue bounced back and forth, neither getting answers that they wanted.

"When did you see Clint last?"

"On the glacier about 10:30. Why? Look, I still don't know why I'm here. What has happened? Is something wrong with Clint or Tony?" she pleaded.

The good guy/bad guy routine had run its course, for now anyway. The good guy, Captain Malloy said, "Ms. Engebretsen—"

"Call me Ericka, please."

"Okay, Ericka. I'm sorry to tell you this but there has been an incident on the glacier that involved Clint. The medical examiner is ascertaining the cause of death."

"What? Died?" she screamed.

"Yes, Ericka, Clint is dead. You delivered food and drink to him and you were the last to speak with him. What do you have to say about that?" Detective Perry demanded.

Already emotionally exhausted from this first-time interrogation, she erupted into tears, with her head in her hands, sobbing. The detective slid a box of tissues across the table to her. It sure seemed real enough to both officers; she was in shock. Tony would disagree if he'd been sitting there.

Detective Perry wasn't finished. "Did you kill Clint?"

" NO!" she exclaimed. "I love him. Loved him."

"Do you have any idea who would have a reason to kill him?"

"No. He is kind and wonderful." Weeping and blowing her nose, she couldn't even think clearly.

CHAPTER TWENTY-FOUR

While Ericka was being interrogated by the police, the medical examiner found no visible wounds. Tony willingly provided the key for entry and police officers had returned with all food and kombucha samples. A technician was already running tests.

Two police officers searched Ericka's apartment while she told them her side of the story at the police station. Nothing appeared out of place. The cat stayed away from them. There were no jars of kombucha. Nor almonds or bagels.

Toward the end of the interview, Malloy was pulled out of the room to take a call and was given the preliminary findings. It was concluded that if somebody poisoned Clint it didn't come from the food or beverages still in his apartment. There was nothing in Ericka's apartment that matched any food items.

Malloy returned with nothing conclusive yet, so she was basically finished with the interview. They needed the lab findings of items in the brown sack.

They didn't arrest her. She has no prior record. Having

nothing to hide, she freely gave them her fingerprints. That act alone convinced Malloy she didn't kill her boyfriend. Detective Wallace Perry was not so sure of her innocence.

Another factor Malloy took into account was that Ericka gave them complete access to her car and offered entry to her apartment. Her only request was to be careful and not let her cat out. Officers found two sets of prints on the passenger front door and handle of Ericka's Audi. Next would be a more thorough search of her apartment.

Malloy learned long ago to trust his gut and his gut was telling him Ericka didn't do it.

Ericka returned to Celebrity Jewelers. Her coworkers huddled around and asked if she was all right. She said that a close friend died. Vinni told her to go home early. It was clear she was having a hard time. She thanked him and replied she'd be in tomorrow afternoon.

The clock on the wall in the store read 6:50. She climbed into her car, feeling exactly the way she had the day she went to the dentist to have her wisdom teeth pulled. Dread.

After sitting there for several minutes recapping the afternoon, she got out of her car and went to a phone booth outside the store. She called Tyrone insisting he meet her at a bar. She knew she looked terrible with puffy, red eyes and didn't care.

Finally, he said to himself, *she's come to her senses*. He was there when she arrived. She pounced on him like a bobcat on a rabbit, almost screaming in a fury that she would never help him again. People at the bar looked at the couple with distain.

"Calm down and shut up," he growled as he manhandled

her into a corner. "If you don't help, I'll tell your employer what you did in Seattle."

"Tell them," she spewed. "I'll just tell the cops all about you," she raged at Tyrone. He grabbed her by her shoulders, pushing her down into a booth. She hissed like a rattlesnake as Leon walked up.

"What's Ericka so het up about, Tyrone?" asked Leon. "I could hear you two ranting and raving when I came in. The manager is going kick both of you out if you don't quiet down."

"Don't ever come near me again or I'll tell the police everything. What we've done previously and how you're trying to get me involved again."

"You'd confess and implicate yourself, *Missy*? That's serious prison time." She hated him and hated him even more when he condescendingly called her *Missy*.

"I don't care, jerk. If you had anything to do with Clint's death, I will kill you." He almost believed her.

Leon sat stunned. He'd never seen her like this before. Unhinged? Maybe. More liked filled with hatred. He questioningly looked at Tyrone who innocently shrugged his shoulders. "She's a whack-job."

Leon asked "What's happening?

She could barely say it. "My boyfriend Clint is dead," she cried.

"What? How?"

"I don't know."

"Why do you think Tyrone has something to do with it? "

"Oh just think about it, Leon, don't be so dense. I told Tyrone that I explained everything to Clint from our days in Seattle."

"What about Seattle?" Leon inquired, truly not knowing much.

"You know, the jewelry funny business, Leon," she snarked.

"*Nooooooo*, I really don't know, Ericka."

"Well, let me tell you." And she did.

Leon asked Tyrone, "She's kidding right? Is this true?"

"Probably. Well, most of it," he admitted.

"Jeez, Tyrone."

Ericka stomped out pointing her finger at him like a gun, "Never again, Tyrone."

Leon uttered, "What in the world, Tyrone? Why are you insisting she do your dirty work?"

"I need money and fast."

"Why?"

"I owe some bad guys a lot of money."

"How much?"

"Fifty grand."

"Like fifty thousand dollars?" Leon almost fell backwards.

"Do you have some to spare?"

"Yeah, like 50, without all those zeros. I can get you maybe $500."

Tyrone spit out a drink of beer he'd almost just swallowed and quietly confided, "I am way over my head in debt from some illegal gambling and looking for easy money to pay off the crime people. That's why I pushed Ericka to help so I can fence the gems and pay off my debts. I'll give her a little."

"I buried my head in the sand and wasn't paying attention to what you and Ericka had going on the side in Seattle," Leon regretted.

"Jeez, I had a plan to get her back. I followed her from her apartment to that stupid boyfriend's place, then to the bakery. I seized the moment to slip poison hemlock into the mason jar when she went into the bakery."

"What if Ericka would have had some of it?" Leon asked incredulously.

Tyrone shrugged his shoulders. "It was a chance I had to take. I needed Clint out of the way because Ericka said he was the only one who knew about our past dealings in Seattle. I need to get Ericka back in the fold. I knew this would frighten her enough to know I am deadly serious about her doing her part of stealing gems."

"Why hemlock?" Leon asked.

Tyrone bragged about all the research he'd done. He told Leon that poison hemlock grows throughout the US. It is very toxic, and he read that animals are poisoned by eating small amounts of green or dried plant. It is also extremely poisonous to humans.

Poison hemlock has white flowers that grow in small clusters. Each flower develops into a green, deeply ridged fruit that contains several seeds. It grows along fence lines, roadsides, along creek beds and irrigation ditches and in other moist places. The hollow stem usually is marked with small purple spots; all parts are deadly.

"I saw it growing in a ditch alongside the road driving into the valley one day. I just pulled over, slipped on a pair of rubber gloves and snipped off the white flowers. It was easy."

Leon sat speechless after Tyrone recited the horrors of hemlock. And at the length Tyrone went to secure Ericka in his illegal business. What would Tyrone do to him now that he was privy to the truth?

Shell-shocked, Leon recalled how he and Tyrone met at a bar in Seattle. Tyrone looked several years older. At 26, Leon figured Tyrone to be around 30. They weren't really best friends, more like drinking buddies. They discovered they both lived in the area for a number of years even attending the same high school but hadn't known each other due to their age difference.

Leon met Ericka at the animal clinic where they both worked. He wanted more of a job, not a career. He wanted to make enough money to pay for extra things like outdoor sports and beer. Now he felt responsible that he introduced Ericka to Tyrone one night at the bar. There were some sparks, but he didn't think it had progressed. Tyrone had other ideas for her, unbeknownst to Leon.

Leon stood up and walked out the door of the bar, the bravest thing he'd ever done. Or stupidest. When he got back to his cottage behind the animal clinic, he called Ericka. Getting no answer, left a message on her answering machine.

"Ericka, it's Leon. I am so sorry. I just left Ty at the bar and he is totally obsessed with you and blames you for not helping him. He's getting further and further in debt. I am afraid for you. He just told me everything, Ericka. He poisoned Clint! Maybe you should go somewhere for a few weeks. *If I turn up dead, tell the police Tyrone did it.*"

CHAPTER TWENTY-FIVE

Anne developed a fondness for Russian stacking dolls and started a collection. With a large community of Russians living along the southeast coast, hand-painted items are plentiful. She was on the lookout for the perfect souvenir. She purchased a precious five-piece, hand-painted wooden Matryoshka doll with four smaller ones stacked inside one another. All five had different scenes from Alaska representing Juneau, Ketchikan, Skagway and Sitka. Each doll has the same face wearing different clothing and a unique symbol that represents its area.

The set spoke to Anne as any art or jewelry must before she purchased it. Anne wasn't a minimalist but by no means a hoarder. She subscribed to the theory that a home should represent the person or people who live there. Her new Alaska stacking dolls would have their place in front of a grass basket with a whale tail carved from whale bone made by local Alaskans.

She knew the exact spot on the opposite end of a wooden shelf where a few treasures from their Venice trip await the Alaska dolls like new friends. A four-inch round, colorful paperweight made from the Millefiori technique, and traditional hand-painted masks were wonderful reminders of their adventures in Italy. Another shelf held her mementos from Scotland and at the other end are keepsakes from Ireland including a favorite, a Waterford crystal Celtic Cross. Some artwork hung on the walls like loyal and constant friends.

After shopping, Peter, Anne, Howard and Pearl encountered Tim and Heather, and all decided to ride the Mount Roberts Tramway to the top. They read: "Through the rain forest the 1,800 foot tram ascends to 3,819 feet in elevation to the top of Mount Roberts."

One cabin held 60 people. Anne thought that about 40 too many. The six of them were the only ones in this tram. Five minutes later reaching the top they ordered huckleberry lemonades at the Tram Bar. They could see the Chilkat Mountains, down the long Gastineau Channel, downtown Juneau, and Douglas Island across the bay.

They went into the cultural center and Raven Eagle Gifts, featuring original art, and one-of-kind pieces from well-known Tlingit artists. Native artists are featured in the complex working on wood, fossilized ivory or silver carvings, making dolls, sewing garments, beading or creating large totem poles out of cedar logs.

Outside, Pearl pointed out soft yellow flowers on deep green stems and delicate white flowers with deep purple centers about the size of a dime. A healthy marmot chewed on stems in a blanket of green clover with sprigs of yellow daisies and other blue and purple alpine wildflowers. The critter was mostly white with gray on its back end. Its ears were charcoal that matched fur around its eyes and muzzle.

One of the things Peter took upon himself to do before any trip was to order laminated pocket guides, some on birds, wildlife, trees and wildflowers; it just depended where they were headed. There were oodles of prickly-stemmed salmon berries about five feet tall with deep cranberry-colored flowers. Some flowers had already transformed into hard green berries about the size of a raspberry.

A blooming serviceberry bush showed off its white five-petal flowers. Eventually it would have purplish sweet berries, similar but not exactly like blueberries at home. Canadian friends attested that serviceberries, sometimes called Saskatoon berries, are much more flavorful.

Deep green, pointy leaves in clumps of five held a delicate four-petal flat flower. According to the guidebook, it is a bunchberry and will produce bright red berries at some point. Bears would have a berry feast up here later in the summer but now they were eating salmon in the rivers.

The view down Gastineau Channel twists to the left winding toward the ocean. Large clumps of arctic lupine transformed rocky areas of the mountainside into an enormous colorful quilt of periwinkle and other shades of blue.

They spotted something making its way through purple violets, parting the flowers like the Red Sea. A blue grouse was moving away from the gawking tourists. They had read ahead of time that some plants should not be handled: death camas, tall with pretty white flowers and poison water hemlock, a green plant that can grow to seven feet with pompom-looking flowers clumped on one stem. They didn't plan to be in any bogs, wetland or ditches where it might be growing.

Looking down at their ship, they saw the sunshine glinting off the swimming pool. A ship was maneuvering out of its place, backing up and heading out. It took about two seconds for them all to agree to ride the tram back down rather than use the hiking trails. It was a hot day with a 91-degree high in Juneau but had cooled off about ten degrees on the mountain.

———

In Ericka's apartment, the blinking red light caught the calico cat's eye. She and Ericka often played a game, Ericka turning a flashlight off and on, bouncing light on the floor or wall. Kirbie would chase and pounce on it.

Restless, the cat jumped on the end table and swatted at the attention-getting light tipping over a card from Ericka's mother that fell and covered the intermittent glow on the answering machine.

CHAPTER TWENTY-SIX

Ericka didn't remember the drive home. Zombie-like, she walked into her apartment and leaned against the closed door. She reached down and scratched between the orange and black patches, Kirbie's favorite spot between her ears. She circled her long tail around Ericka's leg like ivy climbing a fence post.

Ericka fell onto her sofa, pulled her legs to her chest dropping her chin onto her knees and wrapped the log cabin quilt her grandmother made around her and over her head. She didn't want to see light. She hid in darkness until she woke to her cat's familiar meows.

She felt sad thinking about Kirbie and how she took to Clint like catnip, climbing on his shoulder when he sat on her sofa. Rubbing up against his leg, she would purr like a kitten.

She almost chuckled thinking about the first time Clint met Kirbie. "Kirbie, for a girl's name?" he'd asked.

"You'll see why," she replied. "She's a dust bunny magnet."

DELEEN WILLS

Ericka never saw the telephone answering machine—blinking, blinking, blinking Leon's message, like red light, like a flashing stop light, a warning light.

CHAPTER TWENTY-SEVEN

Tony's boss told him to take three days off when he got off the glacier and finished with the police. He felt lost so he ambled around downtown with Ollie. The poor dog weaved in and out as Tony apologized when he bumped into several hurried tourists. He hadn't heard anything from the police. He wanted answers. Had Malloy contacted Clint's parents yet? Maybe there was a message from them on his answering machine letting him know what they planned to do. He reminded himself it had only occurred that morning.

He didn't want to be near people. He stopped at the liquor store on the way back home. He sat drinking, looking out the window. Ollie sensed something wrong and lay at Tony's feet resting his chin on Tony's right foot.

Thinking back, Tony recalled when Clint told him that his dad was a huge fan of Clint Eastwood. His mom not so much. However, she was an admirer of Bill Clinton, so even though one Democrat and one Republican, they could agree on using Clint as a first name.

Clint's mom, Colleen, attended law school in the early 70s before Clint was born. In her third year at Yale in an ethics class, a fellow student, Bill Clinton, with his southern charm, syrupy sweet accent, and sharp wit, caught her eye. He was seriously dating another classmate, so Colleen didn't interfere. After graduation, she returned to her home state, met and married a man who would become tenured faculty at Central Washington University.

She followed Clinton's career as he threw himself into politics. So when her son was born in 1975, she named him Clinton. When William Jefferson Clinton was elected president in November 1992, she reminded her son often that he had been named after a president. Tony had laughed when Clint told him about his mom being enamored with the president of the United States.

The message on the machine from Mrs. Sterling said they'd be in about 9 a.m. in the morning. Thankfully Malloy had contacted them.

Tony called his parents and his mom answered. "I'll get the first flight out in the morning. I'm coming, son."

CHAPTER TWENTY-EIGHT

Peter and Anne visited Northern Lights Bookstore a couple times on past Juneau stops so she knew the way. The bakery was new and a nice addition since they'd been there. She idly picked up one of the older P.D. James' books and saw $2. What a bargain. She hadn't read every one of the books in the series and pulled out the list she carried with her everywhere. It was *Death of an Expert Witness*, book six, written 20 years earlier. This one was going home with her.

She about devoured any of P.D.'s mystery series, starring the New Scotland Yard Commander and poet, Adam Dagliesh. The author became one of Anne's favorites after they visited England the first time. She was thrilled beyond words at one bookstore in London where she found *A Certain Justice*, after just visiting the Royal Courts of Justice, Old Bailey and Inns of Court. Anne had organized educational travel programs for lawyers when working about 15 years in the alumni office at a local law school. The world of law courts and the London legal community was loaded with fascinating interwoven passion and terror. Anne could hardly put it down and mistakenly left it at home.

Anne loved reading, probably because one of her parents read to her before she could on her own. One of her favorite things was to pop into a bookstore, the more unique the better. She loved the aroma of musty paper, which proved its history and value. She enjoyed historical fiction with a dab of mystery and intrigue tossed in, even a murder, as long as it wasn't to descriptive of guts and gore. She appreciated getting to know the characters and wanted to feel like she was right there in the story's region going through what the characters were experiencing in interesting locations.

Her all-time favorite unique bookstore bar none is located in Venice—called Libreria Acqua Alta, or Library of High Water. They discovered new and used books in all languages. But the uniqueness comes not just from the books, but from the very different shelving which were boats, canoes, bathtubs, gondolas, and anything else that floats in which they can possibly insert books and magazines.

The story goes that when the Acqua Alta pushes high water into the canals causing anywhere from inches to feet of water, the boats and bathtubs rise with the water. Some books have been turned into furniture. There are also poles, oars and mannequins to complete the treat for your eyes, and a booklover's soul. Her extraordinary find and souvenir was a small book, *The Grand Canal, Palaces and Families*, complete with photos of every building plus its history.

Peter's cousin, Woodie, an artist, part-time faculty at the local university, and fisherman, lived up dozens of steps in a home perched on the side of a steep hillside. Easy enough to find, so they thought. Anne pulled out the email from Woodie telling exactly where the staircase was located, squeezed between two buildings across from the Native Arts Market. Only 78 steps. Huffing and puffing reaching the top, they glanced down at their ship while catching their breath.

After a tour of his unique home with a million dollar view and taking photos from his front window of their floating hotel, they retraced the steps this time much easier going down and visited his small art gallery. Anne was hoping to find just the right piece for their home. How cool would it be to have a painting from a cousin? Anne naïvely expected to see lovely paintings of mountains and glaciers, bears and moose, breaching humpbacks or maybe a sunset or two. Wrong. The cousin had a fondness for nudes, none appropriate for their home gallery.

The three walked a short distance to Woodie's favorite hole-in-the-wall restaurant where they supposedly prepared the best salmon chowder in Juneau. No local shared the name for fear it would be overrun by tourists. Peter and Anne promised never to tell a soul.

While enjoying dinner, the male cousins several years apart in age with Peter the younger, reminisced about their grandpa. Each summer as far back as they could recall, he would drive from the farmstead at Walterville on the McKenzie River in Oregon, about 2,500 miles north total, going through Fairbanks to the Arctic Circle, and mine for gold. Their grandpa shared a lease with a man named Henry.

Woodie told them, "I was in the Fairbanks area some years ago on a road trip. I was looking at the effects of a series of large wildfires for a painting project. At one point I drove out the Steese Highway one hundred and some miles to the town of Central, so named as it is the center of the Birch Creek mining district.

"On the way to Central there is a junction called Miller House. Nothing remains of whatever it was named after, but

I knew that the mine that Grandpa was a partner in was located somewhere in the area (Mastodon Dome).

"In Central, what appeared to be an old work camp, originally Atco bunkhouses and plywood cookshack, had been converted to a bar and grill/hotel. I had dinner there and asked about the mine owned by Henry Speaker near Miller House. This created a bit of a buzz in the bar and grill. Speaker was one of the more successful miners in the district, and Grandpa was a partner or investor with him since they had mined together in Southern Oregon during the Depression. There is an exit from Interstate 5 near Grants Pass, Oregon, called Speaker Road after Henry.

"I had heard my mother and other relatives often refer to Henry. My mother, as it happens, did not care for him when she first met him in her early teens. She thought that he was 'ogling' her. At the time, he was a 'strapping' (her word) and relatively young man. She met him later with regard to the settling of her father's estate. At that point her adjective changed to 'wizened.' Henry Speaker is the subject of a segment of John McPhee's book, *Coming Into The Country*. He was an interesting guy.

"While at the bar in Central, the buzz created by my interest in Speaker's mine spread up and down the miners at the bar and someone dug up a guy who knew where it was. Stanley Gelvin was a member of a local family of miners who worked in the district for many years, and he gave me directions to the mine. The Gelven family is the subject of the same chapter of McPhee's book.

"The mine is located about 11 miles down a fairly rough road that branches off the Steese Highway at Miller House. It is in the drainage of the North Fork of Harrison Creek, which is a tributary of Birch Creek for which the mining district was named. The Birch Creek district was the location of an early gold rush some years before the Klondike.

"At the time that Grandpa worked with Speaker (summer of 1970), they were operating the last hydraulic mine in North America. Placer mining has lost much of its romance in recent years. These days it amounts to sitting on an excavator digging gravel out of past or present creek beds.

"Speaker was old school. The only heavy equipment he had was an International farm tractor on tracks. This is a small machine with a six-cylinder gas engine. Speaker used it to dig a long ditch at a gentle grade across the hillside above the creek. A settling pond was located above the current work, and irrigation pipe carried the water some distance straight down to the stream bed and through a nozzle looking more or less like a seven-or-eight-foot-long garden hose nozzle mounted on a swivel and counterbalanced with a steel box filled with rocks. This way it could be easily directed by an operator. The 'head' that was built up created a stream of water that could be used to move earth and even boulders away from the bedrock and direct the gold-bearing gravel through a sluice box to separate the gold. This method of mining has been used all over the world and I believe there are people in Latin America using it still.

"Like most older industrial techniques, it relies much more upon skill, knowledge, and physical effort than more mechanized modern techniques. The upside is a far lower overhead. Speaker and Grandpa were in their late sixties.

"I was offered a job but opted to go to Outward Bound Mountaineering School instead. I've often regretted that choice, but I think it was the right one. Both Speaker and Grandpa were known for being a bit difficult at times, and I had heard a rumor of one employee of theirs who quit and hiked out. He must have been pretty motivated.

"My mother also encouraged me to go to school in Colorado, with that look a mother can give that says, 'Don't ask why.' So, I suppose I missed a great opportunity, but I may have saved my relationship with Grandpa."

On their stroll back to the ship, two bald eagles sat back-to-back linked like Siamese twins facing the opposite direction. They could have been taxidermied bookends minus the books.

The ships' lights twinkled like stars. Peter sensed the serenity sweep over Anne. She had been uneasy since the glacier incident but tried to cover it up by being overly cheery. He knew she could hardly wait to tell her parents and brothers about the day's incident, but mostly about the other encounter. Oh and Peggy; she could wait until the morning. Peggy had also been part of the episode at the headwaters decades earlier.

Back in their stateroom, she pressed 9112, her parent's room, then 9435, one brother's room and 8478 for the other. She knew they'd be at the nightly entertainment and left a message, "URGENT, come to our room at 11:00." She paced on the veranda taking deep breaths of sea air.

Each couple seeing the blinking light listened to the messages on their phones hearing Anne's urgent demand. Her mother thought something had happened to Peter. Her brothers thought something had happened to their parents.

Having no clue, the six started walking from the different directions of the ship. A rapid knock and Anne opened the door to her brother Max and wife, Lola.

"Get in here quick," she pulled his arm.

"What's up? What's so urgent?" her normally nonchalant brother apprehensively asked.

"Wait until Mom and Dad get here and Will and Shelley." Lola became concerned with the wait.

Another knock. It was her younger brother and his wife.

"What's up, Sis?" Both brothers always called her Sis.

"Gotta wait until the folks get here."

"So nothing is wrong with them, right?"

"Right. We need to wait for them."

"Well, what's their hold up?"

There was a quiet knock on the door. Amusing was an understatement as Peter watched the expressions on each face while Anne, along with his brief interjections, told them about the boot incident on the glacier.

"Oh dear," her mother said empathically, "not again, Anne."

"It's okay Mom, I didn't see anything really except the top of the upside-down boot. Probably a hem on some pants. Except for the fact that a dead person was attached to it. It is really awful though."

Her younger brother, Mr. Law Enforcement, in his commanding way, asked what the police department was doing and what they had asked her in the interview. Did she sign anything?

Her answers seemed to appease him.

"Jeez, you are a magnet for—" Max shook his head as Will stopped him, "I wouldn't go any further, Bro."

Her dad wrapped her in his comforting arms.

Peter sort of chuckled as he said, "Oh, but wait, there's more, so much more." He motioned with his hand silently encouraging all six to sit, then back toward Anne to take it away, like introducing a leading act on stage.

A silly grin formed as Anne explained she had been asked to go to the police station to give a statement. "You'll never guess in a million years, maybe a trillion, who the captain is and in charge of the case."

With no answers, not even guesses forthcoming, she said, "Mom, it's Deputy Tall, Dark and Handsome, from the Metolius River."

"Deputy Malloy?" Will asked.

"Captain Malloy now," Anne replied.

"Noooooo waaaaaay," Lola dragged out, "*THE* infamous deputy?"

"Yes, indeed," Peter nodded.

"You're kidding, right? How old is he? Like 70?" Max exclaimed.

"58."

"What a small world," her father said, shaking his head.

Anne and her mother's eyes met. Her mom broke into a smile, "How does he look, Anne?" taking her back 29 years and remembering her teenage daughter's first major crush.

"The same. Well, almost," Anne replied. Then she filled her family in on Malloy's life journey.

Just before midnight and still light, they all walked around the top deck reliving the Metolius River caper, as if in-laws, Peter, Lola and Shelley, hadn't heard it enough over the years. Lights all over Juneau were on and another cruise ship departed with deck after deck awash in white lights.

Peter and Anne had missed Russian dinner night but instead had the best salmon chowder ever. Technically still July 3rd, at one minute after midnight, Juneau is the first city in the US to shoot off fireworks celebrating the 4th of July. They cruised out under colorful and loud bombs bursting in air.

CHAPTER TWENTY-NINE

Tony watched the fireworks standing at his window. His window, not their window. Ollie leaned against Tony's left leg, almost like he was supporting him. Tony would never forget the third of July.

With Clint's parents due in early the next day, probably the same early flight as his mom's, he needed to get some sleep. His bloodshot eyes burned. He hoped more beer was the answer.

Who'd tell Clint's favorite younger cousin Caleb who lived in Portland? He introduced Clint to kombucha at a family gathering the previous Christmas. He brewed it in his basement and Clint tried several flavors. It was love at first sip since he was a fan of anything tart, sour and tangy. Clint liked the zippy fizziness and wanted to start crafting their own. Did the last batch of kombucha turn deadly? Had they done something wrong in making the last batch? Did I poison Clint by mistake? And Ericka really didn't know?

Tony recalled how Clint was impatient with his first batch. Letting it ferment for three weeks seemed too long. He started tasting it after a week, pouring a little from the jar into a glass. It first tasted like your average glass of sugary sweet tea but after a week or two of fermentation, it transformed into a tart, effervescent beverage. He checked it each day. Finally, one day Clint heard a soft pop and bubbles flowed to the surface when he opened it. "It's ready," Clint shouted to him. It's supposed to have all kinds of good enzymes, amino acids, and vitamins. There were all sorts of claims for treating ailments. Clint didn't care about any of that, but he had noticed his gut felt better since he'd started drinking it.

It seemed an easy, fun and inexpensive hobby. Clint experimented determining they'd use only caffeinated tea, then decide what their tastebuds preferred: black, green white or whatever.

After batches two and three, they were pros. Clint made quarts of different flavors for friends. Clint decided to branch out and added his favorite juice flavor—blueberry. Tony liked grape. Another batch Clint added strawberry. They wouldn't try this again. Bottles of brown, gold, cherry red, and amber were pretty but didn't mean they all tasted good. Cinnamon was Clint's favorite, Tony's not so much. Clint and Tony stored the colorful concoctions on an open shelf in their water-cooled houseboat.

Tony couldn't sleep. Memories flooded his mind. He had never let Ollie sleep on his bed but tonight he did.

CHAPTER THIRTY

The bright white numbers 2:32 on Ericka's clock glared as bright as the morning sunshine outside her black-out-shaded window. Ericka turned over in bed. She fell asleep but tossed and turned. Kirbie jumped off at some point, unable to put up with the constant movement.

She dreamed someone was watching her. She woke up sweating and in a panic thinking somebody was in her apartment. Some light seeped in around the window, so it wasn't pitch dark. She didn't see anyone. Heart pounding, she reached over to switch on the lamp on the nightstand.

She surveyed the room; she felt like the dream was reality. She looked around trying to find something out of place. Nothing looked suspiciously changed to cause her alarm. Until she looked to the right.

CHAPTER THIRTY-ONE

Anne figured after the day of some of the most unusual circumstances she'd fall asleep in a few minutes. Wrong. After 45 minutes of tossing and turning, she still felt as wired as if she'd drunk three glasses of iced tea after 3 p.m. She gave up and got up from bed as quietly as possible, slipping on a plush robe provided by the cruise line.

Tears sprang to her eyes. She scrunched them shut as she reached in her robe pocket for a tissue then wiped her eyes. She didn't even know this person, but he was still someone's son, brother, husband or boyfriend.

Then she thought about the young man her family discovered in the headwaters of the Metolius River 29 years ago. He was young, only 19 years old. What was his name, she asked herself? Ralph? Randy? Oh, right, Rusty. She cried and cried. It dawned on her that as a 14-year-old girl, she didn't realize the importance of life and what death really meant. She hadn't been touched by death yet.

She wondered as an adult, losing all four grandparents over a five-year period fairly recently, if she was having a post-traumatic experience. Only now did she truly grieve for the boy from 29 years earlier.

Wrapped in a wool blanket sitting in a lounge chair on their veranda, at 3:25, she gazed at the sunrise as it created a brush stroke of pinks and oranges on the white-capped mountains. Anne felt blessed she hadn't missed nature's multi-colored treat. Something caught her attention in the water below. A humpback swam by going the opposite direction. Doubly blessed. She'd tell Peter in a few hours everything he'd missed. Emotionally exhausted, she dozed off in the lounge.

When she slipped in beside Peter and closed her eyes, listening to his regular breathing, punctuated by a random snore, she still couldn't clear her mind for sleep. Sad thoughts kept rushing in. Finally she closed her eyes and slept.

CHAPTER THIRTY-TWO

Tony tried to sleep. He microwaved a Marie Callender's chicken pot pie. Then tossed it in the garbage. He drank three beers. In bed he dozed between subconscious and conscious. Something woke him. He heard water running in the kitchen. He knew it was Clint getting a drink. Something wasn't right. Then he remembered it couldn't be Clint. He was dead. Dead. It was quiet, dead quiet.

Ollie wasn't moving, was he dead too? Tony anxiously reached and touched the warm dog who was breathing softly. Tony let out a moan that woke Ollie who then moved closer stretching all the way, lying right up against Tony's back.

CHAPTER THIRTY-THREE

Something was wrong. The closet door was ajar. Ericka remembered hanging a freshly laundered blouse that she would wear the next day on the outside of the closet. *Where is it?* she said to herself.

Was this all her imagination? Had somebody entered her apartment and was this a way of sending a message to frighten her into silence? Had an intruder grabbed the first thing he could find? A blouse? She frantically searched the closet. It wasn't there. Her first thought was Tyrone. Ericka could feel her heart pounding in her chest, thumping loudly like a determined person banging on a locked door. But then again, she could be imagining the entire thing. She thought not and rechecked the front and back doors. They were both locked.

She couldn't sleep the rest of the night and sat with Kirbie on the sofa back under the quilt.

CHAPTER THIRTY-FOUR

Clint's heartsick parents departed on the first flight from SeaTac airport arriving at the Juneau airport at 9 a.m. They hadn't even thought to look around for Tony's mother, who sat about a dozen rows behind the sorrowful couple. Tony met the three outside of baggage. His fiftyish mom with walnut, tightly permed hair normally looked stylish. Today she looked distressed. They all hugged each other, Clint's mom holding Tony longer than her husband.

They asked to check into the historic Baranof Hotel on Franklin before going to Tony and Clint's place, having to do the unthinkable for their younger son—packing up his personal belongings to take home. They would taxi to Tony's place later.

Tony always used this hotel when family and friends visited. The location was walkable to the State Capitol, St. Nicholas Russian Orthodox Church, Red Dog Saloon, Mount Roberts Tramway, and lots of shopping and restaurants. But this wasn't a social visit and totally different for Clint's distraught parents. They had an appointment to meet with Captain Malloy in the early afternoon. They had return tickets for the following day. Tony's mom would stay at the hotel also, after Tony insisted she'd be more comfortable there.

———

All three grieving parents arrived at Tony's, who had already packed up Clint's clothing for his parents to take home. Clint really didn't have any personal items, just a photo or two of family, toiletries, and a *New Testament* somebody standing on a street corner handed him one day. Tony had never seen him read it, but Clint had written his name on the inside front cover. Mrs. Sterling asked Tony to donate the clothing to the Salvation Army. The rest of Clint's belongings fit into a duffel bag his dad brought along.

The four sat in the living room, solemn and teary, as Tony told them about their unique job, mutual friends and sports they'd done, minus any mention of a girlfriend. Ollie sat with his head leaning against Mr. Sterling's right leg. When they left, Mrs. Sterling told Tony that if he needed anything, to let them know. They wouldn't see Tony again until a funeral sometime later when they could get Clint home. Captain Malloy would be filling them in on laws and protocol for transporting a deceased person.

———

A groggy Ericka showered, dressed and headed to Silverbow for the busy morning crowd. The comforting scents of vanilla, almonds, and honey couldn't distract her. She had to cut her conversation short with Jill because she was not feeling well. She ran to the bathroom and threw up. Jill reassured her that it was the stress from Clint's death or maybe the flu? Jill had heard it was going around.

Locals gathered at the bakery for a sweet treat and coffee, and town scoop. Anyone walking in would smell cinnamon, raisins, biscuits, and ground coffee. They got "the dirt." The "skinny." Local gossip. Today the word was that counterfeit $20 bills were being passed off. Criminals or tourists, the police didn't know yet. Ericka assumed it was Tyrone, that weasel.

Sitting with Jill, Ericka retold her cousin for the umpteenth time how she had met Clint at the original Starbucks on Pike Street.

"I'm so sorry, honey," her cousin said as she wrapped her comforting arms around Ericka, letting her sob.

The idea that her life could be in danger hadn't registered in Ericka's mind. She wasn't being naïve; she didn't want to give in to fear. Because if she did, she would abandon all thought of trying to find out who killed Clint. She had a newfound purpose in life, righting wrongs and exposing the person who thought he had gotten away with murder.

Even though cousins, one would never know by their looks. Jill's round face was the opposite of Ericka's angular one. Ericka's long blonde hair was the opposite of Jill's shining cap of auburn hair cut in a practical, easy style. She was always casually dressed, wearing a plaid shirt and a pair of well-worn jeans.

Jill's favorite colors were lime green and bright yellow. Anyone could see the bakery blocks away and that's exactly what she wanted. The wall to the right of the front door was painted lime green with three horizontal panels of unevenly spaced bright yellow slats of wood. A wood table hugged the wall with three chairs, two yellow and one green. The front door was unremarkable except for the red OPEN neon sign.

The bakery sat nestled between Northern Lights Bookstore and Greengate Studio. The front of the bookstore had been painstakingly painted in swaths of multiple shades of blue, blending into greens and pink then white, supposedly giving the impression of the aurora borealis. This might be the only time people would ever see the northern lights, so the bookstore owner wanted it as she remembered it—vivid and flowing during the winter months.

The bakery window on the left boasted *Best Cookies in Alaska* painted in white. The blocky white-lettered sign against a backdrop of bright purple in all caps read SILVER-BOW. She said it popped.

"Jill, you are so persnickety," Ericka complained. "It drives me crazy. You're so precise on every spoonful of wheat, vanilla, or whatever ingredient you're using."

"Ah, but you do love my sweet treats."

"Very true," but Ericka didn't have the patience for baking; cooking wasn't a favorite either.

Her cousin had purchased the historic building a couple of years earlier and renovated it. Jill's intentions were to host folk singers, movie showings, and who knew whatever else might come their way.

Jill and her husband Scott lived in three rooms above the bakery. Ericka liked the cozy feel of Jill's apartment with one large room for their living space, kitchen and cute four-seat kitchen table. Scott put a swivel rocker by the bedroom window so when Jill had time, she could sit and prop her feet up on the cool upholstered footstool, a real treasure she found at Christopherson's Antiques & More. Or read a mystery novel or travel book from the bookstore, complete with her bay view below.

The other store bookend, Greengate Studios, a gallery where Jessica the owner, who was also a photographer and graphic artist, created her magic. Her love for nature showed through in all of her photographs; not just wildlife and mountains, but wildflowers that no one knew existed until she showcased them.

She also carried about a dozen other local artists' creative items of Forget-Me-Nots encased in glass vases, baskets woven with grasses from the Mendenhall Valley, photographs of birds with the misty glacier in the background, watercolors of moose in a dewy marsh—nothing typical or too touristy like Juneau mugs or t-shirts from overseas.

CHAPTER THIRTY-FIVE

A weary Anne, who had gotten maybe two hours of sleep, read to Peter from the *Gazette*.

"In 1887 Captain William Moore and his young son ventured up the Chilkoot Inlet and built a cabin at the mouth of the Skagway River. Previously unexplored, this piece of land was named Skagway, 'Land of the North Wind,' by nearby tribes.

"By 1896 the word was out that gold had been discovered in the Yukon. Within two years, thousands of stampeders had passed through Skagway using White Pass to reach the gold rich Yukon. Steep and dangerous, White Pass was considered the fastest way to get to the gold. Safer and easier passage could be found by sailing farther north to Norton Sound and traveling up the Yukon River, but many miners chose to forego safety and save the extra time and money this route required. Bones of horses, mules, and prospectors alike lined Chilkoot Pass and White Pass. Prospectors made their way through the mountains, a 600-mile trek across the Yukon's frozen terrain to the Klondike gold fields. Over $50 million in gold was pulled out of the Yukon in just four years.

"Four blocks wide and 23 blocks long, today's Skagway is still little more than a foothold in a gigantic wilderness, but over the last century it has become much more peaceful and civilized. And although the population has dropped to only around 1,000, the town still has plenty of life left. Many of the false-front buildings and plank sidewalks have been maintained through the years, preserving the heritage of the town.

"The grand old Golden North Hotel is a town landmark. Today, the hotel is a living museum—each room is furnished with Klondike period pieces. The Trail of '98 Museum has a collection of old gambling equipment and a number of other historical exhibits on display. Down the street sits the most unusual and photographed structure in town, the Arctic Brotherhood Hall. Covered in hundreds of sticks and logs, the building's façade has been part of the town from the beginning."

Anne was excited to find Peggy and tell her about Deputy Tall, Dark, and Handsome. She punched in the room number on the phone but there had been no answer in her stateroom the first, second or third time so Anne was on the hunt for her. She knew they'd be on the same train ride up the White Pass if she didn't see her before.

Skagway was Anne's second favorite town along the coast-line of Alaska. Situated at the northern end of southeast Alaska's Inside Passage, it blends history with natural beauty, and is the jumping off point for anyone thinking of taking the shortcut over the coastal mountains into Canada's

Yukon. That's why there's a RV park at the end of town and a lot more vehicles in general. Unlike Juneau and Ketchikan, one could actually drive to Skagway through Canada.

But it's the water approach by ship that she'd never get weary of seeing. A tiny town nestled at the base of a river valley surrounded by mountains jutting 5,000 to 7,000 feet straight out of the saltwater fjord was stunning.

The warm temperatures the past week had created new, unnamed and probably temporary waterfalls tumbling into the flat greenish water. They knew they were on the ocean, but it still looked like a lake.

Already docked was Celebrity's *Summit*, a ship they'd had the pleasure of sailing on during a past cruise. The captain expertly moved their ship between *Summit* and the bay. One the other side of *Summit* was a steep mountain where daredevils had climbed and painted their names, class year, ship name and sometimes just nonsense on the rock billboard.

On shore, ship's personnel were dressed as Murray the Moose and Benny the Bear. They cozied in between tourists and had pictures taken. Horse drawn wagons lined up, able to carry six. It was a popular mode of transportation from the ships to town. Peter and Anne preferred walking the easy mile and a half. Sticking up in the backyard of a house like ten-foot tall sunflowers were 21 upside down vibrant blue wine bottles affixed to poles. Tall white flowers almost reached the tops of the bottles. The weather report told them the high would be 86 degrees, another record-breaker.

They walked by the former White Pass and Yukon Railroad Depot, a colorful structure built in 1898 and a big part of Skagway life until 1969, when railroad operations moved to their new building two doors east. The old depot is now the National Park Service Visitor Center. Although the tracks are now on the south side of the building, passenger trains used to chug down Broadway on their way into town from Whitehorse, 112 miles to the north.

———

Standing in line to board the train with most of their friends, who purposely all booked the same time probably filling entire train car, Anne finally spotted Peggy and her husband ahead in line and waved them back to join them. As Peter and Rich looked at the muddy snowmelt river, Anne grabbed Peggy and filled her in on the previous days' activities.

Peggy, flabbergasted said, "Are you kidding me? We heard about a body on the glacier. Really, that was you who found it? Deputy Tall, Dark, and Handsome? No Way! How did he look?" Then Peggy took a breath. She just shook her head back and forth, like she did when they were growing up and she was flummoxed or perturbed with Anne.

———

"All Aboard" shouted the conductor and Anne's friends all stepped back in time into the authentic, vintage car. As they slowly departed Skagway on their two-hour, thirty-minute ride, the train passed a huge rotary snowplow.

The narrator told them about Skagway's rough beginning as they passed by the Gold Rush Cemetery and the grave of the city's most notorious shyster, Soapy Smith. Beginning to climb at elevation zero feet, he told the riders they would climb nearly 3,000 feet in 20 vertical miles and warned them of steep grades and tight, cliffhanger curves ahead.

He said, "By 1898, the town was averaging a steady population of 20,000. Little more than a tent city, it was a rough and lawless place. At times ships dumped supplies on the beach or in the harbor rather than take a risk by docking in the port. Gangs roamed the streets, separating newcomers from their supplies, and conmen helped returning prospectors find ways of dispensing of their newly acquired gold.

"The most disreputable of Skagway's long list of bandits was Jefferson Soapy Smith who earlier had been chased out of Colorado. Smith was a legendary conman who set up his gang in Skagway. For nine months, he portrayed himself as a civic leader, winning the allegiance of not only prostitutes, gamblers and saloon keepers, but also of bankers, editors and church leaders. He earned infamy with his wide array of crooked schemes. He offered telegraph service to fresh arrivals—at $5 a message it would have been a bargain, if Skagway had a telegraph line.

"Crooked gambling and muggings were also favorites. But the scheme that earned him his nickname was that he sold soap wrapped in counterfeit dollar bills and the wrapping was of course, added to the price. Although Soapy conned many people out of thousands of dollars, he wasn't completely unpopular. He gave money to widows and orphans, set up a recruiting office for the Spanish-American War, and was honored by the Alaska governor for his civic efforts. Soapy virtually ran Skagway until things got out of hand, and his downfall came quick and hard.

"After Soapy's gang robbed a miner (a common occurrence) of $2,670 worth of gold in broad daylight and Soapy refused to return it, the locals formed a vigilante committee, the Committee of One Hundred and One to deal with him. Frank Reid, a city engineer, organized a mob to go after Soapy.

"On July 8, 1898, Soapy tried to force his way into the vigilante meeting and Soapy and Frank ended up killing each other in a violent shootout. Soapy was killed instantly. Reid sustained an agonizing groin injury and rallied bravely but died 12 days later. Smith's gang was rounded up and sent to jail. Skagway enjoyed peace and quiet ever since," the narrator concluded.

At mile six and 402 feet, Denver Glacier trailhead, with a derailed White Pass brickish caboose sitting alone like a lost trekker, several people de-trained for their excursion winding through old growth Western Hemlock forest, past Denver Falls, to the upper end of the valley with stunning views of Denver Glacier's hanging blue ice and surrounding Sawtooth Mountains. The train would pick them up on the return trip. Anne and Peter knew about this adventure because they'd done it on a previous trip.

Anne wondered how the workers accomplished all this without modern equipment, mostly man and animal power? The narrator was just about to explain it all to the entire train. He said that between May 1898 and July 1900, some 35,000 workers had a hand, big and small, in connecting Skagway and Whitehorse by rail, and 35 died in the process. She imagined workers hanging from rock faces by ropes, and the 450 tons of explosives it took to blast the line, a good half of it just to get past Rocky Point at milepost 6.9 and 637 feet elevation.

The gentle swaying back and forth made Anne a little drowsy, so she wandered through the three vintage parlor cars to the viewing deck at the back. She stood in awe seeing mountains, glaciers, gorges, waterfalls, water tanks, trestles, and historic signs. The narrator pointed out Bridal Veil Falls to the left at 1,334 feet. The broad waterfalls plunged through evergreens, making a gloriously thunderous sound tumbling into the river.

At mile 12 the train began a huge horseshoe curve. She saw Slippery Rock, the wooden trestle, and wondered how in the world the men constructed this feat with limited resources. Going over the gently-curved trestle, Anne looked forward and saw the three green and yellow engines pulling the passenger cars. They reached Glacier Station at 1,817 feet then went through Tunnel Mountain. At Inspiration Point, they looked out down at Skagway Harbor with cruise ships in the bay, miles of the Lynn Canal, and the Sawtooth Range, obvious how it got its name.

The turn-of-the-century parlor car train seemed to cling to the cliffs in the mountainside. She looked below seeing the old trails that the prospectors used and viewed cliffs in opposite canyons. Over 17 miles up White Pass at Dead Horse Gulch, with the bleached bones of perished gold-rush pack animals scattered below, it was abundantly clear how it got its name, too.

At Cantilever Bridge, passengers peered down as they crossed over the roaring, white foamy Yukon River. The engineer took his time chugging across the trestle. Then they were back in complete darkness in a tunnel. Over 19 miles from Skagway, the words "Trail of '98" are carved into the rocks.

At the White Pass Summit, elevation 2,888 feet, lakes surrounded by hills create the headwaters of the Yukon River. Cotton balls of fluffy snow turned into a lacy blanket of white as the hills morphed into mountains.

At Fraser, British Columbia, each took turns standing by the large wooden sign, "Welcome to Alaska, the Gateway to the Klondike." Then by the "Welcome to Canada" sign, documenting their visit hopping from one country to the other.

Instead of returning by train, their group took a tour bus that stopped in the recreated mining town called Liarsville. The actors are dressed in Klondike-era clothing and visitors hear plenty of lies, but truths also. They all took turns trying their hand at panning for gold. Each came away with a grain that looked about the size of two pieces of sand; in other words, just barely visible.

Several huskies lay nearby waiting for someone to pet them. Sadie had white front legs, a white muzzle and white fur around her face. Her left eye was dark brown and her right, blue, the color of a glacier. It was a bit disconcerting and Anne had trouble concentrating on what was being said as she kept looking at Sadie's blue eye. There was a streak of brown through the middle of her white fur that turned all brown on her head creating a brown cap for the top of her head. The rest of her was all brown including her two back legs. Each husky had its own unique coloring.

"Sweating in Alaska, unbelievable," Peter mumbled, as Anne conveniently nabbed two complimentary bottles of water from an outstretched arm belonging to a friendly store employee. The two sat on a bench looking about a mile down the street at their ship moored at the dock. They never tired of the illusion of a ship cruising right down the main street.

Peter pointed at a van with a window sign promoting Chilkoot Trail Hike & River Float. Several years earlier they'd thought this excursion sounded interesting, unique and quiet, away from the masses.

The shore excursion description read, "After a safety orientation, you will board a van and drive through Skagway to the backcountry deep in the heart of Dyea Valley. You'll travel to the historic town of Dyea to hike the first two scenic miles of the Chilkoot Trail, the centerpiece of gold rush history in Skagway.

"Now a tranquil place of incredible beauty, the trail winds through a lush rainforest alive with birds, animals and wildflowers. Your tour climbs and descends 350 feet over Saintly

Hill. Along the way, your guide will share information about the natural history and Klondike folklore with you. Photo opportunities abound as you retrace the footsteps of the gold-hungry stampeders who forged this route 100 years ago.

"Arrive at the banks of the Taiya River, where your 18-foot raft awaits for the scenic float back to Dyea. Enjoy a riverbank snack of homemade cookies and a hot beverage before returning by van on the 30-minute drive to Skagway.

"Not recommended for guests with physical limitations. Layer clothing. Sturdy shoes are recommended."

The Activity Level graph showed EASY to a CHAL-LENGE and pointed right in the middle at Moderate. "Easy peasy," one said. Her spouse wasn't so sure.

Two others plus Peter and Anne had chosen the hike and float trip. One younger woman clearly a fit hiker, and one guy who probably hadn't walked much. Anne wondered almost out loud to Peter if the guy had read the instructions about layered clothing and sturdy shoes, instead in a gray t-shirt, shorts and what looked like some discount store tennis shoes.

The inappropriately dressed male asked about bears. The guide told him—you just need to be faster than the last person. The guy's eyes bugged out believing the deadpan guide. Others started to laugh. Looking at their small group, they observed he wouldn't be the fastest.

Then Peter recalled how different the hike was from the printed description. Climbing steeply, they were soon swallowed inside huge trees, shaded and damp, crawling over fallen giant trees and roots as big as most moss-wrapped trees, on a trail mostly composed of rocks, clambering up and over boulders, wading a couple of recently formed creeks, before reaching the river two hours later and climbing aboard a yellow river raft. He remembered how the river shone like silver. Anne and Peter survived the unique experience, one they would remember for years.

Anne abruptly stopped Peter and said, "SHHHHHH. I hear bagpipes." Peter had learned over the years that his wife had a propensity, like a sixth sense, for hearing the pipes because of her Scottish ancestry. Many times, he had poo-pooed her and mumbled it was her imagination. He'd learned not to doubt her hearing when it came to Scottish pipers.

And she was right—once again—as they got a block closer, standing in front of Sgt. Preston's Trading Post. In a circle surrounding a white and navy mid-1950s Nash Metropolitan in mint condition was a group of 11 pipers warming up for the 4th of July celebration.

Anne deduced the men would be extremely warm in the wool tartan kilts, but at least the men were wearing cotton, short-sleeve tan shirts. She was never one to speculate whether or not there was more clothing underneath the kilts.

She stood somberly soaking in the haunting sounds that not all appreciated, including her husband who could stand patiently for a bit, but not hours like Anne. She always, always, always, got teary-eyed when hearing the pipes. She figured it must be in her blood. She never made an excuse or blamed herself for being overly sentimental at the tugging of the roots in her Scottish heart, she just let the tears flow.

Standing in the middle of Main Street, Anne was impressed looking at the various modes of transportation: the train, buses, cars and RVs, helicopters, seaplanes, plus fishing boats, yachts, five sailboats, and four cruise ships.

Back on board, Peter put away the *Skagway News* he spotted on a corner newspaper stand. Headlines read: "Tourist Discovers Body on Mendenhall Glacier. Juneau's Search and Rescue removed the body of Clinton Sterling originally of Seattle, Washington. Police are investigating."

Peter announced he would get cleaned up before dinner and Anne replied she'd be back in 20 minutes. It wasn't unusual that she'd take off somewhere. She sought out the small chapel on the fourth deck and entered the empty room. She sat on a padded pew gazing at the wooden cross hanging on the wall. She said a prayer for the person who belonged to the boot and the family and friends affected by the tragic loss.

Pensive, later standing on their veranda, Anne stared straight down at the sapphire sea that matched the sky. A wave of melancholy washed over her. She took a couple of deep breaths then stepped inside their room and plugged in her curling iron to fix her hair before dinner.

They always looked forward to French night. They'd thoroughly enjoyed several European trips that included touring France and found the food to be beautifully prepared and delicious with impeccable service. Anne attempted to enlighten judgmental people, mostly Americans, when she heard anyone giving the French people a bad rap. She'd never met a rude Parisian, only helpful ones as she stumbled through the few French words she tried to pronounce. Even the police officers were patient and kind. She always found that people in different countries spoke far better English than she spoke their language.

Appetizers: Fruit cocktail, Port wine terrine, Escargot bourguignonne, Caviar with garnish. Both ordered escargot.

They skipped soup and salads and went onto the entrée selections: Gruyère ravioli dugléré, Grilled sea scallops, Salmon à l'oseille, Escallops of Alaska king salmon or yummy Côq au Vin. This was a hard choice tonight, but Peter went with the sea scallops and Anne the salmon.

Desserts: Strawberry Mousse Cake, Crisp Napoleon, Cherries Jubilee. Forget the ice creams in favor of Cherries Jubilee not just because of the cherries but the presentation.

A chef wearing a tall white hat pushed a cart with a gas burner on top. In a saucepan he combined water, sugar, cinnamon sticks and lemon rind, that he grated in front of his admiring fans. He explained each step. The sauce boiled until thickened. He added the dark cherries and cooked a bit over low heat with the syrup turning the color of the cherries. He removed the lemon rind and added two tablespoons of brandy over the top and mentioned when trying this at home, it's important not to boil. He turned off the stove.

He lit a kitchen torch, like one would use to brown sugar on the top of crème brûlée. Barely touching the cherries, *poof*, the liquor flamed over the top of the fruit. He used a spoon to baste the cherries with more liqueur and juices until the flames fizzled. The masterful chef spooned the hot cherries over vanilla bean ice cream. Every drop was consumed, and Anne spotted someone running his finger along the bottom of the bowl.

Anne could hear music. "I hear a Brahms lullaby," she announced as Peter reached to ring the doorbell. David opened the door of their spacious, stylishly-appointed suite. Ellen, a fine pianist, was already playing another classical piece on the shiny black grand piano in their spacious living room.

David reported that their butler had just departed after cleaning up an elegantly delivered French dinner served at the black granite table set for eight. He laughed at the over-the-top unexpected service that came along with the suite. They had simply opted for more room for the trip. If they needed the butler for anything, they were to call.

Anne asked what Ellen was playing and her answer was that it's one of her favorites, Beethoven's *Für Elise*. Anne mentioned that she thought she'd heard a lullaby. "Yes," Ellen replied, "I was playing Brahms' *Waltz in A-flat Major*."

David, Peter and Anne sat on overstuffed chairs looking at the mountainous scenery with cascading waterfalls on the way to Haines listening to Ellen's classical melodies. She'd switched to another piece and Anne again, not at all savvy about classical music, asked the name of this selection, and it was Chopin's *Nocturne in E-Flat Major*. Anne felt like she could be in heaven with the scenery and melodies—now if Anne could just get Ellen to take harp lessons.

It was smooth sailing past Scenic Island and David pointed out a squatty lighthouse with an eagle perched on top. "Ellen come see this," David insisted.

CHAPTER THIRTY-SIX

Ericka wandered around downtown going to places she and Clint shared. Vinni told her to take the afternoon off. Back home a few minutes before six, she couldn't wait any longer. Ericka punched Clint's number hoping Tony would be home.

"Hello," flat-toned Tony mumbled.

"It's Ericka." She heard a click as Tony ended the call.

She redialed. It rang at least 15 times until an exasperated Tony picked it up and yelled, "Don't call here again."

"Tony, Tony, don't hang up, I need to—" Click.

"That's it," she said out loud. She ran to her car, climbed in and started the engine speeding to Tony and Clint's place.

She pounded on the door for at least two or three minutes before an extremely red-faced, blurred-eyed Tony opened it. He gotten angrier the longer she knocked. He scanned around the complex and saw a neighbor, standing with her hands on her hips.

"Sorry, Mrs. Clifford," he mumbled.

Tony grabbed Ericka's arm and with a hard tug pulled her through the doorway. She squealed, "Ouch, Tony, Jeez." He cared less if he'd hurt her arm. He looked at the clock on the wall. "You have five minutes." She bent down to pet Ollie and he snuggled between her feet.

Ericka's garbled words tumbled out. He couldn't understand a thing.

"Okay, you have ten minutes," he conceded.

She told him everything she told the police. Sobbing, really the only words he could understand was that she loved Clint. She stopped speaking and rubbed her eyes. Tony turned away. He was crying, too. His best friend was dead. All because of her.

She took a deep breath then added the part about Seattle. He told her she needed to tell the police this additional information.

Ericka told Tony she'd been to their home several times, always when Tony wasn't there except for the three delicious dinners. Ericka knew Tony didn't like her much because of what Clint told him about her shenanigans in Seattle.

Clint hadn't filled him in on the newest developments of their relationship. But she had a key. Tony saw that clearly Ollie was used to her as the dog nuzzled her arm now on her lap.

"Clint loved Ollie and my Kirbie," she whispered.

"Kirbie?"

"My cat."

"You're nuts. Clint only liked dogs."

She nodded, "Except when it came to Kirbie."

She glanced around and the place looked different. What had changed? Clint wasn't there. She could see the ships lined up at the dock below and one in the bay. It was a busy tourist day in the capital city.

Ericka told him, "I am going to the police station tomorrow after I finish my shift at the bakery. I'm Jill's only help, and the mornings are crazy busy. I will be there by

11:45 at the latest. Then I'll go to my shift at the jewelry store."

She told him about the dream the night before feeling so real like somebody was in her apartment. And she felt positive a blouse was missing. Was it a dream or maybe a premonition? Or was somebody actually in her apartment? She was very tired because she hasn't slept. "I'm afraid to go to my apartment."

"Clint loved you like a brother. I know you blame me for this."

"Yes, I do, Ericka." He blinked several times, trying to process the newest revelations.

"I do, too," once again tears springing into her eyes. "I'm not sorry I loved him but now wish I never met him. He was the kindest man I've ever known. Except for my father and brother. We were on the right track. He knew my past yet saw a future for us here. I haven't done anything illegal here. I'm done with the chills and thrills. I was so immature. When I up and left I didn't tell Tyrone or Leon. I just left. But they found a piece of mail somehow with a forwarding address and came to Juneau. Ty has been pressuring me to get back into business with him and I continue to refuse. Clint knew it all."

Tony admitted, "Clint didn't tell me all this. I knew you were seeing each other for some time."

"We saw each other often but at odd times due to our schedules," she said with a sad smile. "We'd become quite, well very, close."

Tony didn't ask how close. No wonder Clint seemed happier the past several months.

He looked at the clock on the wall. "Time's up, Ericka, just make sure you tell Captain Malloy everything you've just told me. If you don't, I will."

"I will, I swear. Tomorrow after my bakery shift is over."

Sitting on the sofa she rested her head and instantly fell asleep. Tony left her there as he processed everything she had just revealed. He decided it was okay to leave her there for the night. As he put a blanket over her he saw tears streaming down her cheeks. He wondered if people really cried in their sleep. Ollie settled in at her feet, leaving Tony on his own.

He had either the world's best liar, a murderer, or a completely misjudged, innocent woman on his sofa. He wondered if Ollie's sixth sense was totally discombobulated and he'd been hoodwinked, too.

He also wondered how Clint's parents would feel, and his mom, no less, if they knew Clint's girlfriend was asleep on his sofa.

CHAPTER THIRTY-SEVEN

Anne's parents strolled on the top deck in short-sleeve tops, enjoying the scenery of the Lynn Canal while cruising toward the small town of Haines. Only one ship at a time could fit at the dock.

Forty minutes later coming into the bay, the sight looked dreamy, dotted with the white houses and colorfully painted businesses appearing through pines and firs with white mountains out their back doors.

Several years earlier when Peter and Anne visited Haines on their second Alaska cruise, they had enjoyed the Potlatch alder-baked salmon dinner. Then they sat enthralled by the Chilkat Dancers at the performing arts center sharing their culture and legends through traditional storytelling dances. Their costumes are authentic reproductions of traditional dance items, most of which were made by the young people themselves. Anne remembered it like yesterday.

Each dance was explained before the performance.

-The Bear and Raven dance is the most famous, based on historical traditions. The chief is killed by a huge brown bear. The warriors discover his body and inform the women, who come to carry his body home in his Chilkat ceremonial blanket. The warriors, in searching for the bear, kill many bears until the Raven informs them who the bear is with human hair still in his teeth.

-The Chilkat blanket dance is about the famous blankets and how they are worn in a competitive dance with each clan choosing its champion to uphold the honor of the clan, either Eagle or Raven. The fancy footwork was exhausting even to watch.

-The Farewell dance is where each dancer is given the chance to present his own step or to show off his costume or a piece of artwork. This dance is used by all Northwest tribes, with their own variations.

Everyone in attendance was enlightened, educated and entertained by this outstanding program.

This trip the couple signed up for a jetboat Chilkoot River cruise. Riding a short distance on a bus, the vegetation was green and lush, like everywhere else they'd been.

The owner and captain named Darby told them about the area as they scooted across the top of the water in the powerful yet quiet, uncovered boat making it easy to spot wildlife and perfect for photo opportunities.

They had just moved away from the river's edge when a bald eagle flew down and nabbed a good size fish in its talons and flew off. Bald eagles are easy to spot in the trees with their white heads and tails.

Looking back at the river where they'd just been, it widened out and mountains loomed behind them. A field of low gold grasses led into a pond. There stood a moose, head down grazing all the marshy goodness it could. It looked up as rivulets flowed from both sides of its mouth. The moose stood in the sun's glare, but Anne took a photo anyway.

Cottonwood trees were in full bloom, heavily laden puffs drifting in the air. The season started later in Alaska. Anne and Peter had already gone through the cottonwood tree blooms at home. Both had allergies especially to these floating chunks of what felt like wood spikes in their eyes. Peter rubbed his eyes from the bothersome minuscule toothpicks.

As they rounded a corner the captain stopped. He had a story to tell. He had grown up living in Haines and attended schools there. A few years ago his best childhood friend named Jack moved to Juneau. Jack remained single all his life but thought of Darby's family as his own. He flew his two-seater *Sea-Rey* often to see Darby. They'd fished, hunted and did about everything together.

Darby was devastated one day to get a phone call from one of Jack's neighbors saying that Jack dropped dead outside his back door. It was a tremendous loss for Darby.

That day he needed to be by himself. His wife understood. He got in his boat and meandered the river, trying to come to grips with never seeing his friend again. And not getting to say a proper farewell. As he maneuvered staying in the middle of the river, he noticed something off to his left. It was a bald eagle. It flew level with him for what Darby thought was a half mile.

Then he shut off the motor mid-river, drifting with the easy current. The eagle circled and landed on the front of his boat.

Darby stated, "Now I am not a religious man, but that eagle got my attention. Jack always talked about the feeling he got flying with birds, especially eagles, when he was in his little seaplane." Darby said he stared at the eagle. He blurted out through his tears, "Jack is that you?" The eagle looked right into Darby's eyes and flew off.

The next day Darby returned to the same place in the river as the eagle paced him then landed on the front of the boat, just like the day before. Darby didn't know if he should be nervous or believe what was happening before his very eyes.

Back home he told him wife. She reminded him of Indian lore and beliefs. She said, "Well, dear, it very well could be Jack. Just go with it. Who's to question such a gift?"

Darby said each time he comes to the area, several times a week, the same eagle shows up. One skeptic male patron said, "Obviously it's because you feed it something." Darby replied, "No sir, not true. It's unlawful to feed the animals and birds."

Anne believed every word Darby said but knew that even though Peter hadn't expressed his opinion verbally he was inwardly a nonbeliever in unproven stories like this. Darby explained they were now sitting in the exact location of the first encounter. Flying toward them was his eagle. Anne felt shivers up her spine. She poked Peter hard.

Right in front of their very eyes, the eagle landed on the boat. Darby didn't feed it anything. But he spoke in a calming voice and called it Jack. The passengers were silent except for clicking from camera buttons taking photos of the unexplainable phenomenon. Anne thought, *why not?* When Darby started the motor, Jack soared off. Passengers just looked at each other. A few with eyebrows raised, others with contented smiles—clearly believers like herself, and two with skeptical looks. She took a sideways glance at Peter watching his expression go from skeptical to quizzical. She had pretty much convinced herself that visitors from some other worlds had created Stonehenge and Machu Picchu, so why couldn't an eagle be Jack?

Around every bend, the mountains looked different and Anne told herself to stop taking photos of each one, gorgeous was gorgeous. They floated by a huge cottonwood with mom or dad eagle feeding an eaglet. Darby explained that both parents shared feeding duties. Ending the adventure on the riverbank, Darby's wife delivered thermoses of steaming hot cocoa and platter-size molasses cookies, still warm from the oven.

––––––

Cruising out of Haines, the sun dropped until it finally vanished from their sight yet leaving the cloudless sky fairly light. Just because they could no longer see it hidden behind mountains, the sun would not completely set due to the time of year. The flat ocean reflected a soft pinkish-orange glow.

Peggy and Anne strolled the top deck arm-in-arm, just as they had many times growing up. Both husbands had already retired for the evening. Best friends since junior high, they wanted some "me" time. Even though still light, the moon appeared low in the sky. Peggy asked, "Do you remember all of our camping trips to the Metolius River and how we'd sit outside late at night and watch for falling stars and Sputnik, and Jeff's mom would tell us all about the constellations?"

Together they stood leaning against the railing talking about stars and planets. Anne had known from their childhood that Peggy would grow up to be a teacher. She had indeed, and coming up on 20 years of teaching second-graders.

At the midnight buffet, Anne and Peggy thought they couldn't eat another morsel after dinner. Taking photos of seafood in every shape, design and color, she simply couldn't pass up something similar to shrimp but tasted like lobster called langoustine. She had it when they visited Scotland and it was finger-licking delicious.

CHAPTER THIRTY-EIGHT

With Ericka asleep on the sofa, Tony stood in the same spot as he had the night before gazing at the water. There were no fireworks and it had been one entire day since Clint died. A long, horrible day.

He recalled their flight from Seattle to Juneau. Clint's first flight ever. His back was glued to the seat as they took off from SeaTac on an Alaska Airlines flight to Juneau. Clint had kept his nose pressed to the window almost the entire trip except when lunch was delivered and when he downed three Dr Peppers. "As many as I want?" he asked Tony. "Yep" was the reply.

He saw for the first time from 20,000 feet recognizable mountains like Mt. Adams and Baker, the white-capped Cascade mountains, and lots of water. Flying right over the San Juan Islands he poked Tony reminding him of the time they kayaked in Friday Harbor.

About three hours later, Clint's white-knuckle hands grasp the armrests at a grinding noise as Tony dramatized the jarring bump when the pilot lowered the landing gear.

Clint's wide-eyed, sucking air reaction was exactly what Tony hoped for. He laughed at his friend.

They flew out over water and back toward land. Clint could see how city streets were laid out in a grid below. The buildings got larger and he could tell they were descending, then the asphalt runway appeared. Over the runway, the ground came up toward the belly of the plane, and there was a jolt as the wheels touched down. They bounced up then settled back down again, this time meeting the runway smoothly and taxiing toward the airport buildings.

Tony said, "You can breathe now, we're on the ground." Clint reached to unbuckle his seatbelt, but Tony shook his head and pointed to the illuminated seatbelt sign. "Wait until the sign goes off. We need to stay seated until we reach the gate," Tony instructed Clint.

It didn't take long to taxi to the gate, then another few minutes while the jetway was locked into position. Finally when the seatbelt sign went off, they stood up with other passengers to retrieve their items from the shell above their heads, both grabbing a duffel bag.

Tony let a torrent of unshed tears flow freely, mourning the loss of his best friend, knowing he'd never have more memories like Clint's first flight. He believed now that Ericka had nothing directly to do with Clint's death but indirectly she was still responsible and guilty. He was still so full of outrage he speculated how to make her permanently disappear. That reaction frightened him. He let her sleep and he dozed off and on in his bedroom.

CHAPTER THIRTY-NINE

"**W**ake up, Ericka, WAKE UP," he stood over her. She woke with a jolt. She heard Tony's voice telling her to go talk to the cops. Ollie jumped off the sofa.

"What time is time?"

"About six."

"I slept longer than I thought. I usually get to work at 5:15."

Lying there she experienced an almost paralyzing sense of dread. She knew with certainty that something was going to happen today but couldn't know what. She could feel something unpleasant in the offing.

Quickly she washed her face, brushed her finger over her teeth then ran her fingers through her hair. She straightened her slept-in clothes the best she could.

"Thank you for your kindness. I'll let you know after I've told the police everything."

"You don't need to tell me anything," he replied, still in a grumpy mood from lack of sleep, "Just do it."

"You are, I mean…were, the best friend Clint ever had." She looked like a lost puppy as she closed the door.

She lifted her hand to wave goodbye as a dark swell of grief overwhelmed her, like thunderheads rolling in and blotting out the light. Tony had already closed the door.

She sped home, put out fresh water and food for Kirbie, took a shower, washed her face and added a dab of moisturizer under her puffy bloodshot eyes, brushed her teeth, pulled on a flowy blue top and beige slacks. Hanging on the back of the bathroom door was her blouse. Good grief, she thought. Had she totally overreacted? After giving herself a quick spritz of Diamond, her favorite perfume, she ran to her car. She couldn't shake that overwhelming feeling of dread. She would still have bet $200 that somebody had been in her apartment.

Jill had gone to the bakery even earlier than normal. She usually enjoyed these few quiet early morning moments, sitting down with a second up of coffee and thinking about the day ahead.

Ericka showed up 40 minutes later. Jill looked surprised to see her walk in. Jill took one look at her and her cousinly radar was on full alert. "Oh Ericka," she said several times as her cousin retold her dream from two nights earlier and how frightened she still was. She'd spoken with Tony last night, and she'd just come from staying overnight there. She felt safe there. She still didn't feel well, maybe she had the flu. "Could you be preg…" Jill started as Ericka stopped her midword, "No!!!"

She told Jill that after her shift she was going straight to speak to the police. Receiving a supportive nod from Jill, Ericka knew her cousin fully agreed with her decision to speak with the authorities about everything.

CHAPTER FORTY

W ay too early, Anne woke checking the clock—4:57. Peeking out the heavy floor-to-ceiling curtains, a small boat was skimming its way on a calm sea, not too far from the ship speeding right toward them. They had cruised enough for her to know it was a pilot boat delivering the pilot who would be with them for the day cruising through Glacier Bay.

She stepped out and watched it slowly turn and gingerly edge itself against the ship, careful not to come in contact with the vessel. As the ship's wake thrusted the boat upward, a man jumped into the ship's open door on the second floor and disappeared.

Beyond the boat a humpback was traveling in the same direction as their ship. Anne watched it for some time in the glow of the sunshine on the ocean. She felt so blessed to be sharing space in time with such a magnificent creature. She went back to bed for another two hours.

Anne flung open the curtains. This was one of those monumental days that no one wanted to miss. They were dressed and had jackets laid out on the bed, with cameras, binoculars and sunglasses at the ready. Anne's excitement was infectious. She was already pointing out coves and inlets perfect for animal habitat, scouring the shoreline with their spotting scope for bears and watching for the first ice chunks.

Their TV was set on channel 36 which would broadcast everything LIVE all day. At 7:10 the cruise director announced, "Good morning. Here's a little history on our way to Glacier Bay. When Captain George Vancouver first set eyes on the small five-mile inlet that was Glacier Bay in 1794, he described a 'sheet of ice as far as the eye could distinguish.'

"By the time naturalist John Muir visited in 1879 with a group of native Tlingit, who called the bay their ancestral homeland, the ice had retreated enough to begin exposing one of the world's most majestic wildernesses. You are in for a remarkable, unforgettable day," he ended, promising to notify passengers if wildlife was spotted from the bridge.

At 7:15 their ship arrived at Bartlett Cove. They could tell the ship had slowed down somewhat. Three rooms of friends plus Peter and Anne stood on their verandas watching another small boat approach from an inlet. Anne had already told Peter what he had missed watching the pilot boat and whale earlier.

Markings on the side of the vessel showed it was the National Park Service. Two people moved from the top deck one floor down to the side of the rocking boat. As it moved right alongside their ship, the first man leaped into the open door. Then the second one. Their commentary would begin in two hours.

The mountainous scenery was already stunning, but nothing compared to what was ahead. They'd been here before when it was overcast with typical coastal mist. At the end of the bay, the clouds had parted, reflecting sunshine off the white-crowned giants.

Today was already bright and sunny with a few light and wispy clouds. But that could change; they were in Alaska after all. But they'd need sunglasses probably the entire day. And probably not even need to layer their clothing.

She had energy to burn. Peter suggested they go to the buffet for breakfast. She was in her element and loved Alaska, especially on days like today. Anne said, "I'll be back in a flash. I'm going down to speak with someone at Customer Relations to sign us up for a bridge tour. I'll meet you at the main entrance to the buffet."

"Roger that," Peter acknowledged.

She trotted from their stateroom down the long corridor then turned right onto the staircase. She walked down from deck nine to four and stood patiently in line, overhearing comments like: "The TV isn't working. The sliding glass door glass is filthy. The toilet flushed in the middle of the night by itself." Now that was a first for Anne.

Walking down ten flights of stairs, two per deck, was one thing but the thought of going up 14 to the buffet was a no-go. She was the only person in the elevator when it stopped on deck five. A man maybe ten years older entered and greeted Anne, politely asking the typical question—"Having a nice trip so far?"

Before she could courteously reply, "Yes and you?" he continued, "I don't mean to be overly friendly, but you smell just like my grandmother when she baked cinnamon cookies. The vanilla aroma has taken me back to my childhood summers spent on a lake in Michigan with my grandparents."

"What a lovely memory," Anne replied. "I must have doused myself a bit too much this morning. But it's fine, I've heard this line before."

He chuckled and questioned, "No, no, it's just right. What's it called?"

"Estée Lauder Youth Dew. It was created in the early fifties and used first as bath oil. I found it years ago at the fragrance counter and it became my signature perfume," she explained like he deserved some history.

On the quick ride up she told him of other Youth Dew encounters. One was about a man who stood a bit too close while she selected green peppers at the grocery store. He apologized for being forward, but she smelled just like his mother. He revealed that as a child, he and sister stood outside knocking on the locked bathroom door as his mom soaked in their tub in the fragrant bath oil, her only relaxing time of the day. As an adult, he bought a bottle for his mother every Christmas. He thanked Anne for bringing back such a fond remembrance. His mother passed two years earlier. Anne looked at the man with tears in his wonderfully honest brown eyes and quietly replied, "It was my pleasure. Truly."

She told the story to the elevator stranger like it was yesterday. He said, "I totally get it." They both stepped to the rear as three passengers entered when they stopped at deck eight. "The best though," she said, "was a man in an elevator who said he picked up the earthy, warm spicy scent immediately. It reminded him of an ex-girlfriend and transported him back to his college days. He got this funny grin on his face and confided he'd been thinking of her lately. Maybe this was a sign to reach out to her. I wished him well and thought he should indeed act on his intuition. I reassured him that such an action would certainly impress her."

They reached the 12th floor, after stopping at six, eight and nine, and walked off together, Anne wrapping up her

Youth Dew encounters. He said, "Enjoy the rest of your trip and thank you for the memories." Peter waiting outside the main entrance asked, "Another new friend?"

"Oh, just another Youth Dew encounter." He nodded his head. He'd heard the random stories and he, too, loved the earthy, woody, cinnamon scent. "Did you tell him about the woman in the bathroom?" She laughed and said she'd forgotten that one.

They entered the buffet for early breakfast and joined a table of strangers, one couple from Wales, one from Australia and the other from Sweden. All were chatting as Anne and Peter joined them.

―――――

At 8:45, while they were outside on the top deck gawking at the incredible scenery, the cruise director interrupted and reminded everyone to keep Glacier Bay pristine for future visitors and generations by doing their part: "Do not throw anything overboard. Take extra care that loose clothing, hats, and other items do not blow overboard. Do not feed wildlife or birds. Avoid disturbing wildlife. Please respect your fellow guests' experience of this majestic place."

Switching topics he said that mountain goats are the true mountaineers, so to spot any they had to keep an eye out, looking high on steep-sided cliffs and rocky outcrops. They typically live in groups or bands. Peter searched with his binoculars as they watched around Gloomy Knob, one of the mid-Channel Islands in Glacier Bay where the critters notoriously hang out. He pointed to several light brown globs moving stealthily on the ragged rocks that only those with massive lenses or binoculars could prove were goats.

Miles of breathtaking scenery passed by. Strategically thinking ahead, Peter suggested they eat early, around 11:30, and be on the top deck when reaching Margerie Glacier about one o'clock. It sounded fine to Anne, but it was still just mid-morning.

Puffins are just one of dozens of different species of diving birds commonly seen in Alaska. Both tufted and horned develop their characteristically bright bill color in the summer months, presumably to attract the best possible mate. Supposedly, some were at the entrance coming in, but they hadn't seen any. Anne had high hopes of seeing the black and white clownish-looking birds reportedly in Yakutat Bay and Prince William Sound.

CHAPTER FORTY-ONE

Almost nine. Two hours, 30 minutes until Ericka's shift ended at 11:30. During a short break at 9:30, she called Captain Malloy and said she'd be in by 11:45 to provide more information. She breathed a sigh of relief yet still felt antsy. Jill watched her anxious cousin out of the corner of her eye hoping her further testimony would be exactly what was needed to help find the person who murdered Clint.

CHAPTER FORTY-TWO

Around 9:45, Dr. Canoy called Malloy, "Crime lab report finds no issues with bagels or almonds. However, tests conclude poison hemlock in the kombucha, enough to kill something as big as buffalo pretty quickly. Poor boy, didn't have a chance and didn't taste a thing. Awful way to go, though." He explained some of the side effects: trembling, lack of coordination, convulsions, rapid and weak pulse, then respiratory paralysis, coma, then a quick death.

Poor boy indeed, but my lucky day, Malloy thought, with a key witness coming in again and conclusive lab results of a poisoning.

CHAPTER FORTY-THREE

After the revelations Ericka told him and that she would be sharing with police, Tony decided he couldn't just sit around. Mr. and Mrs. Sterling's visit had shaken him. His own mom couldn't do anything to make him feel better. He appreciated her coming so quickly but insisted she fly home. She reluctantly agreed.

He needed to be doing something, anything. Maybe he could help find the guy named Leon. He'd let the cops find Tyrone. "If Leon is as innocent as Ericka thinks, hopefully he'll spill his guts," he said to Ollie. Ericka said Leon worked for an animal clinic. The police were doing their thing, but he felt helpless. So why not help out?

"What do you think, Ollie? Can we help the cops out?" He'd talked more to Ollie in the past 48 hours than ever before.

Around 11:15, pacing the floor then taking Ollie for a walk, Tony had an epiphany. He'd find Leon if he had to go to every vet clinic within 100 miles. He'd either talk some sense into him or pound him into the ground until he talked. Ericka would do her part at 11:45, so he'd do his.

He placed the Juneau telephone book on the kitchen table and turned to Veterinarians then Animal Clinics in the yellow pages. He was surprised there were so many. "It's not like its dairy or cattle country and not that many horses either," he grumbled to Ollie.

He started with clinics and made a list looking at a map.
    #1 Southeast Alaska Animal Hospital
    #2 Juneau Veterinary Hospital
    #3 Valley Veterinary Clinic

Now he just needed a legitimate-sounding excuse to find Leon. He'd go with the typical, "We have a family emergency" scenario. "Let's go Ollie," as his dog jumped into the back seat. With no one in the front where Clint usually sat, Ollie moved next to Tony.

———

At the first clinic he swung open the door and approached the receptionist saying, "We have a family emergency and I'm looking for my cousin Leon."

"Who?"

"Leon.

"Are you sure he works here? I've worked here for two years and I don't know a Leon."

"Oh sorry, I guess not." He'd keep going until he found this Leon guy.

"Strike one, Ollie."

CHAPTER FORTY-FOUR

At 11:34, Jill hugged Ericka and asked again if she wanted her to go along to the police station as moral support.

"No, I'm good but thanks, you've got the lunch crowd coming in soon."

"It's never as busy as the morning rush."

"I know, but really, I can do this." Ericka fought down a rising sense of panic.

"I love you, Cuz," she turned back to Jill and waved as she rushed out the back door to the alley where her car, along with other stores' employees, parked their vehicles.

Preparing a variety of the most popular sandwiches ahead of the noon rush, Jill stood at the stainless steel work-station in the kitchen, drinking a quick cup of vanilla iced chai. Juneau would have record-breaking temperatures today and the bakery didn't have air conditioning. It wasn't needed in most locations of Alaska.

As usual it had been a busy morning so maybe lunch wouldn't be too hectic. She was totally distracted, like Ericka. To make it worse, Ericka probably had the flu, throwing up in the bathroom. She felt so sorry for her sweet cousin.

Someone pounded on the back door, "HELP, HELP, OPEN THE DOOR." Jill snagged the tray of bagels saving it a nanosecond before it landed, doing her best impression of an outfielder diving for a fly ball. She ran to the back and opened it up to her friend Jessica, who owned the art studio next door. "JILL, CALL 911," she shouted, "somebody's hurt out here."

"What? Who?" a confused Jill responded.

"Just call now, Jill!" Jessica barked.

Jessica could see long blonde hair streaked with red. She didn't look any closer and didn't want to jump to conclusions. She blocked the doorway so Jill couldn't see behind her.

Jill ran to the only telephone and punched 911, blurting out there was a body in the alley behind her bakery between Northern Lights Bookstore and Greengate Studios.

The dispatcher said her name was Loretta and kept Jill talking, reassuring her police were on their way. She asked, "Jill, how do you know there is a body behind your bakery?"

"The woman who owns the shop next door, Jessica—" she answered.

"Jill, did you see the body?" the dispatcher asked with their question and answer dialogue continuing.

"No, I haven't been out there."

"So you don't know who it is?"

"No."

"Okay, stay put. Are you okay, Jill?"

"I guess," listening for the wail of the police cruiser's siren. Jill could hear sirens getting louder and louder.

"Hang up now, Jill. You've done really well. Now go to the front and meet the police officers. Do not go into the alley," was the dispatcher's final instruction.

***

What seemed to take forever probably turned out to be three minutes as Jessica stood guard over the area. She also heard the sirens getting closer.

With no parking spaces in front of the bakery, two white Ford Crown Victorias and one Taurus came to a screeching halt, stopping traffic on one side of the street. Officers came pouring out of the vehicles: Fitch, Kruse, McFeeters, and their only female officer, Ruby Wood. Captain Malloy pulled up in an Explorer.

Three went around to the alley as two officers entered the front door where they found the owner of the bakery completely shocked by the happenings in the alley behind her establishment. No, she hadn't been out there. But Jessica, the shop owner from next door was, and she's the one who told her to call.

Officer Wood stayed with Jill and started looking around. She asked everyone to stay in the building. The captain asked Wood to call Detective Perry.

Captain Malloy walked through the bakery out the back door.

Jessica blurted out, "I'm the one who found her. I am so afraid that I know who it is."

"Who you think it is?" Malloy asked.

"It's Ericka. Jill's cousin. I just don't have the courage to look."

Ericka, the woman in his office two days earlier because of the suspicious death of her boyfriend Clint with an 11:45 appointment today, was lying on the ground. He didn't need

Jessica or anyone else to ID the body. He knew who the victim was.

Jessica burst into tears. Malloy opened the door of the bakery for her. She collapsed on a chair in the corner. She felt nauseous and dizzy, so she put her head between her knees. She couldn't look at Jill. Someone gave her a cup of sweet tea to sip. "Best thing for a shock," she heard a kind voice say. When Jessica finally looked up, Jill saw her eyes were puffy and cheeks cinnamon red. She was wearing black capri pants under her white artist jacket smeared with colorful oil paints.

———

Malloy called Dr. Canoy, "We have another body, Doc. Please come to the back of the bakery."

Malloy found Jill standing at the cash register and asked her to sit down. He had something to tell her.

Sobbing, Jill exclaimed, "I brought her here. This is my fault."

Malloy sympathetically said, "It's not your fault. Could you make sure no one moves anything or cleans up? We need to wait for forensics to get here and for the ambulance to remove the body."

"The body? That's my cousin. Who'd want to kill Ericka?" Jill blurted out.

Her world stopped. She could hear the *tick, tick, tick* sound of someone's watch. A revved-up vehicle *vroomed* by. *Tap, tap, tap*, who was tapping fingers on a tabletop? *Splash*, she heard water ricocheting in the sink. A *splat*, like somebody dropped a fresh tomato on the countertop. Why was she hearing all these sounds?

Yet she couldn't hear the man sitting right in front of her. His mouth was moving but she only heard the *tick-tock* of the metal bear clock on the wall. People walking on the old wooden creaky floors and opening and closing the squeaky door which she never noticed until now. She put her hands over her ears and closed her eyes as the *fizz* from someone opening a bottle of Coke about sent her over the edge, almost causing her to run out the door screaming.

She hopped up, "Oh no, what about Kirbie? I can't take her. We have a high-strung Schipperke named Charley."

"Don't think about that right now, Jill."

"But somebody needs to feed and take her," she cried.

"Maybe a neighbor will take her?"

Captain Malloy saw Jill going into shock as the medical examiner and an ambulance arrived. Knowing how hard it would be for her to see them work on the deceased, he said, "I think you should go to the other side of the bakery and don't come outside."

She about collapsed on a padded bench by the front window. A cup of hot sweet tea was placed in front of her. "Sip it. Best thing for shock," she heard someone say.

Giving Jill something to do would give her a purpose. Malloy asked her if she could help list the names of the folks inside so they could be questioned. Jill barely whispered, "Okay but you better find out who did this. I want whoever did this to pay, big time." She had the list completed in five minutes.

Clay learned long ago not to offer any false hope, instead a nod of his head. It always reassured the person on the receiving end and left the feeling that the murder would be solved in record time, like a two-hour murder mystery movie.

Clay shook hands with the medical examiner. The bald, medium-built doctor looked at the police captain carefully. He noticed a definite increase in stress-related illnesses such as ulcers and high blood pressure among his patients in summer.

"Out here, Doc," Malloy said and opened the back door for the medical examiner. He squatted at the body turning to the captain saying, "This happened recently, probably in the past 15 to 25 minutes. She is still warm."

They were cousins. Jill thought back to all the family humor and drama over the years. Even though Ericka had an older sister, she really thought of Jill as a sister, being closer in age and temperament.

If Ericka's beginnings weren't so funny, she'd cry. Ericka's mom Martha was addicted to the weekday soap, *All My Children*, starring Erica Kane, played by Susan Lucci.

The series started in 1971 and Ericka's newly married parents, Nels and Martha, started their family with their first child being conceived on the sofa on her dad's lunch break from the bank. He often came home for lunch, her mother would laugh years later, slightly distracting her from her favorite soap.

She swore all three children's lives began that way. She never felt guilty about watching it at noon for one hour; she had to have lunch, too, when jointly they decided she'd be a stay-at-home-mom.

When asked why her name wasn't spelled the typical way, Erica, and like the TV character, her clever mom explained it was too common, but by adding the K, it was a combo of the star's first name and initial of her last name, Kane. Her mom was proud of her creativity. Oprah Winfrey's favorite soap was also *All My Children*, like it added credibility and justification to her mother's addiction.

Two older siblings, a brother Jeff, born in 1972, now a banker; a sister Brooke, born two years later, worked at a college. Ericka was born in '76, and really did nothing important. Her older siblings were goodie two-shoes; she was not. She had a rebellious side, maybe because she was the baby. They let her get away with too much.

Ericka's middle name was Rose. She felt grateful it wasn't Juniper, Sunbeam or Buttercup. Rose was tolerable. Moonbeam, it would have been so like her mother for her third child.

As a freshman in high school, Ericka was taller than all the boys in her entire school. She stood five-foot ten, and had wispy, light blonde hair with azure eyes. She was athletic and excelled in track. When some boy, or girl for that matter, made a blonde joke or questioned her, "Do blondes really have more fun?" or called her a "blonde bombshell," it would only be once. Her mood changed the color of her irises. She would stare the sorry excuse for a person down with her cold, steady, unblinking Nordic eyes. Then she'd turn and walk away, never paying them any attention again.

Her older siblings towed the line, but she was her parents' wild child, and ran with the rough crowd. Jill was close to Ericka not just because of their age, but similar personalities and common likes and dislikes.

Ericka had gone through a defiant streak, trying out the goth look. Jill about fell over when Ericka showed up at age 16 at a family function wearing a black skirt, lacy black top tinged with deep purple, fishnet stockings, precarious stilettos, and a leather band around her neck with silver spikey things. But the drama of the dark eyeliner, black nail polish, dark lipstick and black streaks in her naturally blonde hair drew the attention Ericka was seeking—drama. That was it

for Jill, as she pulled her favorite cousin into her grandpar-
ent's bedroom asking, "What the heck, Ericka?" If it wasn't
heartbreaking knowing her cousin was gone, she'd laugh at
all of Ericka's shenanigans that occurred a few years earlier.

Jill knew Ericka was no dumb blonde. She'd gone to
community college and taken a course to become a veterinary pharmacy technician, an intensive 18-week program
where she received her certification after taking the national
board examinations. She aced the program and exams and
worked at a good job in a veterinary clinic. Mostly she
blended ingredients and chemicals to make medicines.

She'd told Jill she enjoyed her coworkers and met a really
nice guy named Leon. He invited her to a bar for a drink. He
introduced Ericka to an acquaintance named Tyrone, a
buddy, she surmised. Ericka's immediate reaction was that
they were like oil and water. During the cousins' first
conversation and a few later, Jill learned red lights and stop
signs popped up in Ericka's mind to stay away and avoid this
guy but she hadn't.

If either Ericka or Leon had asked for a letter of recom-
mendation from the owner of the veterinary clinic, Dr.
Sammie Larson, she would have given them both glowing
endorsements about their honestly, integrity, hardworking
ethic, being on time, and that she could trust them with
anything.

Ericka was pretty, a knock-out, and guys always looked at
her. Sometimes she'd look back. With a string of boyfriends,
some more serious than others, at age 21 she was glad she
hadn't gotten pregnant. She didn't consider herself loose, but
she wasn't a prude either. Her mother would understand.
Her father would not.

Her mom loved music, always playing it in their house.
"Build Me Up Buttercup" was her favorite song. But her
mom's all-time favorite group was ABBA, the quartet from

Sweden. Ericka grew up singing along with her mom, "SOS, Super Trouper, Take a Chance on Me" and "Tropical Love-land." Ericka could sing "Dancing Queen" before she said three words in a row, according to her dad.

Things like this shouldn't happen. Young women shouldn't die. What in the world would Jill tell her aunt and uncle? How would she tell them their youngest daughter was dead? How did people get through it, she pondered, crying even harder. And worst was the fact she'd been murdered. It would be hard enough to accept the loss of a child in an accident, but how did you deal with the knowledge that somebody had killed your precious daughter on purpose?

Unable to sit still any longer, Jill pushed the chair back and stood up. She reached for a sponge and began wiping down countertops. Pacing back and forth, scrubbing and rescrubbing the same countertop, she finally stopped. She needed to get a grip for her family.

An hour later, after Jill had been interviewed by the police, reinforcements came to help with interviewing the rest of the patrons. Jill put most of the leftover bagels and mugs of coffee on the counter for police officers. She gathered her purse and put three bagels in a bag and walked up the flight of stairs.

What now, she thought and decided she'd call her cousin Brooke, because she was the most responsible and would know how to handle this situation. Ericka's older sister acted like an adult when she was six years old. But not this time. Brooke wept along with Jill, 1,200 miles away. Jill hung up, flopped onto her bed and threw a blanket over her head and sobbed.

The crime scene investigators were collecting blood samples and DNA evidence from the ground around the car where the body lay. They scoured the area for footprints, placing markers indicating evidence, taking detailed information on how a weapon entered Ericka's body, and prepping the body for its trip to the morgue.

Two officers walked up and down the street asking questions of shop owners and any by-standers who might have seen or heard something helpful. The officers fanned out, searching trash cans and climbing into large dumpsters. They searched underneath bushes and shrubs blocks away.

About an hour later, Malloy heard his radio crackle; a knife was found in a dumpster seven blocks from the scene. It was wiped clean. But he knew it could be anyone's knife. After dozens of photos were taken of the knife and location, Officer Kruse bagged it. They continued searching an additional three-block perimeter then called it quits.

CHAPTER FORTY-FIVE

Leon was having a difficult time keeping his mind on work. He kept hearing Tyrone's voice laying out the past couple of years of crimes. The entire situation was giving Leon a major headache. How could he have missed all this?

He forgot the golden rule as a pharmacy tech—*Wear Gloves* when mixing medications and chemicals. He was helping with an elderly patient, a cat, with thyroid cancer problems. The owner couldn't get her pet to take oral medication so Leon was concocting a topical cream that hopefully the owner could apply. Cats are notoriously difficult to give oral meds to, so he mixed the pure drug chemical into the topical cream that hopefully would be rubbed in the cat's ear flap twice a day. The directions would include that anyone applying the ointment should wear gloves.

He mixed timoxizide HCL, an anticancer drug, with the clear ointment. When he accidentally bumped the jar of chemical and the powder puffed into the air like a cloud, he swore. He slammed the windows closed between the lab and the office, threw on his super-duper protective ventilator mask, and waited for the powder to settle before he started to clean it up. He hoped he hadn't inhaled any of the pure chemical.

Thankfully he had the sense to shut the windows to the office immediately. Anyone standing nearby could have inhaled the chemical and become ill.

Leon felt sick earlier and now worse, much worse. As soon as he finished the ointment compound he told Darrel, the tech in the front office, about a supposed family emergency and left the building. He walked to his place, heated up a can of Campbell's Tomato Soup, added a handful of crumbled of soda crackers, then plopped down on his couch. He fell unconscious before his head hit the pillow. Red soup poured onto the floor.

CHAPTER FORTY-SIX

Ollie heard, "blah, blah, blah," as Tony said, "Strike two." Then at the third one, the technician said, "Oh sure Leon, but sorry, he's out today, some kind of an emergency.

Quick-thinking Tony replied, "It's the same family emergency. I've flown from Ketchikan to see him. I don't even know where he lives now, Darrel…" reading his name on the oval badge. He muffled other words so fast the tech couldn't track him.

"Slow down, Buddy. He lives out back in the cottage. He's our 24-hour on-call guy. If his orange Chevette is there, so is he. But I don't know because of the family emergency."

"Thanks, Darrel," Tony waved, going out the door like they were best buds.

Tony motioned to Ollie to come as he leaped out of the window trailing Tony. "Bingo, Ollie." Around the sprawling animal clinic, he saw that the rust almost matched the original deep orange color of the two-door hatchback.

The small log cabin actually looked rather cool to Tony, and a place he'd be satisfied to live in. The bright summer sunshine produced several long droplets of glistening pitch.

He knocked hard on the door. "Leon, it's Tony. We have a family emergency," thinking if anybody heard him, it would be legit. Ollie ran around the corner of the house.

No answer. He put this ear against the door, hoping to hear something. Anything. Tony swore out loud. Tony didn't cuss much, but the past couple of days changed that. And his drinking habits. Fortunately he was tall enough to peek through the window at the top of the door. He saw a chair and tiny kitchen table. He walked to the small front window and looked in. Nothing but a bed and dresser.

Around another corner, Tony spotted a bench with Ollie standing on his hind legs peering in a window. Ollie was making an odd, mournful sound, not a full bark. This window allowed Tony to see more of the living room area. Leon was on the sofa and there was blood all over the floor!

He ran back to the front door, "Leon, Leon!" Tony shouted. Ollie barked. He pounded more on the door. Still no answer. Tony turned the unlocked handle on the door and barged in. As the door flew open, Tony ran over to Leon being careful not to step in the blood. "Wait a minute," he said when he noticed crackers in the red stuff. "Oh, thank God," when he noticed the tipped bowl and spoon.

Tony shook Leon. His arm dropped like a rock when Tony lifted it. He was unconscious. Leon was soaking wet from sweating. Beads of perspiration dotted his flushed face like measles. Even his bushy auburn hair was flat on his skull.

Tony raced to the black phone on the wall and punched in 911. "I'm behind the vet clinic and my friend Leon is unconscious. Please send help. And it's extremely important you tell Captain Malloy it's Tony calling about Leon."

"He's out on a call right now but I'll get him the message," was the reply from the dispatcher. It had been a busy morning, one like no other for Loretta.

Tony covered Leon up with a brown and tan crocheted afghan that was draped over the back of the only chair in the room. He grabbed two towels from the bathroom, doused them with cold water and placed one on the back of Leon's head and neck, then one on his chest. He'd learned that in first aid somewhere or maybe it was on ER, one of his favorite TV shows. He noticed Leon wasn't all that tall, maybe five-eight or nine and thickset, like he could have come from hardy stock, working on a farm.

Tony shook Leon again and got no response. He help-lessly waited and paced making sure Leon was still breath-ing, as if he could do anything if he stopped. It seemed like forever but soon he heard the blaring of the sirens.

Medics checked Leon's hazel eyes and pulse. Tony heard one say, "He has a weak heart rate." They sped off to the hospital as Tony explained to Officer McFeeters what he'd been up to. The reply suggested Tony stay out of the police business, but thanked him.

Tony said, "Yeah right, and somebody might want to check him for whatever killed Clint."

Not knowing what else to do, and for whatever reason feeling slightly responsible, Tony showed up in a waiting room at the hospital. Ollie stayed in the car with the windows halfway rolled down. Tony would stick around until he got a chance to speak with Captain Malloy about Ericka's testimony. He wasn't surprised when he saw him run through the automatic opening doors. He was surprised that the captain looked like crap.

Malloy saw Tony and said in a low, clearly concerned voice, "I'll be back to speak with you after I get an update on Leon. I need to tell you something Tony."

An ER doctor and two nurses worked feverishly on Leon, not even knowing what was wrong. Captain Malloy told the doctor what had transpired with Clint's death and that somehow these two men could be in contact with the same person so having no external wounds, they assumed it could be poisoning or drug overdose so were pumping his stomach.

Malloy had said, "Do anything you need to, just keep him alive. I need him."

A flexible tube was inserted through Leon's mouth, down his esophagus, and into his stomach. Despite the name, he wasn't actually getting his stomach pumped at all. Instead, the procedure was more like a washing or irrigating process that rinses out the contents of the stomach using water or another solution like saline, then removed by siphoning, taking out the contents of the stomach along with the liquid. They also took a blood sample for a rapid test, and urine for analysis. They needed answers fast.

The ER doctor had contacted Leon's employer who was on the way with the compounds Leon was using. The doctor assured Malloy that Leon wasn't in serious danger now and would likely wake soon. He was responding to IV's and his eyes were much clearer.

Not knowing whether it was an overdose, accidental or intentional, or if he ingested a poison or whatever the situation, Malloy had already decided to let Leon assume anything he wanted in hopes he would share whatever he knew about the entire situation.

Malloy told the doctor, "I want to be there when he wakes up. Nobody talks to him but me. I've got to speak with the man in the lobby. That's where I'll be."

Captain Malloy had almost reached Tony seated in the lobby when the ER doctor pushed through swinging doors calling Malloy's name, "Stay put," he instructed Tony, as Clay walked toward the man dressed in white.

"I'll be back, Leon is awake. Stay here, I must speak with you. Don't leave this room." Malloy told him.

"Okay, I'll be right here," Tony responded, thinking it was odd that Malloy wanted him to hang around.

After regaining consciousness, Leon remembered mixing the cancer drug without wearing gloves. Certainly an anticancer drug, when absorbed into a human, could cause all sorts of issues. However, Leon believed deep down that Tyrone tried to kill him. He was sure Tyrone wanted him out of the way since he'd told Leon the entire sordid story with explicit details.

The doctor checked Leon's eyes again, still unusually dark but better, he observed. Reports indicated Leon got sick from a combination of chemicals at work. He was probably allergic to one drug in particular but wouldn't have reacted if he had worn gloves.

Feeling a little better, Leon's eyes were still rather watery or maybe teared-filled. The doctor agreed he could speak with law enforcement and Leon told Malloy and Detective Perry everything, having nothing to hide. Leon helped a lot, but they needed evidence to go with the motive. Tyrone somehow had kept naïve Leon in the dark in Seattle and even when moving to Juneau.

Leon thought moving to Alaska sounded like a lark, something different. Leon enjoyed outdoor sports and fishing, so it was perfect for him. When asked why Tyrone wanted Leon to come with him, he replied, "I dunno. Maybe I was supposed to be his wing man, his right-hand man, but he didn't need me. He had Ericka doing his dirty work in

Seattle and was convinced he could control her to do it here, too."

———

Leon hadn't learned the truth until the other night and called and left a message on Ericka's answering machine. Leon revealed where Tyrone lived in the Mendenhall Valley in a shack on the right side of a dead end street. He'd only been there a couple of times. He normally met Tyrone at a bar. His last name—Olsteen. His place was a broken-down house with flaking paint on the front door, Leon recalled.

"He drives an old beater, a 20-year-old dark green truck, if you can see it through the rust," were Leon's final words about Tyrone.

It now made sense to Leon why Tyrone has a rolled-up sleeping bag in the back of his truck. He's on the move, hiding from those he owes money. Malloy asked about weapons and Leon hadn't ever seen any but felt pretty sure Tyrone was armed.

———

Now Malloy needed evidence from fingerprints to prove Tyrone had access to Ericka's backpack and poisoned Clint. The crime lab guy called twice in one day. They had pulled and matched prints from the knife and Ericka's apartment door. The mason jar had a good solid print on the glass but the lid with its ridges was smeared so had nothing usable. Then they found prints on the handle of her car's passenger door. All belonged to the same person. This was all well and good, but they needed something to compare it with. Malloy would ask Officer Kruse to start running Tyrone's name through the database and hopefully they'd find some priors on him.

———

Malloy delayed telling the recovering Leon about Ericka's murder. There needed to be a better time. Leon was feeling bad enough and pretty guilty about not stepping in sooner if he'd only known.

CHAPTER FORTY-SEVEN

The park ranger dressed in forest green announced that when Captain George Vancouver first surveyed this area in 1794, he sailed by an icy shoreline. One hundred years later naturalist John Muir was able to canoe 40 miles up a fjord left by melting glaciers. Today we can sail 40 miles beyond Muir's campsite up into a bay formed by retreating glaciers.

He continued that the park once had been called Thunder Bay because of the roaring sounds made by falling ice that is the result of glacial retreat. Situated about 90 miles northwest of Juneau, this grand collection of tidewater glaciers is a wondrous blue ice land that encompasses 3.3 million acres. The waterways provide access to some of these 16 glaciers, a dozen of which actively calve icebergs into the bay. He added that it is also a land comprising three climate zones and seven different ecosystems supporting an amazing variety of animal life: humpback whales, Arctic peregrine falcons, seals, black and brown bears, marmots, eagles and mountain goats.

In a narrower passage, the cruise director pointed out several mountain goats on rocky cliffs and toward the mountaintops. They were easy to spot; they just looked for the moving dirty cotton ball. With binoculars, they could see them climbing sheer cliffs. Playful seals treated sightseers to antics of water aerobics.

The park ranger said that John Hopkins Glacier is a 12-mile long glacier and begins on the east slopes of Lituya Mountain and Mount Salisbury and trends east to the head of Johns Hopkins Inlet. Up the inlet is a white glacier touching the sapphire water with all-white Mount Orville and Mount Wilbur in the background, named after the inventors, the Wright brothers.

People who dressed in winter parkas, hats and gloves were soon stripping them off. The aqua water turned sapphire then back to aqua, depending on depth and glacier melt. The park ranger pointed out one brown bear on shore.

As ice chunks became visible, the excitement level felt electric. One icy floating island held two baby seal pups and mamma. Margerie Glacier grew larger the closer they got. The entire feeling of the passengers changed. People who'd been jabbering with excitement became calm and serene. The sheer magnificence of the experience stunned some into silence and awe. The glacier reminded Anne of a coconut cream pie with dozens of stiff peaks of fluffy meringue.

Peter was glad they'd be viewing glaciers and not on land for a while, keeping Anne from encountering a newspaper with updates. She had sworn people were pointing at her and she was positive she'd heard one person whisper way too loudly, "That's the woman who found the body on the glacier."

Standing at the front of the ship not wanting to miss a thing, Anne breathed in deeply. Margerie was a remarkable cobalt blue. Layers of delicate clouds drifted between the ship and mountains, slicing the peaks into thirds. Sunbeams bounced on shimmering water. Chunks of ice bumped up against the side of the ship creating a groaning then scraping sound. The bay was littered with millions of pieces of ice of different sizes and shapes. They heard loud fizzes and pops coming out of the floating ice chunks. Peter said it reminded him of eating Rice Krispies as a kid, the same snap, crackle and pop.

As if someone lifted a large hand, what few clouds there were evaporated. Only the tip top of the mountain cap was hidden. Oohs and aahs showed appreciation of nature at its finest. One woman standing next to Anne exclaimed she's seen *National Geographic* programs of Glacier Bay, but they were nothing compared to experiencing it in person. Anne nodded silently in agreement.

———

A waiter pushed a metal beverage cart offering complimentary hot chocolate. Anne asked if he'd heard of a "Heidi," hot chocolate with peppermint schnapps they'd had in the Swiss Alps the summer before.

He replied, "No ma'am, we don't have Heidis; we have Snowshoes in Alaska."

"But I have something else I'd like you to try. If you don't like it, I'll give you a complimentary hot chocolate with the peppermint. I guarantee you'll love it." The butterscotch schnapps lingered on her tongue then warmed her throat. Hot Scotch was the second-best hot chocolate Anne had ever tasted.

———

Not often did Anne need a break from people. It was usually Peter who retreated to the privacy of their stateroom when he'd had his fill of the general public. She took her second hot chocolate, this time a Snowshoe, and told Peter where she'd be. He followed. Their neighbors were already on their veranda in lounge chairs soaking up the sights and serenity.

The captain couldn't shut engines off, but he did something to make it quiet. The only motion they felt was when he turned the entire ship in a circle for anyone standing on their veranda, so that at some point Margerie would be off their deck. And that's exactly where Peter and Anne stayed along with Sherrie and Joel.

They came up with a system of watching for the glacier to calve by splitting up the glacier into quadrants. Sherrie pointed to movement as a tall chunk of glacier fell, then they heard a tremendous boom like a cannon, silencing their conversation. They knew that if you looked where you thought the noise was coming from it was already too late. The calving or breaking of ice starts first, then you hear the noise. There were several displays of calving that created a round of applause above and below them.

———

Peter announced hunger pangs and Anne acknowledged the need for protein, so they darted into the dining room instead of the buffet where many were in line.

They spotted Anne's parents and her dad's 10th Mountain Division Army buddies and joined their table. They skipped soup and salad and went right for the hot entrées. Anne ordered sauerbraten, a German pot roast served with spaetzle. Her dad was already eating the same thing and it looked and smelled delicious. Peter ordered the wiener schnitzel. Both heavy meals, this would get them through until dinner.

Well, maybe with a snack in the afternoon as they were doing a lot of running up and down stairs and back and forth from bow to stern.

By one o'clock the vantage point from their veranda was directly in front of Lamplugh Glacier. This glacier is thinner and lower so they could see for miles as it winds down through rocky hillsides. Also, it is the bluest glacier, but rocks cause it to look grimy.

Anne read to Peter from the ranger's handout. "This glacier flows out of the Brady Icefield and trends north for sixteen miles to its terminus in Johns Hopkins inlet. It's almost a mile wide and the ice face rises to about one hundred fifty feet. The flow rate is estimated at about one thousand feet per year. The central part of the ice face is currently receding by calving.

"It's eight miles long in John Hopkins inlet, seventy-six miles northwest of Hoonah. This glacier was named for English geologist George William Lamplugh, who visited Glacier Bay in 1884."

Anne was bemoaning to Peter about leaving this magnificent bay as she noticed an arm slinking around the frosted plexiglass wall separating verandas. A hand was holding a small plate with a bite-size hunk of maple walnut fudge. "Gosh, thanks," Anne appreciatively replied, happily consuming most of it before offering a smidgeon to Peter.

Kathy added, "Try this one." A slab of peanut butter fudge was passed over. Peanut butter sort of dribbled out of Anne's mouth. "How about this one?" "Yes, please," handing a piece of butterscotch to Peter, finally sharing. Then another sample, green mint fudge, made its way around, ending with rocky road.

"What'd you do Kathy, buy out the candy store?" Peter laughed.

Her husband Mike answered, "You should see the variety of popcorn she got. Not just caramel—dark chocolate, peppermint bark and yogurt. That's coming your way soon." Anne learned from previous adventures that Kathy bought fudge and popcorn anywhere she could.

Kathy, their own Fudge and Caramel Popcorn Queen, bought five types of fudge and four types of popcorn they generously shared with their appreciative neighbors, Phil and Sharon, on the other side, too. Once Anne learned about Kathy's propensity for sweets, she knew who she wanted as a neighbor on any voyages they'd take together. She would put up with Mike's tomfoolery that was offset by Kathy's confectionary generosity.

The navy and white Holland America's *Statendam* passed them entering Glacier Bay as their ship departed. A few hours later the rangers left the ship at Bartlett Cove, just reversing their delivery, mammoth ship to little boat.

Cruising farther, they again saw another small boat coming their way. The pilot boat arrived and scooched up against their ship right below their balcony. Many on their verandas watched the Glacier Bay pilot jump from the open door of the ship onto the bobbing motorized vehicle. The boat pitched away from their immense vessel creating its own white wake behind it.

Anne announced she'd be back soon. She zipped through the buffet area going from one side of the ship to the other when the cruise director announced a humpback on the port side. She swore she felt the ship tilt left as hundreds did the same thing she did. Luckily the gelato station had just opened. She selected limone, lemon in English, two scoops of her favorite chilly Italian delectable delight. It was a lot of sugar but then they had more excitement coming up and who knew when she'd eat dinner. Then she remembered one of her travel mottos, *What happens on the cruise, stays on the cruise.*

CHAPTER FORTY-EIGHT

At the hospital in Juneau, Tony looked his watch; it showed 3 p.m. He'd gone through all the magazines on the tables and in the rack since Malloy had left strict instructions to stay put. He had thumbed through *LIFE* magazine with Prince William on the cover with the caption, "The Boy Who Will Be King." On the cover of *TIME*, the headlines read in bright yellow bold and block style, "Kiss Your Mall Goodbye," boasting that online shopping is faster, cheaper and better. Plus hot stocks and brash billionaires.

At 3:15 Malloy was sitting down next to Tony, thanking him for his part in finding and rescuing Leon, who was recovering nicely and had been a tremendous source of information.

"Sure thing," Tony replied. "Happy I could do something. I am feeling pretty useless. Ericka told me this morning she was going to speak with you after her shift was over at the bakery. Have you seen her? She told me her entire story last night about Seattle and more recently here with those jerks Tyrone and Leon; that's why I had to do something," he said with a sort of innocent apology.

Solemnly Malloy started to speak, "Tony—son—listen, um, this morning about 11:45, Ericka was mur—" Tony couldn't comprehend his words. He just watched the captain's lips move silently.

CHAPTER FORTY-NINE

The ship made a beeline to their next stop. Anne had read to Peter earlier that, located on Chichagof Island in the northern end of the Inside Passage, the Icy Straight sits 1.5 miles from Hoonah, 22 miles southeast of Glacier Bay.

The historic Hoonah Packing Company had been the area's economic engine. That changed when the commercial fishing industry began to decline in the early 1950s. The facilities were used only for maintenance of the fishing fleet. Logging provided a welcome boost and became the core of the local economy until it disappeared in the mid-1990s.

Southeast Alaska not only has scenery galore, but opportunities for adventures at every stop. This area seemed to have higher than normal towering evergreens that blanketed its steep mountains. The forest has been pushed back in places by the seaside community. Hoonah, on Chichagof Island, is surrounded by the Tongass National Forest. This was their first time visiting this town.

Anne was eagerly anticipating this stop. She would be doing something that she assumed would be once-in-a-life-time. Not terribly risky or thrill-seeking to many, it was to her. Peter made it clear he wasn't going. His reasoning was that one of them needed to stay on Mother Earth for parental inheritance purposes. Pearl agreed with Peter and would stay behind. Howard, always up for an adventure, signed up to go with Anne. They would ride the world's largest ZipRider, a zipline. She was hooked when she read she would fly at speeds exceeding 60 mph, soaring 300-feet above the rainforest below.

While getting ready, the phone rang. Pearl was sick. She had seen the doctor who diagnosed the contagious norovirus that was known to spread quickly so Howard was quarantined with her.

Anne and Howard were bummed, but it didn't dissuade Anne. She checked in for the two-hour adventure, kissed Peter farewell, "Maybe our last," he muttered, as she boarded a refurbished school bus and headed out. She sat behind a woman in her fifties and adult daughter both with straight blonde hair and fair complexions. Anne assumed they were from some Scandinavian country. As they conversed, she realized they were speaking English with a heavy accent similar to British but not exactly the same.

The driver narrated as they passed through the tiny village of Hoonah, the main street lined with weathered wooden homes. A beat-up red and white Chevy truck was parked in front of a gray house.

He pulled over at several overlooks offering spectacular vantage points of the tiny village, their ship in the bay, Port Frederick and Icy Straight. It was a clear afternoon, so he pointed out the towering peaks of Glacier Bay in the distance.

On the drive up Hoonah Mountain, a moose trotted out of high brush on the right to a grassy field on the left. It munched tender leaves on the bottom of a tree. Shrieks of excitement rippled through the bus as a bear and her cub lumbered off the road to the left, fortunately on Anne's side of the bus.

After 35 minutes driving up the side of a mountain, 1,500 feet in elevation, reaching the top, all disembarked and walked a quarter of a mile through towering old-growth rainforest to the zipline launch pad. One thing that synched this ride was it was one-way down, no switching from tree to tree. Plus, the seats were flat and wooden, not a canvas harness. Each line was 5,300 feet long with a descent of 1,330 feet in 60 seconds, going 60 mph. She couldn't wait.

Anne watched as several groups went before her, one person per seat, four across, flying down the mountain. Two of the ziplines were not being used. She also noticed several people stepping out of the line and returning to the bus.

Chatting with the mother/daughter duo, Anne discovered they were from South Africa. The three exchanged pleasantries and stories about the trip so far. All three stuck together and vowed to take photos of each other.

Upon reaching the tower, they received a safety briefing and organized people into groups of three or four. After the briefing, several more returned to the bus. Anne felt even more exhilarated watching people soar over treetops reaching the beach in a minute.

They were next up. The three women would descend at the same time. Anne had on her fuchsia windbreaker so Peter could easily spot her and hopefully take a few photos. Proof of her accomplishment.

Anne sat easily into the two-foot-wide, one-foot deep wooden seat. An employee strapped her in at her shoulders and waist. With feet sticking straight out resting on the closed gate, it reminded her of horses at the starting gate of an important race.

Someone counted down: *Three, Two, One*. The gate door dropped down and Anne was zooming over 1,000-foot-tall firs. The Christmassy-tree smell hit her first, like getting into a car with the overwhelming scent of one of those green tree-shaped air fresheners.

It felt like riding a magic carpet over emerald wall-to-wall carpeting. Exhilarating was an understatement. With the slight turn of her hand she could rotate her seat left or right. Within seconds, she felt comfortable and pretty darn proud of herself. She glanced over at the South African duo with blonde hair flying straight back. Feeling confident, she held on with one hand and started snapping pictures with the other.

Flying in the openness at 60 mph, the bay was getting closer by the second. She saw their cruise ship. About three-quarters down and now closer to the landing pad, she noticed Peter standing atop a boulder taking pictures. She waved with only one hand, as he yelled, "Don't wave! Hang on!!" Such a worrywart. She felt a slight jolt as the brake activated, then they came to a full stop in the building on the beach.

His report of watching the bright pink dot atop the mountain zooming down with hair flattened, looking like Rocky the Flying Squirrel, was hilarious. He was glad she was back in the arms of Mother Earth. She wanted to do it again.

While Anne was experiencing a thrill-of-a-lifetime, Peter had wandered along the shoreline watching kayak excursions heading out. He thought back several years to the time he and buddy Chris kayaked for the first time off San Juan Island. They followed a guide along the coastline, saw seals, fish, lots of birdlife and lush scenery. But the most memorable and still laughable was when the guide suggested that they try a bite of kelp. Skeptical Chris, a meat, potatoes man, refused. Peter was game and reached in and pulled off the top of some green wavy weed. He took a bite, as Chris cringed. "Well?" Chris asked. "It's okay and salty." Since Peter hadn't vomited or died, Chris figured he'd try it just to be able to say he did. He concurred it was okay and salty, but never again.

———

Peter strolled around the renovated cannery, home to about one dozen Alaskan-owned shops offering a selection of native arts and crafts such as Alaska salmon, handmade soaps, local native remedies and logoed items. He resisted another cap but instead bought a classy forest-green fleece pullover.

He picked up a local newspaper where the headlines read, "Body Discovered by Tourist on Mendenhall Glacier." He purchased it for 50 cents and tucked it away for Anne to read later. There wasn't anything to report at this point, just a body discovered. Next of kin were being notified.

———

They didn't know if they'd return to this town or not, so they crammed as much as possible into the time. Their late afternoon outing would be spending a few hours exploring the scenic and remote Chichagof Island in a small group tour that showcased life on the tiny island of 750 residents. Their local guide told them about the Alaska wilderness and wildlife and that the island had the largest concentration of bears on earth.

They rode in a chopped-off school bus through the village then down a narrow dirt, pot-hole-filled road. A guide at the front of the line and one at the back both carried high-powered rifles. This didn't necessarily reassure Peter, but Anne felt safe enough. Remember, she winked, "It's the one that runs the slowest."

Walking on an elevated, spongy boardwalk through bushes well over their heads and leaves so huge they looked like they'd been transplanted from Jurassic Park, they came to a wooden landing well above a river.

Before walking to the edge, Anne could already hear a loud chomping sound, like bones crunching. A huge brown bear stood in the middle of the shallow river, his paws grasping a salmon. He took a bite out of the middle, tossed it aside, and grabbed another one. More crunching, biting and tossing. Another bear wandered upstream but stayed some distance from the first.

Peter set up their portable spotting scope and focused on the bear. The lens was so powerful Anne felt like she was eyeball to eyeball with the animal and its meal. Along the bank several bears were trying to catch salmon. Peter turned to Anne and said, "Do you remember that Despair demotivator called Ambition? The one with the picture of the open-mouth bear and a fish about to leap in? *Ambition, the journey of a thousand miles sometimes ends very, very badly.*" They both enjoyed this type of dry humor.

The bears would stay until so full they could hardly waddle off. An osprey turned on high currents waiting for its time to dive for salmon.

Back at the ship, the couple cleaned up and headed for dinner. At this point in the cruise, most in their group could no longer eat something from every course and a bit of the novelty had worn off. Both Peter and Anne had gotten more selective. She'd have an appetizer if it was shrimp cocktail or something else extraordinary. No more soups, skip the salad, on to the entrées: Cajun fried catfish, Peter stopped perusing the menu. Creole shrimp, Anne didn't need to read further. However, roasted tom turkey complete with apple dressing, giblet gravy, cranberry sauce, and grilled sweet potato patty did sound appealing. Thanksgiving in July. She switched.

Anne observed her sister-in-law Lola stealthily gliding from table to table like a female James Bond. She was up to something, which meant fun. She watched Lola covertly slip a piece of paper to their sister-in law Shelley. Lola moved to another table sneakily handing something to Anne's nieces Kelly then Katy.

Then Lola circled behind Anne and surreptitiously passed her a folded note. On top it read, "**FOR YOUR EYES ONLY**" in bold uppercase lettering, obviously something of great importance. Intrigued, Anne opened her note hiding it in her lap.

Karaoke
10:10
Starfish Lounge, Deck 10
Silence is Golden!

Anne gathered that was code for "Don't Tell Anyone." She looked up as four sets of female eyes stared at her. She did a thumbs up as did the other four women in her family. Only Katy noticed the slight trepidation on her aunt's face.

Dessert offerings were: Strawberry shortcake, Apple pie à la mode (Peter's favorite dessert), Marble chocolate terrine with raspberry coulis or ice creams. Anne passed on dessert, feeling somewhat, well a little guilty about the earlier fudge extravaganza, along with gelato. When asked for her dessert choice she replied, "Nothing, thank you." The waiter frowned.

While other desserts were being served, a white plate with the word "Nothing" written in swirly calligraphy dark chocolate with artistic hearts appeared before her. It was picture worthy.

———

The Diamonds were the evening entertainment in the three-story theater. This popular vocal quartet from Toronto, Canada had 16 Billboard hit records in the 50s and early 60s. Wearing bright blue blazers and black slacks, they boogied across the stage, choreographed perfectly. The audience overall was older than Peter and Anne, with most rocking and rolling to "Little Darlin, Silhouettes, The Stroll, Doo Wop, Zip Zip, Tenderly, Ka-Ding-Don," and some renditions originally sung by other popular singers.

———

While on their veranda, nonchalantly Anne informed Peter she was meeting Lola and Shelley for a beverage around 10. These two women were the closest she'd ever get to having sisters. Except for her Sisterchick, Sue, a dear forever friend.

The five Rollins women huddled around a table in the corner of the Starfish Lounge planning their debut and showcase number. Whatever they decided to sing, Kelly, the songstress of their family, would be the lead, the rest would be backup. Anne suggested "Rock the Boat." Shelley said what about "Girls Just Want to Have Fun?" It was unanimously decided to perform Sister Sledge, "We Are Family."

Now onto planning the synchronization. "Just sway left to right," Lola instructed. Anne, born with no rhythm, needed it simple especially if she was expected to sing, too. "Can you move your arms back and forth, too?" Lola hesitantly asked Anne. "You mean plus sway left and right at the same time? And sing?"

"I take it that's a no?"

"A big NO!"

Kelly and Katy had been on their high school dance team. No problem for them. Lola and Shelley could do it. They talked about adding a few more dance steps. Anne said adamantly NO, she knew her limits. It was supposed to be fun, right, not a contest.

Lola, somewhat competitive, admitted a prize was involved. Anne gave her the "really?" stare. Lola went to the front of the room and wrote down the song and just like that, The Sisters Rollins quintet was formed.

They sat through a horrible rendition of the Willie Nelson and Julio Iglesias duet, "To All The Girls I've Loved Before," both parts sung by a nasal-sounding young man, totally off-key. Everyone felt embarrassed for him but apparently he was unfazed and tone deaf. Another young man, who should have been a professional singer, belted out "New York, New York," better than Frank Sinatra, and a woman in her later years sang "Rock Me Baby," the Ike and Tina Turner version.

The newest American vocal group, The Sisters Rollins, were announced. All five strutted up the two-step riser as the music started. Kelly read off the prompter singing and dancing around the stage with her back-up singers swaying evenly behind her. She turned and joined the background sisters singing the familiar chorus, "We are family yeah, yeah..."

Everyone in the room stood during "Get up everybody..." which could have been construed as a standing ovation, the "Sisters" laughed afterwards. They vowed to stick with the motto, *What happens on the cruise, stays on the cruise*, except no one had seen Katy's twin brother slip in the back. He followed her after she'd made up some lame excuse for her sudden departure. She was never good at subterfuge.

As second place winners, they each were presented with a cruise line key chain. Mr. New York, New York received a bottle of champagne.

CHAPTER FIFTY

Tony lowered the shades. He lay on the sofa with a damp towel over his face. Four beers or maybe five by now hadn't helped him fall asleep. Some doctor at the hospital felt sorry for him when Malloy filled him in on the entire situation. The doctor gave Tony three yellow capsules, one for the next three nights to help him sleep. Tony was tempted to take one right then. But unfortunately he'd read the instruction: "Do not mix with alcohol" after consuming the beer.

First Clint and now Ericka—the woman who'd slept on this very sofa the night before. He couldn't grasp it all. He wanted it all to go away or to wake up from a bad dream, a nightmare. For some reason he had a flashback to about ten years earlier as a kid in junior high when he watched one of his parents' favorite Friday night TV shows called *Dallas*. A popular character named Bobby Ewing—supposedly very dead, run over by a speeding vehicle, returns. Maybe this was like that entire television season, just a horrible nightmare.

Kirbie crawled on the top of his fridge, away from Ollie,

who slept on the floor. Tony's arm draped over the edge with his hand resting on his dog's back. He heard the phone ring. His mother called to check on him and left a message on the answering machine.

CHAPTER FIFTY-ONE

Waking up early with light seeping through the curtains, Anne had the feeling she was missing out on something. Peeking out, the bright morning sunlight temporarily blinded her. She didn't want to wake her husband, yet she badly needed to be on their own private bit of the world, their veranda. She wrapped herself in a blanket, separated the curtains and quietly slid open the door.

Having been here before, she knew that in about two hours they'd be cruising past North America's largest tide-water glacier. She recalled it being about 90 miles from the entrance of Disenchantment Bay and the glacier. They would be entering Yakutat Bay soon and that this massive glacier could be seen from 30 miles away.

She looked toward the shoreline and mountains with a few broken low clouds above. She couldn't stand it; Peter needed to see this even though they'd seen it twice on previous cruises. Each time they came, it looked different depending on the month and weather.

As their ship sailed along the southwest coast reaching Ocean Cape, the point of entry to Yakutat Bay, she watched as a boat got closer and closer. Two men, one pilot and one ranger jumped aboard right below their stateroom. They were about two hours from Hubbard Glacier.

About 20 minutes into the bay, she spotted the first chunk of ice, undoubtedly from Hubbard Glacier. The lump looked like a whale with its tail up towing a bird. This was just the beginning of hundreds of icy shapes they'd see. She spotted many seals playing among the islands of ice. Numerous bald eagles perched on the drifting icy masses in search of fish. How in the world could Peter sleep through this, she wondered?

"That's it," she exasperatedly said out loud pushing the door open not so quietly. But Peter was already in the shower, and fortunately the night before Anne had put out an order for room service to deliver breakfast to their room.

Minced ham and scrambled eggs, a fruit platter and pastries arrived as Peter stepped out. Flinging open the curtains he could see icy blobs and mountains cut in half by a ribbon of thin clouds. However, the clouds were disappearing, disbursing streams of sunbeams onto the smooth water. It would be another hour or so until they reached the glacier.

Anne decided to dress up for Hubbard, wearing her new blue sapphire and diamond pendant that slipped onto her Omega necklace, and matching two-stone drop earrings. The pieces complemented her sapphire and diamond wedding band purchased for their anniversary two years earlier. When Vinni had shown the blue sapphire pieces to her in Juneau a few days earlier, she knew the set would be a wonderful reminder of sapphire blue water, white glaciers and snowy mountaintops and sapphire blue sky.

While eating, Anne read between bites, "Stretching over 90 miles from the core of the twelve-million-acre Wrangell-St. Elias National Park to the head of Yakutat Bay, Hubbard Glacier is one of Alaska's largest and most unpredictable. It's a staggering 76 miles long, six-and-a-half-miles wide and 1,200 feet deep. Its blue face is more than 400 feet high, about as high as a 37-story building.

"Rarely do these walls of ice do anything unexpected or newsworthy, but in 1986, Hubbard Glacier made the news by surging forward to block off Russell Fjord from the sea. Water began to build behind the glacier at a rate of 210 million cubic feet per minute creating a rising freshwater lake. Flooding became a serious concern. In the weeks that followed, the tremendous flow slowly overwhelmed the massive wall of ice and the newly formed lake cascaded into the ocean. This incident with Russell Fjord has not deterred the six-mile wide, 300-foot-high face of Hubbard Glacier."

Donning jackets, binoculars and cameras they headed to the top deck. The park ranger explained how to tell the difference between seals and sea lions. Steller sea lions are easily seen in Alaska because they are often lying on buoys. Since seals do not have articulated flippers that bend like elbows, they cannot climb up on buoys or piers. They can drag themselves onto flat surfaces like a small iceberg or hop onto boat if a whale is near.

The ranger answered questions as well as giving a commentary through the ship's communication system. He explained the entire glacier life process, how and why thunderous calving happens, why there is blue ice and why the water is turquoise. They learned rocks grinding against each other underwater causes glacier "flour."

The ship stopped roughly a half mile from the face of the glacier. During the two hours they were fortunate to see about ten calvings. The blue color of the lower layers of ice looked amazingly bright, and the upper layers were extraordinarily jagged and dirty. The captain turned the ship around so everyone could have a full view of the sheer magnitude of the glacier whether on a deck or standing on their own private veranda.

It was a phenomenal sight. Standing there hearing the sounds and seeing the ice fall, Anne felt awed by the power of nature. She would never tire of seeing this marvel. The extensive calving due to the high daytime temperatures was sensational timing for both photography and live action.

Because of close proximity to Hubbard, looking across the top deck at a group of people standing opposite of them, it gave the illusion they were superimposed on the glacier. The captain said the week before they had to stay two miles away due to heavy ice melt and winds. Today it was calm, and he was getting them as close as he could, bearing in mind all safety regulations.

Pops, creaks and moans emanated from the mass of ice. Chunks calved, creating shouts of glee from grateful onlookers. One small orange boat, with four crew wearing waterproof clothing, patrolled the waters around their ship watching for dangerous icebergs.

The right side of Hubbard Glacier looked cleaner and white. The middle third held more rocks. As it traveled down it pulled gravel and boulders along with the ice. The left side was also gray from the gravel but looked bluer. The range of mountains to the left were covered in so much powdery snow they could barely see land or ridges. It looked like a humongous cozy, fluffy cotton blanket.

The captain announced that this was the closest he'd been able to get to the glacier this cruise season. Ice was low, and winds were calm, making any danger minimal. The small orange boat cruised in front of the ship toward the glacier showing just how impressively wide the glacier really is.

Peter caught a motion out of the corner of his eye. He picked up the video camera and filmed as they watched a colossal chunk of ice, several stories high, lurch forward in slow motion. But it wasn't one chunk. It was more like seven or eight dominos stacked on end, pitching forward slowly, one at a time. Then everyone heard the tremendously loud cannon boom, always after the fact. Those that looked in the direction of the noise missed the calving. They watched the newest iceberg's ripple effect move quickly across the open water to their ship. It caused just the slightest movement.

Only 3,000 feet from Hubbard, the captain voiced his amazement, and the closer they got the mightier it looked. The six-mile-wide glacier stretched on and on and was so lengthy Anne couldn't get it in one photo. Because of the length, Hubbard calves often. Peter pointed out that a few of the larger icebergs had stowaways; seals were hitching rides.

Pea soup was delivered on the deck at 11:00. It was about the last thing Anne would ever eat, that and liver. She requested hot cocoa instead, upgrading to a Snowshoe.

They cruised many miles before the icemelt completely disappeared. Departing Yakutat Bay, they sailed along the coast passing Cape Decision and then on to Sumner Strait. The distance back to Ketchikan was 420 nautical miles.

CHAPTER FIFTY-TWO

A fter a fitful night of restless sleep, Jill recalled a few days earlier when she and Ericka were having coffee before Ericka left for the jewelry store. She ran her fingers through her hair and tucked it behind her right ear. The gesture was a holdover from her childhood and a telltale sign that Jill was about to finagle some hidden truth out of her.

Ericka didn't like keeping secrets, especially from her cousin, her best friend. She shared some things about her past in Seattle that almost nobody knew except Clint. Jill just shook her head. Ericka had reassured her those days were behind her.

Jill called Captain Malloy explaining she had more information and was asked to return to the police station. A cup of hot coffee was waiting for her and she sipped it carefully. Detective Perry, she noticed, had opened his file and was clearly ready to begin.

"Now Mrs. Harrison, about yesterday at the bakery. Please repeat for me everything you told Captain Malloy."

Mrs. Harrison, Jill thought. The last name sounded oldish, like her husband's mother, not her.

"But I've come with additional information that I just remembered," she insisted.

"Yes, we will get to that," said the detective, pursing his lips and making a tiny scribble on his yellow pad. He had a slight lisp, she noticed, and his upper lip was elongated sort of like the muzzle of a dog.

She looked at him closely, thinking what a serious man he must be and such a contrast to Captain Malloy, who had rolled up his sleeves, looking almost grandfatherly, and listened to her intently. The captain had a fine head of glossy walnut-colored hair with more than a few distinguished strands of silver where the detective had black, thinning hair.

She filled them in on what Ericka had told her with Clint knowing the facts about her extracurricular activities in Seattle.

"I see," said the detective, compressing his lips and making more scribbles on his yellow legal pad. "That should be all for now," he said dismissively.

Jill was a mess. She couldn't think straight at work, so friends helped out. And Ericka's parents were flying in that afternoon.

Trying to distract herself, she attempted to read, then dropped the *People* magazine in her lap. She leaned back closing her eyes and told herself to breathe deeply and relax. Her shoulders were killing her. It's where she carried all the stress of her world, in her shoulders and neck. Her eyes refused to stay shut, and then her legs twitched. She needed to get up and move. She stretched and walked to the front window looking at the water in the bay. More cruise ships and more people. She couldn't deal with any of it right now.

Malloy called Dr. Canoy, just checking in. The medical examiner said, "In addition to a blow to her head from falling after the stabbing, there are older bruises on Ericka's arms like she was defending herself, fending someone off at some point. I don't feel there is any reason to do an autopsy since the cause of death is obvious. I'll call you when I get the results of the blood and tox tests that have gone to the lab. It's not official yet." Before Malloy could say thanks, he heard the click on the phone. Canoy was never one to waste time or words.

CHAPTER FIFTY-THREE

Peter and Anne met his two sisters, Ashlee and her husband Brant, and Julee with her husband Wyatt, for lunch in dining room at 11:30, right when the doors opened. It was his sisters' first Alaska cruise and they could now see what Peter and Anne had been talking about for the last several years. Brant and Wyatt were enjoying the scenery and wildlife. Julee asked Anne if she always wore her lavish jewelry cruising and Anne sighed, "No, just for Hubbard Glacier." They had learned Anne's quirks over the years and didn't even ask why. Anne ordered Quiche Lorraine and Peter requested the Viennese veal goulash.

Hundreds sat that afternoon watching an ice carving demonstration at the pool. The artist started with a large block of ice. He had sharp knives and two handheld chainsaws. Guesses during the half-hour process were all wrong until the eagle's wings took shape. When completed, he asked if anyone had any questions. A person asked, "What happens to the ice sculpture when it melts?" Anne and Shelley walked away chuckling.

Several from their group had tickets for the same tour of the bridge. They were impressed by the number and variety of instruments and controls, most in different colors. They were told that all newer ships are equipped with the most modern navigation-integrated bridge systems and safety devices. An officer pointed out different sensors, gyrocompass, speed log, satellite navigation, global positioning, Loran receiver, radars, weather station, depth-indicating system, autopilot, voyage management system, and much more. And believe it or not, the good old-fashioned round wheel that they let passengers touch. On the bridge there are always at least two qualified officers on duty, a senior and junior navigator.

Somebody asked, "What's a knot?"

"It's a measurement of speed equal to one nautical mile per hour and is used for measuring the speed of ships and boats. A nautical mile is equal to 1.15 land miles. The word "knot" is derived from the ancient sailor's practice of gradually trailing a knotted rope over the side of the ship and the number of knots fed out in a specific period of time indicates the ship's speed."

Another person inquired about "Port" and "Starboard." The answer: Port is left, and starboard is right.

One man asked, "How come I have a starboard stateroom and a port hole?" Patiently the officer answered, "A possible derivation of these two words goes back to the early days of sailing ships. There was a certain kind of ship which had a steering board suspended over the side and this acted as a kind of rudder. As most people are right-handed, the steering board was suspended over the right-hand side of the vessel and so this side became known as the steering board side. This was eventually abbreviated to Starboard Side. When these vessels came into the harbor, it was safer to berth with the left-hand side of the ship against the pier, thus avoiding any possibility of damaging the steering board. Therefore, the left-hand side of the vessel became known as a port side. However, you have a porthole, or window, not a hole on the port side. Confusing, I know," he laughed.

For the second formal night both repeated what they wore earlier in the week. Anne switched to the fuchsia top under her spangly jacket. She hoped to see the mermaid again. She was slightly disappointed to see the same woman wearing a fashionable black, knee-length leather skirt. Her flashy top shimmered with thousands of pearls.

Anne looked at the glittery outfits her friends and family wore, halting her gaze on her grinning 17-year-old niece Katy. She wore a one-of-kind stylish skirt they had purchased together one year earlier in London while on a whirlwind educational student trip to Europe. With several hours of free time after touring Westminster Abbey and the Tower of London, they selected shopping. Auntie Anne wanted to purchase a special gift for her niece.

The duo had walked into a trendy store on the second level of Covent Garden, one of London's most popular shopping neighborhoods, where a young woman was happy to help Anne's six-foot-tall gorgeous niece, who easily could have been a runway model. Katy tried on a half dozen eye-popping outfits, none quite right for her. Then she waltzed out wearing a darling lightweight olive, billowy, gathered parachute skirt. "See, with the ripcord all the way around?

The skirt can be longer, or I can cinch it up for a shorter look. It's a ripstop nylon like what's used in parachutes to make it strong and heat-resistant." Auntie Anne asked why a heat-resistant fabric would matter in a skirt and both laughed. "I'm wearing it to the prom, and it's designed by Riley and made by Poshmark," Katy closed. And that sealed the deal.

That night for dinner, Anne planned to skip any juice choices or appetizers. The chilled strawberry soup was tempting but skipped. No thanks for any salad. Peter selected the sautéed sea bass, and at Shrimp Provencal, Anne stopped reading the menu.

Desserts: Black Forest cake. Swan Chantilly with apricot sauce. White chocolate mousse. Ice creams. Anne ordered the swan. Sitting next to Cathy, Anne observed the waiter deliver a crème brûlée, without her even asking for her dessert choice. Anne asked, "Again?" The reply was, "Every night. And there's only one more night left." "Can I please have one, also?" Anne begged, "We're running out of time."

The late-night entertainment was the Not-So-Newlywed Game. Peter headed to their room and one nice thing about being on a cruise ship, it's safe and easy to get back to your room. Anne went exploring and dropped into some of the shops. Then when she walked by the three-story theater, she could swear she heard a familiar voice. She pushed open the door and low and behold, her parents were on stage. They had been selected as one of the couples to answer questions about how well they knew each other. Or tried to predict what the other would answer.

Anne was sucked in, almost enthralled hearing things she'd never heard before and really never wanted to know about her parents. Especially the last question, for a whopping 25 points. Where was the most unique place they had ever DONE it? As in "done it."

The women answered first with the husbands in some secure location, like the cone of silence. Anne's mother didn't even hesitate. Anne was floored. Her father didn't waver and had the exact same answer as her mother in a second flat. Memorable, Anne guessed, but never ever to be forgotten in her memory banks. Anne's parents won first place getting every answer the same. Anne never asked how her parents were chosen but suspected both brothers played a part in volunteering them.

———

Anne stopped by their room nabbing Peter for the Chocolate Buffet Night. The ice sculptures included the Statue of Liberty, a ship with masts, an eagle, a bear with fish in its claws, and the salmon jumping out of the water was melting with water droplets looking like twinkling diamonds.

A chocolate cheesecake frosted in yellow with chocolate swirls had four butterscotch mice placed around the cake. A dark chocolate cake was topped with poufy three-inch-wide curls of black and white fondant used for firmness. Desserts, all chocolate in dozens of shapes and sizes, lined two long tables. She was very grateful for her digital camera.

Peter dozed off three second after he hit the sheets, about 12:30 a.m. Anne was standing on the veranda as a humpback swam by. She wanted to yell like she normally would at the close encounter but didn't. Who could sleep with the endless possibilities of wildlife sightings? Not Anne.

Once Anne tucked herself gently under the cozy blankets with Peter fast asleep, she realized she wasn't as tired as she'd thought or at least should be. She reached for J.A. Jance's latest book, *Rattlesnake Crossing*, a murder mystery she bought at Powell's Bookstore at the airport. Soon she was absorbed in the latest adventures of Sheriff Joanna Brady and her skilled, seasoned deputies based in Arizona. Before she realized it the clock read 2:31. Light crept in through the blackout curtains. She knew she was missing something outside.

CHAPTER FIFTY-FOUR

Poor Tony was groggy most of the time from drinking, and his mother empathized through her long distance daily telephone calls. She offered to fly him home to Tacoma once the police said he could go. Parents are never supposed to have favorites, but truth be known, which she wouldn't ever say, Tony is her favorite.

Ericka's parents were met by Officer McFeeters at the Juneau airport and taken to the police station. Malloy thought about the two sets of grieving parents, both in just a few days. Captain Malloy told them the facts. He drove them to the Barnoff Hotel for an overnight stay. Malloy asked Tony if he felt up to talking with them about Clint and Ericka. He did not.

Guilt-ridden Leon called his parents explaining what had happened and asked for temporary housing. He turned in his resignation.

———

Tyrone showed up at the bar he and Leon frequented. Leon was nowhere to be seen. Questions swirled through Tyrone's head: Had Leon talked to the police? Was a police officer in the bar right now stalking him? After a third beer he wondered if he should sleep in the back of this truck another night before returning home. Had the police located the knife he tossed in the dumpster? Should he have thrown it into the bay? Did he leave enough food out for his dog? He ordered another beer.

CHAPTER FIFTY-FIVE

Having only a half-day in the town of Valdez, Anne could see why it was called the Switzerland of Alaska with the alpine meadows and snowy peaks. These mountains looked even taller than others they'd seen the past week.

This being a first-time stop for them, Peter paid more attention to his wife's morning historical and geographical presentation courtesy of the *Gazette*.

"Resting in the valley at the head of Prince Williams Sound, the town got its start in 1898 when gold seekers discovered the harbor was the perfect spot to launch their expeditions into the gold fields of Fairbanks.

"Named by a Spanish explorer who discovered the harbor over 100 years earlier, the town grew rapidly in the glow of gold fever. Within a few years, the gold fields were exhausted but Valdez maintained its place as a supply port for Alaska's heartland. In the early 1990s, the army established a base and General Wilds P. Richardson constructed the 365-mile Valdez Trail. It eventually became Alaska's first paved road.

"In the years that followed the gold bust, life slowed into uneventful bliss. Supplies were delivered by the ship, loaded onto trucks and driven north. At 5:30 p.m. on Good Friday 1964, the calm ended. The earthquake measured 8.5 on the Richter scale. The water from Prince William Sound was heaved up in a tidal wave that crashed over Valdez, destroying the waterfront and town. The destruction was so total, with surprisingly few casualties, that residents decided to rebuild four miles away on safer ground.

"Four years after the town's destruction and rebirth, a second shock was felt. Oil had been discovered on the North Shore of Alaska. The oil men were faced with the same dilemma that slowed prospectors nearly a century before. How do you get people and supplies over the mountains and across the frozen terrain and how do you get the treasure out? Within a year the answer was conceived and designed— the Trans-Alaska Pipeline.

"Stretching 800 miles over three mountain ranges and under 350 streams from the North Shore to Valdez, the pipeline was the most daunting and expensive privately funded engineering feat. It was completed nine years later in 1977, the final bill-$8 billion. With the facility pumping out one to two million barrels of oil each day, the cost was quickly recovered, leaving the oil companies, Valdez, and the rest of Alaska to bask in the newly founded wealth."

The couple discussed the infamous grounding of the *Exxon Valdez* oil tanker ten year earlier carrying over 53 million gallons of oil with about 10 million spilled at the entrance of Prince William Sound, where they had just cruised. Anne asked, "Do you remember all the video on TV of the heavy sheens of oil covering the Sound? And the black blobs on birds, seals and other wildlife? Then the big storm a few days later that pushed the oil onto rocky shores. What a horrific mess."

Off on another lark, Anne organized an outing, calling it a sibling's escapade. Both of Peter's sisters and husbands, and Anne's brothers and wives, slipped their sunglasses on as they disembarked the ship for a tour of the Valdez area.

After a short drive, they arrived at Valdez Glacier. Peter left the motorcoach first, leading the way toward the glacier. Tons of rocks and gravel on the left side made for a dirty glacier but easy hiking. The right side was clean and blue. The glacier created its own lake where people were walking the parimeter. The lake sits at the base of two mountains where one gently rises up one side with another one directly behind, dressed in a white draping cape.

This would be their second glacier walk in a week. Anne stood solemnly thinking of their earlier walk on Mendenhall Glacier and wondered about the person she'd discovered. She pondered how Captain Malloy was coming along with the case. Peter's sister Julee put her arm around Anne and asked how she was doing. "I'm fine, thanks, just thinking about earlier in the week."

"Well, of course you are," Julee said sympathetically. "My guess is you will think about it for quite some time. And this has undoubtedly brought back some childhood memories from that body your family discovered on the river."

Anne nodded her head affirmatively, "It was such a long time ago, 29 years but right now it feels like yesterday." She looked at her brothers, now adults. She had a flashback of their childhood, camping once when she was perturbed at something the little bozos had done. She mumbled something about them being twerps. Her mother assured her that those little rascals would one day become her best friends. Men she could depend on the most. She couldn't even imagine them as men at that point in their young lives.

But her mother was right. Again. They turned out to be wonderful fathers, and even better brothers. She needed to tell them both how proud she was of them. Her feelings seemed more urgent right now. She'd tell her parents that night how much she appreciated and loved them.

They tramped firmly on the icy mass not needing spiked boots. It wasn't as slippery as Mendenhall Glacier. Anne picked up several agates and one mossy-green jasper for their rock garden at home. This had become a vacation tradition, if permissible and legal. She scanned for signs that might specifically tell people not to remove items but saw no warnings anywhere. She'd certainly learned her lesson.

She had returned some sacred black sand to the ocean in Hawaii after getting spooked by some holy woman admonishing anyone removing it from the beaches. Not knowing the sacredness while strolling the gritty black sandy beach, she had filled a small Kodak film canister with the scratchy stuff, for safe-keeping. She planned to do something crafty with it at home. A few other friends did the same thing. All hearing the same shaman, four women were now alarmed. Not wanting to tempt the gods or have something horrible happen to them on the cruise or the flight home, she would follow instructions by wrapping the sand in a tea leaf.

"If someone had removed some black sand, where might that person find a tea leaf?" she repentantly inquired. The reply, "The buffet uses them for ornamentation."

She laughed on her tea leaf search trying to remove one without being noticed. Even though not superstitious, she would return the grainy sand to the loving arms of Mother Earth, or in this case, mother ocean, respecting culture. Anne tossed her sand-wrapped tea leaf into the water apologizing to the gods for her ignorance and begged forgiveness. She vowed at this point in their travel lives to study up on culture and societal nuances ahead of time.

The three other culprits said their peace and tossed the sand back where it belonged. One friend dramatically tossed it over her left shoulder with her right hand. "It's not salt like in good luck," Anne pointed out. The wrongdoer replied that at this point, it couldn't hurt. The women left the side of the ship laughing, noting it would make a great story years later.

Lola thought a snowball fight would be fun and amusing until Max playfully walloped her in the back with a hard-packed ice ball. The snowball fight was over before it really began.

Back on the bus, they drove Richardson Highway entering Keystone Canyon. Anne stared out the window at sheer mountains, searching for Dall sheep their bus driver had mentioned could be along the ridges. They saw dozens of waterfalls, some thundering down the mountainsides, some trickling.

But one by far was the most spectacular. Water tumbled down 600 feet in a giant stair-step fashion. Driving on the bridge over the fast-moving whitewater, Anne could see water pouring over boulders. Their bus driver pulled off at a large turnout where everyone could get a magnificent view of white water tumbling from Bridal Veil Falls.

Julee mentioned that this was the second Bridal Veil Falls this cruise. Her husband added that there is also one in Oregon in the Columbia River Gorge.

The bus driver pointed to bands of rust-colored rocks in the side of the ridge. "Now see these slow moving white dots? Grazing Dall sheep," he said. Through binoculars, they could see the massive curling horns on a band of rams. Four ewes and their babies were feeding on steep slopes away from the males.

Shouting diverted their gaze as some hardy souls, or fools, depending on one's point of view, were kayaking in the swift white-water of Lowe River.

On the bus, they crossed the milky river again and pulled over at a second viewpoint. Horsetail Falls spilled over the top and at its crest was an outcropping of rocks that splits the falls sort of in half, plummeting over more black boulders much like steps for a giant, disappearing behind lush green shrubbery.

Turning in a complete circle, all they could see was mountain after mountain mostly covered in snow. The lower areas and pockets that were free of snow were packed with green trees and low bushes. Someone pointed out three rafts racing by in the rapid current. Not a single person from the rafts waved, they were hanging on for dear life.

"No way," wide-eyed sister-in-law Shelley, exclaimed.

"I couldn't agree with you more," Anne responded.

"In a heartbeat," her brother Will chimed in.

Returning to the ship, Peter and Anne rode the elevator to the top deck and stood at the front, looking back over the length of the ship toward Valdez. The top deck was lined with people on chaise lounges. The swimming pool and hot tubs were filled with passengers who would have never guessed they were in Alaska. From their vantage point, the mountains looked like they were just yards off the back of their ship. Several glaciers filled ravines in the mountains.

They watched as mountains got smaller the farther away they sailed. This might have been the most spectacular scenery of the entire trip but then Anne remembered she'd thought that about Haines, too. Then Juneau and Skagway, also. This was the main reason she couldn't get enough of the coastline of Alaska. She'd been bitten by the Travel Bug so many times and Alaska was one place that helped heal her soul.

Anne pointed out a narrow river of ice that looked like a white flowy ribbon coming from some unknown source. Peter reminded his wife that the small ice flow is referred to as "rice" and comes from a glacier.

Over lunch, Anne read the information about their upcoming adventure. This would be their first time into this fjord, so Peter listened attentively.

"Located within Prince William Sound, College Fjord is home to six calving glaciers. The fjord's steep cliffs rise above the water and the area is covered with stands of giant trees. The area is a haven for wildlife, including the largest animal on the planet, the blue whale, weighing in at 150 tons.

"Containing 26 glaciers, College Fjord has one of the highest concentrations of glaciers in Alaska. The fjord gets its name from the fact that each of the glaciers is named for a university or college in the eastern United States. On one side of the fjord the glaciers are named for all-female colleges with glaciers on the other side named after previously all-male institutions."

Standing on the top deck, Anne could see the entire range of mountains with six glaciers on one side, five reaching the water. Between the white and blue of the glaciers, miles of trees broke the uniformity of the white.

Several black heads bobbed in the water. They weren't seals or tree stumps. Peter grabbed his binoculars then announced, "Sea otters!" More were sleeping on ice chunks as they approached College Fjord.

She'd read that the two largest tidewater glaciers are Harvard and Yale. They both originate from the same icefield. Harvard is the last of five glaciers in a row, separated by miles of trees and mountains. One glacier abruptly ended about a third of the way from the waterline with rocks and dirt meeting the seawater.

Back in their room, standing on the veranda, Anne took a deep breath. She loved the smell of the sea air. She could smell sugar, too. She looked around the frosted plexiglass barrier as a guilty-looking Kathy's mouth was full of gooey saltwater taffy. Her purple teeth stuck together, she uttered "Waaa a iece?"

"Yes thanks, I'll take two of those purple ones. Huckleberry?" Anne laughed as Kathy nodded her head affirmatively.

That night Anne and Peter had dinner with their nephew Nathan, nieces Katy and Kelly, plus her husband Darren. Anne's parents and her dad's 10th Mountain Division buddies and wives, Walt and Joan, Don and Alice, were at the table next to them laughing and having a marvelous reunion.

Tonight's dinner was one of their favorite food groups— Italian. Along with the typical juice selection, the appetizer selection included mozzarella antipasto, mussels in a sun-dried tomato sauce, and a few other things of no interest to Anne. One time on a cruise Anne ordered three appetizers and a bowl of watermelon gazpacho, just because she could. Skipping appetizers, salads and soup, they went onto the entrées: Alaskan Coho trout fillet. Peter read no further. Anne didn't either at Scampi Oreganato, shrimp in a sauce of basil, garlic and oregano butter.

Desserts: Tiramisu, Peter's go-to at any Italian restaurant. Anne asked for key lime pie and got it.

A familiar feeling hit Anne like a ton of bricks. Denial. This was their final night on board. It had been a glorious cruise with friends and family. Except for the body Anne discovered on Mendenhall Glacier and the extreme emotions that went with that day. They had to pack tonight. But their adventure was far from over.

CHAPTER FIFTY-SIX

S lowly opening the curtain for the final time, the coastal hamlet of Whittier awaited their arrival. Those going by bus to Anchorage and flying to their various final destinations would have a spectacular drive through the Kenia Peninsula viewing more mountains, along rivers and lakes and probably would see wildlife.

Peter and Anne had said their farewells the night before as they'd be some of the first off the ship while most would be eating a final breakfast onboard.

Anne, Peter and their group of ten friends, along with dozens of other cruise passengers, were continuing aboard a train for 300 miles taking them on a nine-hour adventure—final stop Denali Depot in the national park.

The brochure promoted the ease of getting off the ship, walking across the tracks and boarding the luxury rail cars offering panoramic views. There is a full-service dining car with made to order cuisine and an open-air observation platform to experience the great outdoors.

They stepped into the first class luxury car Teklanika and found their seats. The window for Anne, always the window. The cushioned seats reclined with plenty of leg room even for over six-foot Peter and really tall Joel. Domed windows extended over their heads for unobstructed views.

As the passengers were settling into the comfortable seats on the train to Denali, in Juneau Dr. Canoy called to inform Captain Malloy that Ericka died of a knife wound in the back from a jagged-edged knife like a serrated type, piercing her arteries and heart. Blood results found no alcohol or other illegal substance.

Malloy contacted Officer Kruse and instructed him to go back over to Ericka's apartment to see if he could locate a set of knives.

Forensics had discovered a fingerprint on her apartment's front door handle matching Tyrone. However, they were acquainted so he could have been there before.

The Denali Express departed Whittier in dazzling morning sunshine at eight o'clock sharp and within two minutes entered a pitch dark, two-mile long tunnel. Only the interior train lights provided illumination. There was no light at the end of the tunnel for quite a while. When exiting, there was a line of traffic, vehicles waiting to go through the one-way tunnel. They were training across a 14-mile wide isthmus.

Their rail car guide, Dalton, introduced himself and trainee, Skylar, with a toast, "Raise your glasses to new faces, new places and new adventures." Anne heard lots of clinking of champagne glasses. Dalton explained that the tunnels were constructed during WWII to supply the military in Alaska along with a port, rail terminal and other infrastructure.

He told them, "As you travel across Portage Valley, keep an eye out for bear in the streams and moose in the open grasslands. Much of this area was covered by Portage Glacier which has receded to form Portage Lake." They could see it on the left before entering the second long tunnel.

Since they departed before having breakfast on the ship, Peter's grumbling stomach indicated it was time they move to the dining car for their first meal of the day. While perusing the choices, they ordered a Moose Mary, a version of the classic Bloody Mary but with a slice of bacon. Peter's motto of "Everything's better with bacon," held true once again.

Heather and Anne appreciated the attention to detail with white tablecloths and matching cloth napkins, china and silverware. A bud vase holding a purple mini-iris added a splash of class and color next to the white salt and pepper shakers. The wall of windows allowed passengers to continue viewing the glorious sights and watch for wildlife. The ladies took the window seats as Tim requested one with easy access for a possible quick getaway not wanting to miss a photo op.

The menu showed the choices for breakfast: Alaska King Crab Cake Benedict, Reindeer Sausage Breakfast Burrito, Bagel Breakfast Sandwich, Cinnamon Roll with house-made icing, Skillet Scramble, Steel cut oats or Flapjacks.

Peter and Anne shared a large cinnamon roll with an

avalanche of warm cream cheese frosting, melting like a warming glacier. Each ordered a different meal to share a few bites. Peter normally ordered something that wasn't prepared at home and he was sure that Anne would certainly never cook anything with reindeer or any number of other animals or birds. He said, "Reindeer sausage breakfast burrito, please."

Anne was morally opposed to eating certain things like reindeer, whale, puffin, and previously cute little lambs, until she had her first bite of lamb in Scotland. Sadly, her moral compass had been compromised. She ordered the Crab Cake Benedict.

After a yummy breakfast, Anne and Peter walked to the outdoor platform and stood mesmerized at the low feathery fog that hovered then shifted over cooler ponds, creating its own unique look. Returning to their seats just in time, Dalton was concocting a delicious drink for a mid-morning treat. He offered an ice cream beverage called a Mud Slide, actually a milkshake-on-the-rocks for adults. One couple across from them had two each.

It was hard to stay seated and there were no reasons not to run back and forth to the outside platform taking loads of photographs. Tim and Anne were the most active with the cameras. They both took zillions of mountains with glaciers in the background, and ones of tree-lined beaches with their exact mirror images reflecting in the smooth lakes.

Even though they'd seen glaciers and breathtaking scenery, this scenery changed with variations in vegetation and lakes. Anne pointed out a beaver on a small lake. Standing on the outside platforms, when the train curved to the left, Anne could see all the way to the engine car. They rode on a wooden trestle above a river hundreds of feet below. Lodgepole pines doubled their length with their reflections in the still lakes.

As they continued toward Anchorage, Turnagain Arm became visible which Dalton said they would follow the rest of the way into Anchorage. This area is influenced by a unique natural phenomenon called a Bore Tide or a Tidal Bore. This natural wonder occurs when the leading edge of the incoming tide forms a wave of water as it travels up the arm. This wave can be six to eight feet tall, traveling at ten to 15 mph and is most pronounced during extreme low tides either side of new or full moons.

The Seward Highway hugs the dramatic shorelines of the Arm, and Anne announced that this had to be one of the most beautiful stretches in America. The sprawling flats of Turnagain Arm stretched like a marshy dotted plain to the opposite shores of Cook Inlet, where mammoth sloping mountains abruptly stopped the flat's expanse.

Zipping back and forth between their seats and the fresh air on the outdoor platform, Anne implied she'd worked up quite an appetite and 11:45 wasn't too early for lunch.

Back in the dining car, the lunch menu included: Seared wild salmon with quinoa summer salad, Alaska fish tacos, Award-winning reindeer chili, Turkey club, Seafood salad sandwich, Cheeseburger and Chef salad. Anne looked at the desserts first. This would determine what she'd select for lunch. Sweet treat choices: Triple vanilla bean cheesecake, Fruits of the Forest pie—medley of strawberry, apple, raspberry, blackberry and rhubarb à la mode, and Chocolate lava cake with vanilla ice cream. Normally there would be no competition with the warm lava cake, but the warm forest pie won.

One unnamed spouse had the reindeer chili and reported it was quite good. He was ignored by his wife. Twice in one day her food moral compass had been smashed by extenuating circumstances of others. The seafood salad sandwich was delicious. Both had their own piece of forest pie à la mode.

While lunching, they traveled past Potter Marsh Bird Sanctuary on the right and Rabbit Creek Rifle Range on the left. Entering Anchorage, the train slowed as loudly-clanging crossing guards went down stopping traffic. They crossed Dimond Boulevard which is named for an early Alaskan politician, judge and champion for the Alaska statehood cause, then rejoined the coast briefly before pulling into the train depot. Downtown was visible up the hill on the right with the Port of Anchorage to their left. Anne couldn't wait to get out of the city and back into the wilderness.

Leaving the big city behind, they started into Matanuska-Susitna Valley that locals like Dalton refer to as Mat-Su. They were about 35 miles north of Anchorage. Dalton told them some history and stories about locals who grew record-size cabbages, heads of lettuce and squash, along with other vegetables displayed annually at the Alaska State Fair. He suggested when they get home to check out the *Guinness Book of World Records* because some Alaskans are in the record books for their gigantic vegetables because of days with long hours of sunlight.

He informed them that the Mat-Su Valley was carved by glaciers leaving thousands of lakes. The Mat-Su river and lakes are the spawning grounds of Chinook, Silver, Sockeye, Pink and Chum salmon. He held up his left hand with palm facing them and explained an easy way to remember types of salmon: Chum, rhymes with thumb. Sockeye, because it's number one. King because it's the biggest. Silver, for your ring finger. Pink, for your pinky finger.

Their train didn't go fast so gave ample opportunity to take in the scenery and a chance for photos if someone spotted wildlife. They occasionally checked their copy of the *Rail Gazette* map route. By 2:15 they were sampling carrot cake, cookies and ice cream. Anne wondered if they would be in a diabetic coma by the time they reached their destination.

Commentary by staff was informative, especially pointing out things of interest along the route. Dalton was a bottomless pit of history, information and silly Alaskan jokes. Several miles before reaching a stop at Talkeetna, he told them that the town began in the late 1890s, with the construction of a trading station and later the Alaska railroad. Today it is a hot tourist spot and the starting point for mountaineers who climb Denali. Stopped at the train crossings, four-wheel drive vehicles lined up loaded with people and their gear strapped to the top.

Dalton said that in 1935, as part of the New Deal, 203 families from the midwest travelled to Alaska and started the Matanuska Valley Colony. Families were chosen specifically from the states of Michigan, Minnesota and Wisconsin, due to their similarly cold winter climates.

As their train rolled to a stop, some passengers disembarked. The Talkeetna Mountains were on their right with what they assumed was Chulitna River on the left. Pulling out, Dalton explained that the river splits in half and Chulitna is farther away. The river closest to them is the Susitna River. A single engine red and white airplane flew parallel along the Susitna River, tipping his wings toward their train. Several times along the way they could easily see both rivers flowing side by side. Skylar excitedly pointed out Denali in the distance. She remarked how fortunate they were as it was normally shrouded in clouds.

Dalton, their mobile mixologist of fine beverages, whipped up a specialty combining hot chocolate and coffee, with a dab of amoretto, Irish cream and whiskey. Anne's insides felt all warm and cozy like being wrapped in a soft fleece blanket sitting in front of their fireplace at home. A range of mountains reflected its mirror image of several glaciers, dozens of ravines, and many waterfalls in a calm lake. Camera clicks drowned out the clacking of the train wheels. Almost. Dalton pointed out where the Susitna River veered to the right, or east, as the Chulitna River would follow them through Hurricane Gulch to Denali.

CHAPTER FIFTY-SEVEN

Over 600 miles south, Officer Kruse called Malloy reporting that in Ericka's apartment on the kitchen counter sat a six-slot wood block that held a set of knives. One was missing from an empty slot. All the other knives were straight-edge. He was bringing it back with him.

Malloy was pleased that Dr. Canoy had determined the type of murder weapon and now knew with a high percentage of likelihood that the knife discovered in the dumpster was the one. Looking at the knife set, it didn't take an expert to see the match of the murder weapon to the set of knives, minus one, from Ericka's kitchen.

CHAPTER FIFTY-EIGHT

About 90 minutes out of Talkeetna, Dalton gave his passengers notice that those wanting to get photos of the Chulitna River, down 300 feet, should head to the observation platform. They all hurried out for a space at the outside railing.

Hurricane Gulch was dead ahead. The bridge rises 296 feet above Hurricane Creek. The bridge is a marvel of engineering, according to Dalton. The engineer slowed the train, giving everyone plenty of time to enjoy the view and snap dozens of photos. Dalton told them that the bridge is 918-feet long, both the longest and the tallest Alaska Railroad bridge. For eight years it was the tallest bridge in the entire United States.

Construction of the arch bridge began in early 1921. The first steel was erected in June and the first passenger train crossed it on August 15 of the same year, and the project was difficult and expensive. Both sides were constructed at the same time using an aerial tram crossing the gulch. Nearly 1,000 tons of steel went into the arch plus an additional 530 tons were used to construct the approaches.

Anne peered over the edge seeing a ribbon of white water meandering through the ravine. Stands of fir trees created an intermittent green canopy over both sides of Hurricane Gulch.

Before they knew it, their nine-hour train adventure would be over. Dalton alerted them that they weren't far from Denali Depot and to please start collecting belongings. And not to worry about luggage, it would be waiting for them in their rooms at the lodge.

About six o'clock their train pulled into the historic Denali Depot, then they boarded a luxury motorcoach for a short ride to their accommodations at the Denali Wilderness Lodge. They efficiently retrieved a welcome packet, including a colorized map of the complex.

Their meal choices all looked inviting at either the Lynx Creek Pizza & Pub, River Run Espresso, Grizzly Bar & Grill, King Salmon Restaurant, or Rapids Bar & Grill. They decided to hold off on dinner until later after eating and drinking most of the way from Whittier to Denali.

As a couple of women had their noses pressed against the Fox Creek Studio window, a spouse announced that there would be sufficient time later to investigate unique shopping. However, Sherrie and Anne couldn't pass up Milepost 238.5 featuring the Christmas Cabin, in other words, souvenir Christmas ornaments. Sherrie and Anne reached for the exact same ornament. Sherrie gifted Anne a matching moose. They vowed to recall this special trip together when the moose was placed on each other's tree.

They popped into the Grizzly Bar because their signature beverage, a Wildberry Twizzler, just sounded fun. The fruity combination of fresh cranberry, raspberry, blueberry and blackberry with some type of alcohol plus club soda, tasted light and refreshing.

The Cache Fine Jewelry boasted furs and handmade moccasins and mukluks. The Ice Box sold wood bowls and baskets and wood carvings. The Trading Post displayed stained glass, glass beads, blown glass, knit items and beaded jewelry. Anne purchased a three-by-eight-inch glass wall hanging of painted Alaska Forget-Me-Nots against shades of green with blue sky. Sugarloaf featured sweet treats, and Peter got a cup of coffee and couldn't resist the smell of the freshly roasted cinnamon glazed nuts. A life-size carved wooden bear stood outside the hotel complex and shops.

Around eight o'clock, majority ruled and the group of 12 went to dinner at King Salmon restaurant overlooking the Nenana River. People stopped to look at the unique metal chandelier made of hand-blown glass salmon. Out the windows stood giant trees, flourishing blooming bushes, grassy meadows and more mountains.

Appetizer choices: Scallop bites, Coconut-crusted halibut, Pear and bacon flatbread, Wild salmon fritters, Crab, shrimp and cod cocktail.

"These are just the appetizers?" Sherrie said.

Soup and salad starters: Alaska salmon chowder, Caesar salad and Spring greens.

Entrée choices: Sea salt-accented king salmon, Alaskan halibut, Chimichurri grilled salmon, Prime rib, Bering Sea crab trio, New York strip, Brick chicken, Pine nut linguine and Fireweed salmon salad.

The crab trio won hands down for Joel and Peter: Jumbo king, Dungeness and Opilio, served with drawn butter. The triple crab was picture worthy, especially the humongous legs. Anne ordered the pear and bacon flatbread, the salmon chowder and grilled salmon.

After dinner and strolling around the complex, Joel and Sherrie departed. Joel had an 11:30 tee off time. 11:30 p.m. Sherrie went along to share the unique experience. He'd have bragging rights that he golfed at midnight in Alaska in the daylight.

Anne texted Sherrie about 30 minutes after his tee time to see how things were going. Her reply read, "He is standing at the first tee still waiting. A hungry moose is munching on the grass and apparently isn't in any hurry to get off the nice, lush first green." That would become Joel's go-to golf story for years.

While Peter slept soundly, Anne stood at the window, their first in eight nights on solid ground. The brightness wouldn't let her sleep. She knew she might miss something. Like the moose that strolled through the grounds out their window. She took pictures to prove to Peter in the morning. This was the farthest north they would be.

What amazed Anne up was the sunrise at 3:31 a.m. and sunset at 12:20 a.m. Almost 24 hours of light. Even using clothes pins to keep the curtain shut tight, she could see lots of light coming through the top and bottom. It didn't even dim to dusk. She should have brought duct tape.

CHAPTER FIFTY-NINE

The next morning they started a new day with a Sourdough breakfast buffet at the Wilderness Lodge. They embarked on their half-day trip to Mile Thirty riding in a school bus with the most knowledgeable guide they'd ever had anywhere in the entire world. The driver kept his eyes on the bumpy road while scanning the wide open grasslands and forests for wildlife.

In a green meadow were a caribou couple, one with a large antler rack. Anne spotted movement in another grassy field. An antler rack from a moose traveled through the tops of the grasses. They never saw the actual moose's body.

At Savage cabin, they took a step back in time. Long nails pounded into the sides the house were used to deter bears from trying to get in. They saw the doghouse for Cinder, the husky. The local guide shared history and culture at a living history presentation at the cabin.

Ranger Fritz Nyberg wrote in 1927, "It's not fair to the rangers to ask them to patrol in the freezing weather…and then have to spend the night out in the open under a spruce tree."

The sign at the cabin read, "Even during the short summer months, the subarctic can be a harsh environment. Imagine conditions in the winter: sub-zero temperatures, gale-force winds, blinding snow, overflow ice and darkness."

The guide continued by saying that spruce trees, like a big one close by, were a welcome sight to the first rangers on winter patrol. Shelters were few and far between, so spruce trees with large flaring skirts provided protection from the elements.

Years later, these trees continued to provide shelter in the form of cabin walls. The round logs made walls and were sawed into planks for flooring, roofs, tables, shelves and shutters. The smaller poles became roof supports, chairs and tables. Natural materials such as moss were chinked between logs and provided additional roofing insulation when mixed with dirt.

CHAPTER SIXTY

At the police station in Juneau, Malloy and others were comparing photos and evidence that had been collected. For the murder of Clint, the jar of poisoned kombucha had a solid print around the middle but not on the lid. Ericka's car's passenger side door handle had a print. The knife they believed was used in killing her found in the dumpster had a viable half print. The doorknob into Ericka's apartment had a fingerprint. Each one belonged to Tyrone.

They had solid statements from Leon about what Tyrone confessed to doing to Clint. They had Tony's statement about what Clint had told him and what Ericka told him before her death. Even Jill corroborated Ericka's story. It was all tied to Tyrone.

Being shorthanded, a couple of off-duty police officers volunteered and were checking out Tyrone's house off and on. No one had seen him.

CHAPTER SIXTY-ONE

About 1,000 miles north, on the gravel road they drove a few miles then pulled over at Mountain Vista. Their guide pointed out the first glimpse of the day at Denali, poking up over a mountain range. Anne took several pictures of green brush and scarlet flowers with Denali in the middle.

The sign read that they were at 12.8 miles of their 30 miles to the Teklanika River. Still seven miles away, Denali appeared in the distance to its staggering height of 20,310 feet. For comparison, the mountains appearing as a high point in front and to the left of Denali are ten miles away and 6,000 feet tall. They drove over a river that wound its way through a meadow. Some smaller trees where broken in half from busy beavers.

Stopping at Primrose Ridge, a rocky point, a local native woman shared culture and history. With her backdrop of spectacular mountains and watching for wildlife, Anne was easily distracted. She tended to wander off as she wanted to do now taking photos of wildflowers and mountains.

Back on the bus, alongside the road a mama and baby moose munched bushes and berries. Her big brown eyes looked at Anne in her window seat, eyeball to eyeball. Mama was grayish brown and looked like she needed a good brushing, like Peter would give their golden retriever. Her baby was more milk chocolate in color.

They drove over Riley Creek which was more like a wide river. Snowmelt had enhanced its size greatly. Stretching their legs at a pullout overlooking a wide expanse like a solid green blanket, Anne spotted periwinkle arctic lupine swaying slightly in a breeze. Dainty, four-petalled white flowers about the size of Anne's small fingernail, called Mountain Avens, were wedged between rocks. An alpine azalea looked like theirs at home but more petite. Returning the same way they'd come, again eyes were canvasing open fields for anything moving.

———

Back at the lodge, Peter picked up a newspaper and read: "Female found dead in Juneau." He read it and recognized the first name of the girl they'd seen in Celebrity Jewelers who had been led away by the police. Now she's dead, too? Good grief, he thought, what in the world is happening in Juneau? He would not tell Anne and ruin the rest of her vacation.

———

Cathy and Anne took a hotel shuttle to the Denali Heritage Center. Greeting them was a floor-to-ceiling mural of the valley and mountains, with life-size animals, eagles, bears, wolf, moose, caribou, Dall sheep and mountain goats.

One hilarious display held a Jurassic Park-size mosquito with a plaque that Anne read to Cathy: "Mosquitoes deserve your love. In late spring, adult mosquitoes become a food source for many birds. If you like birds, you should appreciate mosquitoes.

"In late summer, the berries begin to ripen. Bears love them—so do humans. If you like bears or berries, spare a kind thought for mosquitoes. They feed on plant juices. They're important pollinators of many subarctic plants, including plants that produce berries. The next time you swat mosquitoes, think of the birds and the bears that depend on them."

The friends meandered through an informative display of historic black and white murals showing times gone by. On the drive back, a moose and her baby indifferently ate tender leaves on young trees, not caring in the least about the bus full of excitable tourists.

Dinner had been so outstanding the night before, several returned to the King Salmon for another eagerly expected remarkable meal. Anne and Peter shared salmon cakes and repeats from the prior night. They saved room for an ice cream cake wedge about ten inches tall, with whipped cream on the wedge side and two dollops of vanilla ice cream.

Behind the bar hangs an American Flag that looked a bit off. Upon closer inspection, this flag has 49 stars and is an authentic US flag fabricated during that seven-month period between Alaska and Hawaii gaining statehood.

An official yellow Alaska highway road sign showed an outline of a mosquito with a person caught with its feet.

CHAPTER SIXTY-TWO

They just couldn't stay away from King Salmon so that morning before heading to Fairbanks they went for breakfast. Anne selected the frittata and fresh fruit, while Peter had Smoked Salmon Benedict.

At two o'clock that sunny afternoon they boarded a motor-coach driving through more stunning countryside. They followed the Nenana River toward Fairbanks then saw the Chena and Tanana rivers. In about three hours they were in Fairbanks.

After pulling into the Fairbanks Riverside Lodge, luggage was taken and deposited in their rooms as the 12 friends went to the Riverview Deck for food and beverages over-looking the Chena River.

Anne picked up the Fairbanks *Daily News-Miner* in hopes of finding out something about the glacier body incident. Now seven days later, certainly there should be something newsworthy.

The headline that caught her attention was: "Murder in Juneau." Not a surprise. But the next two sentences stunned her. "A body was found behind the Silverbow Bakery, possibly an attempted robbery. The deceased, Ericka Engebretson, worked part-time at Celebrity Jewelers and the Silverbow. If anyone has any information, please contact Captain Malloy at the Juneau Police Department." It was dated three days earlier.

"Peter!!!" she hollered, bursting into tears, as he and their friends surrounded her knowing something was amiss. Secretly they'd all been watching her since the glacier incident just making sure she was doing okay. They had decided that someone would be with her at all times, in case she needed anything. Her female companions encircled her with care and support.

A *toot-toot* diverted their attention as all six women, still huddled with Anne in the middle, walked en masse taking baby steps to the railing above the river. By now they were all laughing hysterically, with tears running down Anne's cheeks.

The white two-story Tanana Chief paddle boat motored by. The people on board waved and they waved back as it carried on its course downriver just as lingonberry mojitos were delivered along with a variety of tantalizing treats from Trackers Bar & Grill.

Walking around there were plenty of warning signs about moose. "Meeting Moose: The Do Not Enter Zone" was the scariest. "Violating a moose's personal space or zone can have dire consequence. Adult moose use their deadly hooves to defend themselves against wolves and brown bears. Learn the moose's warning signs so you can avoid a dangerous encounter."

Warning signs: "Raised hackles, ears back and flattened, lowered head, stomping hooves, clicking teeth and licking lips are all signs that a charge and trampling could likely be imminent. Be observant, recognize these danger signals and you may escape the consequences."

Walking around the complex, bright pink wild roses were in full bloom on lush tall bushes. They entered a small one-room hunter's cabin with snowshoes hanging on the front by the door. A small wooden structure with one door perched on top of sturdy ten-foot tall stilts, read "Bear Cache."

A gravel path led through a canopy of aspen trees with pink roses lining the way. Gravel revealed probably moose poop, none were experts on wild animal droppings. Pretty blue and purple bells that Anne's wildflower guide showed were harebells. A pealing paper birch bark rustled in a slight breeze.

Joel, Sherrie, Peter and Anne ducked under a tree limb drooping over the entire pathway. While reading a display about the pipeline history they all heard a rustling in the grass nearby. A moose was about to trample them to death, Anne was sure. Out popped a gray bunny which seemed risky with all the predators around. Fortunately she hadn't blurted out prematurely about the probable moose attack before seeing the harmless rabbit.

Sherrie read a sign about Reindeer and Caribou. Even though they look different they are the same species. Caribou are large, wild elk-like animals which can be found above the tree line in Arctic North America. Because they live on lichens in the winter, they are well-adapted for the harsh arctic tundra where they migrate great distances each year. Caribou cows and bulls both grow distinctive antlers, and bull antlers can reach four feet wide.

Reindeer are slightly smaller and were domesticated in northern Eurasia about 2,000 years ago. Reindeer were introduced into Alaska and Canada during the last century.

Both have unique hair, which trap air providing them with excellent insulation. These hairs also help keep them buoyant in water. They are very excellent swimmers and can move across wide rushing rivers and even the ice of the Arctic ocean.

A thermometer on the fencepost read 64 degrees. It was almost 11 p.m., winds calm, humidity 35%, air quality good, and sunshine almost 24 hours.

Sitting in his office in Juneau, Malloy checked on the progress of matching Tyrone's current prints with his past. It was taking longer than he liked. It always did.

Sitting in his office in Juneau, Malloy checked on the progress of matching Tyrone's current prints with his past. It was taking longer than he liked. It always did.

CHAPTER SIXTY-THREE

The next morning, Peter and Anne went to The Edgewater Dining Room and checked out the breakfast buffet offering an omelet bar, eggs cooked to order, bacon, reindeer and link sausages, potatoes, biscuits and gravy, a waffle bar, oatmeal, assorted pastries and fruit, cold cereals, plus coffee and juices. They selected a lighter fare of fruit, granola and bacon, always bacon.

They meandered through the Discovery Trading Post as they waited to board the four-story *Discovery II* sternwheeler, renovated and refitted one year earlier. A large brass plaque dedicated to Captain Jim Binkley honored his work as a sternwheeler captain, servicing the river. He wore a captain hat and aviator sunglasses, his trademarks.

Anne read a brochure explaining that *Discovery II* is current with all US Coast Guard regulations and run by the Binkley family. There are no other sternwheelers from the era still in operation today, so it holds a unique place in the heritage of navigation along the riverways of the Alaskan Interior.

The sternwheeler had a wheelhouse, canopy over the Texas deck, the galley, a snack bar, then down one deck to the gift shop with seating around the windows. Down one more flight of stairs to the main deck, with more seating and big windows, the engine room, and another galley.

Several from their group stood at the back admiring the craftsmanship of the 14 paddles turned by direct drive. They needed 20" draft for the paddlewheel and rudders.

Anne and entourage headed to the top deck. Their host, also the guide, explained that the Binkley family's steamboating tradition goes back over 100 years and five generations to the Klondike Gold Rush. He became a respected pilot and boatbuilder in the north.

His son, Captain Jim Binkley, Sr., followed in his father's footsteps and piloted freight vessels on the Yukon and Tanana Rivers in the 1940s—journeys of about 2,000 miles roundtrip. As transportation systems changed in the north, railroads and airplanes began to carry much of the freight. By the early 1950s, the last of the steamboats were retired.

Noting the coming changes in the freighting business, Captain Jim and his wife Mary began a river excursion business in Fairbanks in 1950. They purchased a 25-passenger boat from the Episcopal Church. In 1955, he built the company's first sternwheeler, the 150-passenger *Discovery I*, in his backyard.

Captain Jim and Mary respected and admired the native cultures and wanted to share their appreciation of those cultures with the many people who were coming to Alaska. Mary served as guide, hostess, office manager and researcher for the business.

Jim and Mary had three sons who all worked on *Discovery I*, learning the ways of the river and the visitor industry from their parents. The sons each became a United States Coast Guard-licensed riverboat captain.

As the business grew, so did the fleet. In 1971, the 300-passenger *Discovery II* was put into service built on the steel hull of the last freighting sternwheeler on the Tanana and Yukon Rivers. By the 1980s, plans were being made for yet another vessel. In 1986, *Discovery III* was built near Seattle, and shipped to Alaska in 1987. It began service in July of that year.

The guide introduced the Binkleys working onboard and explained that each of their 11 grandchildren was given the opportunity to work on the boat starting at age five. Like their parents, the fourth generation started at the bottom of the company and worked their way up. Eight grandchildren earned their US Merchant Marine Officer's Licenses. One, Kai, had just made marine history that very year by becoming the youngest female to be certified by the US Coast Guard as a sternwheeler riverboat Captain.

Downriver, a floatplane pilot did a couple of "touch and goes," and broadcasted by radio over loudspeakers he explained how he navigates the challenges of landing in a river.

The sternwheeler stopped alongside a mushers' camp called Trail Breaker Kennels, established by David Butcher and his wife Susan, best known for her participation in the Iditarod Sled Dog Race winning four times within ten years. With David himself a Yukon Quest champion, they had a toddler daughter together.

Dozens of dog houses were surrounded by a dirt track. One husky, Sheba, had a litter of four rambunctious six-week old pups. One of the dog handlers had her arms full of brown, tan and white furry pups and she described how the kennel operates and how they train their dogs, what food they eat and a day in the life of a dog.

Often they'd see a boat tied to some tree or bushes and plenty of moose antlers above front doors. There were many tall tiny huts on stilts to keep food away from bears. A man was drying salmon on racks.

They cruised by the Wedding of the Rivers, where the Chena and Tanana rivers converge. It was flat and open, and they clearly could see the merging of the rivers. Mountains were miles away. The captain turned the vessel and reversed course. Several reindeer were chomping on grass. Their antlers were in black velvet. In the distance, mountain range summits were haloed in snow.

Their floating transportation pulled over to the bank and docked at Chena Village, resembling the original Chena Athabasca Indian village of the early 1900s. The guide explained that villages similar to this appeared along the rivers after steamboat captains began bringing prospectors in search of gold in the late 1800s and early 1900s.

Alaska native guides welcomed them ashore. Guests sat on log benches watching a demonstration by a young native woman who sat on a small wood deck of a tall building. Hides were hanging along the walls—wolf, weasel, red fox, beaver, and white fox. Caribou antlers hung above the door.

Peter and Anne meandered around a cabin with green grass and weeds growing from the roof, matching the shrubbery surrounding the entire building. Anne petted a reindeer whose head stuck through a hole in a wire fence while it munched peacefully in an area of ancient trees. Then at the fish camp they viewed a ripping rack, salmon drying rack, and fish wheel.

Peter thought the skeleton of a 1956 *PA-18 Super Cub* was cool. The frame was made from extremely lightweight chrome-molly tubing and weighs about 175 pounds. The skin of the aircraft is a thin sheet of fabric with special coating. It could be equipped with skis in the winter, pontoons in the summer or tundra tires which allowed it to land on rough terrain.

They went into the log cabin of Chief Silas, from the original Chena village, seeing the cache and fur display. Outside, not far from the trading post, they viewed a lush garden with colossal vegetables then a salmon smokehouse. They peeked inside a trapper's cabin seeing garments, hides and moose antlers.

Anne stood in front of the display about an extraordinary woman. She read: "Susan Butcher is best known for her participation in 'The Last Great Race'—the Iditarod Sled Dog Race. But Susan was more than a champion of long-distance races. She came to Alaska to live the simple life, the life of a pioneer woman. She epitomized a lifestyle many dream about but few dare to live."

Anne walked around viewing photos and reading the entire history of Susan on display in the building. "She was born in Massachusetts and at age 23 moved to Alaska. One year later she moved to the wilderness in the Wrangell mountains, 100 miles south of the gold rush community of Chisana. The following year she began training for her first Iditarod. The next year she moved to her homestead in Eureka and runs her first Iditarod sled dog race. She comes in 19th. She also established Trail Breaker Kennels.

"In 1979, she joins fellow musher Joe Redington, Sr., in making the first ascent by dog team of Mt. McKinley, North America's highest peak. That year she comes in 9th for the race.

"In 1980 she meets David Monson while he is training for the 1981 Iditarod and she wins 5th place. In 1981, 5th again. In 1982, 2nd place. In 1983 she and David climb Mt.

McKinley with Seven Summits Expedition. And she's 9th place. Between 1981 and 1984 she continues to participate in Iditarod Long Distance Races. She wins 2nd in 1984. In 1985, Susan marries David Monson, a lawyer from South Dakota who traveled north in 1977 to find his own dream in Alaska.

"In 1986, '87 and '88 she is the winner of the Iditarod sled dog race three consecutive years. Another win for the couple, David wins the Yukon Quest, a 1,000 mile sled dog race from Fairbanks to Whitehorse, in Canada's Yukon Territory. Susan comes in second in 1989. In 1990 she wins first again for the fourth time. In 1991 the couple builds a cabin in Fairbanks.

"In 1992 she is 2nd, in 1993 she is 4th, 1994, 10th. In 1995, baby Tekla joins the family."

There were several blank walls so more history could be added. Anyone standing at this display couldn't help but be in awe of this remarkable woman.

Scenes as they cruised the river were of a dilapidated fishing boat and sprawling ranch-style log homes. Peter pointed out a floatplane parked on one side of a dock with a boat tied on the other. Blue, red, white, green and black Adirondack chairs sprinkled colors on the green lawns of many homes.

Back on the bus they followed the river stopping for a snack at a store and greenhouse. A green and white sign read: "Please do not throw your cigarettes on the ground, the mice are getting cancer."

CHAPTER SIXTY-FOUR

Tyrone was becoming more paranoid. He wasn't eating much but drinking enough to keep his strength up and moving. The nights were chilly, but he continued to sleep in the back of his truck, sure his cabin had been wired by police. He'd only been home to feed his dog.

In a liquor store one afternoon, he was positive two undercover cops were following him. He tried to stay calm, not drawing attention to himself and drove slowly from the parking lot. The guys in the truck turned in the opposite direction. Leon hadn't shown up at their usual bar and Tyrone didn't really care.

Maybe he was overreacting. Maybe Leon hadn't spilled his guts. Maybe Ericka's death scared her boyfriend's room-mate into silence. Maybe the dude didn't even know her. There was no way Leon would have ratted him out. Maybe, maybe, maybe, he rationalized, he was in the clear.

CHAPTER SIXTY-FIVE

At the Fairbanks airport, a polar bear and grizzly stand life-size in huge glass enclosures separated by a boxy tram on rollers advertising exciting tours and an authentic Alaskan over-100-year-old hot springs resort. From the ceiling hangs a wood bi-wing plane, with open cockpit and two tiny wheels looking like they would be better suited for a bike.

Twelve friends flew from Fairbanks to Anchorage with majestic Denali showing off its impressive magnificence in a clear sky. A river cut through two mountain ranges with snow on the tops of most peaks. It snaked for miles and miles until Anne couldn't see it any longer.

At the Anchorage airport, they all stood by the huge moose in the middle of the complex for Anne's final group photo. Wood-carved Canada geese flying down the corridor going to gate B were impressive.

Anne pointed out a first—seeing a vending machine with

socks, gloves and hats by The Buffalo Wool Co. The sign read: "There is no bad weather, only inappropriate clothing."

They boarded the Alaska Airline flight for the four-hour flight home. Anne had the window seat and poked Peter to lean over to see all of the College Fjord glaciers. She took photos of the entire fjord from 20,000 feet and got eight glaciers in the picture.

The captain pointed out Bering Glacier, the largest glacier in North America. It spans 2,000 square miles. Then the captain drew their attention to Malaspina Glacier, the world's largest piedmont glacier at the top of Yakutat Bay. He said it was such a clear day he'd point out remarkable landmarks and scenery that he normally couldn't, and apologized ahead of time to anybody who wished to sleep.

They could see Margerie Glacier with the Grand Pacific higher up. Juneau and Mendenhall Glacier were in full view which caused Anne to wonder more about what was happening with the case. She saw what looked like little ants flying in the sky, actually helicopters, landing at mile two—business as usual—like nothing tragic had happened a week earlier.

Ketchikan was visible, one of its 16 days of sunshine per year. At 30,000 feet with her nose pressed against the window, she sat amazed at the scenery and bodies of water, some powder blue deepening to cobalt. A few minutes later the pilot announced they had left Alaska and were now over Canada. She spotted little villages in valleys, more water than she would have ever guessed, and serpentine roadways—every minute of the flight was a visual delight.

The captain reported that they were flying over Vancouver Island with Victoria at the end tip. They flew over the San Juan Islands in Washington State and just past Seattle descending for the remaining 30 minutes into the Portland International Airport flying by Mt. Adams, Mt. Rainier, and

Saint Helens. Familiar Mt. Hood, and the entire Cascade Range greeted them home to Oregon.

Upon arriving home after any trip, the first thing was always hugging their golden retriever who would have to readjust to their return after being spoiled for two weeks by doggy-sitter and longtime friend, Sharon.

Anne walked into her blue and white kitchen and wondered if cooking or baking would help distract her thoughts of the double murder they left behind in Juneau. Probably not, she concluded.

CHAPTER SIXTY-SIX

Anne hadn't slept well. Thoughts spun round and round in her brain like a load of laundry in the dryer. The clock showed 4:30. Questions troubled her brain. Fully conscious, she gave up at five slipping out of bed quietly not to disturb Peter.

Anne signed on to her computer anxious to review her thousands of vacation photos. First she deleted the junk mail. She saw nothing from Malloy. As she was ready to sign off, she heard a *plink* that indicates you have mail. Anne assumed it was an ad for something she didn't need but she was curious. It was ten after five in the morning, West Coast time. Then she recognized "malloy@jpd."

Captain Malloy filled her in as much as he could and where they were in the process. She would have preferred more details but was thankful for this much. He promised to send another update once it had been resolved but had no idea when that might be. He didn't mention anything about Ericka's death. Anne concluded he'd have no reason to know they had met Ericka while making jewelry purchases. It was after their encounter at the police department.

The final line was short and sweet: "I hope you had a nice time on the rest of your vacation even though an unpleasant surprise on the glacier. Clayton Malloy." She chuckled, not "Sincerely, Clay;" "Cordially, Clay;" just his full name.

Anne clicked Reply and wrote, "Thank for you this update. By the way, we met Ericka at the jewelry store. I was heartbroken to read about her death when we arrived in Fairbanks."

Waiting wasn't Anne's strong suit. She was a tad nosy about what was going on. She checked the Juneau newspaper website for snippets of information several times a day. Plus Anchorage and even Fairbanks. Days of no news turned into a few weeks.

CHAPTER SIXTY-SEVEN

Captain Malloy and his team high fived each other when they received word that the fingerprints from the mason jar that Clint drank from were found in the database. They already matched the print from the passenger car door and the serrated knife used to stab Ericka.

It was a perfect match to a man residing in Seattle—Tyrone Olsteen. Of course, they knew he wasn't in Seattle but lurking somewhere around Juneau. Officer Kruse called the Seattle Police Department and within two hours he received a photo and fingerprints via fax. Finally the man they'd heard so much about from Ericka, Tony and Leon, and they had his prints confirmed. He had several prior arrests but never murder.

Several days later, after the grand jury convened in the criminal matter, it handed down a true bill of indictment. They concluded there was enough evidence: the knife as a murder weapon, the jar with the poison kombucha, the matching fingerprints from various items and locations, and motive. The district attorney sent it to Judge Munson to sign the actual arrest warrant. That afternoon Malloy got what he'd been hoping for—a warrant to take Tyrone into physical custody and present him before the judge. They also knew there was a high probability he wouldn't come willingly.

———

Tyrone lived by himself down Trapper Lane, at the end of the single lane, dirt road. They wouldn't have the element of surprise on their side.

Several officers had the house and area where Tyrone lived under surveillance. They'd trampled through brush into a slummy area way out in the woods checking out possible routes for them to surround his shack. They hadn't seen him or his vehicle. Just a dog with a healthy bark.

———

Early on Saturday, August 1, almost one month after the deaths of Clint and Ericka, with plans made and reviewed, discussed again, modified and readjusted, officers dressed in bulletproof vests spread out in various locations ready to move and arrest Tyrone.

The day was gray. A cloudy day. Officer McFeeters led the motorcade of police vehicles including Officer King on a motorcycle. As the procession drove by Mendenhall Lake, McFeeters noticed the gray clouds blending with the milky gray water. He couldn't tell the difference between the low clouds, fog and water.

The motorcade would go in silently; no sirens blaring, no lights flashing. Several officers would walk in by foot hopefully preventing an escape through the thick woods.

———

Tyrone returned home a few days earlier, convinced nobody was looking for him. No one was trailing him. But he was still sleeping fully clothed like he had when he camped out in the back of his truck.

His German shepherd mix Brutus started barking. It wasn't unusual. Brutus was observant and growled at a squirrel or owl. He wasn't vicious but a darn good watchdog. However, Tyrone's sixth sense told him danger was near. He grabbed his wool jacket then ran out the back door. He saw a tornado of dust and knew trouble was driving down his road. There would be no escape in that direction.

He hopped on his souped-up Honda motorcycle and raced off through the forest. As he looked back he saw two police rigs pull up to his house. He wound through dense trees, slowing down then speeding up, mowing down bushes and anything else in his way. He finally reached Ninnis Drive. Now on pavement he picked up speed to Montana Creek Road. At the split, he swerved to the right onto Skaters Cabin Road then came to a screeching stop at the dead end where he dumped his bike.

In the distance, he could hear a motorcycle and the wail of the several sirens getting closer by the second. He took off on foot running as fast as he could. Heading toward West Glacier Trail, he wished he hadn't ditched his bike so soon, having to stop to catch his breath. He could hear a dog barking, probably that police dog he'd heard about that could track anyone or anything.

He knew he had to get into water so the dog couldn't pick up his scent. Mendenhall Lake wasn't far away. Water—he'd be safe, and he was a good swimmer. He swam a lot in lakes and streams in Washington. He could hear radios squawking so knew the cops were near. Daylight was creeping through the foggy forest, but he could see the lake. He kept running, knowing the dog would lose his scent if he could get in the lake. With two murders, he knew they'd find him guilty. He'd end up on death row or decades rotting in prison. After spending what time he had in jail in Seattle he knew he wouldn't go through that again.

One officer yelled, "Tyrone, we just want to talk."

What do you think I am, stupid? Tyrone thought.

He stopped, pulled out his pistol from the back of his jeans, and turned to fire at them. He shot three times and bullets zinged by hitting trees and foliage.

Officer Kruse stopped, took aim and fired back. Tyrone fell when the bullet grazed the outside of his right leg.

The officers heard him shriek in pain. Tyrone was still able to walk and there was no way he'd give up. He just needed to get to the lake. It wasn't far, he could make it. Swimming was easier than walking.

McFeeters hollered, "Hey Tyrone, we'll help you, just stop running."

Stumbling through heavy undergrowth, Tyrone reached the end of land. At the edge of the water, without hesitation Tyrone jumped into icy Mendenhall Lake. The coldness took his breath away. No lakes at home were ever this cold. His heart raced three or four times its usual rate. It felt like it was pounding on the outside of his chest. He felt small muscle spasms from his waist down. His arms were trembling.

His natural instinct to save himself clicked in with one kick per arm stroke, then two kicks, then he repeated it a several more times. He tipped his head gasping for air, with his head going back into the cold water, holding his breath as long as he could. He spotted and swam toward a partially submerged log and hoisted himself the best he could. His legs dangling in the water started to ache but oddly now his right leg didn't hurt from the gunshot wound. He felt in the jacket and found he'd kept his gun dry enough should he need it again.

Two officers at the side of the lake both knew they would not be jumping into the glacier-meltwater. One radioed for the police zodiac, anticipating this area could be a possibility for Tyrone's attempted escape. The watercraft headed up the lake.

McFeeters again shouted for Tyrone to return to shore. They'd help him. "It's cold, Tyrone, you're going to freeze to death." Tyrone fired off a shot in their direction. "Don't shoot back, it's no use," one said to the other. Other officers, plus Malloy, converged at the water's edge.

The log was floating downstream, too slowly for Tyrone. His eyes darted around looking for a chance to get across the lake. A large chunk of ice floated by and he grabbed it. He figured he could hide on the opposite side as it floated away from the police. Simple, he rationalized, he'd hop off when it reached the other side of the lake. He'd never felt so cold.

Police watched Tyrone's desperation and there wasn't much they could do.

"Did you see him go from the log to the iceberg?"

" I've never seen that before."

" Jeez, gutsy move."

Tyrone had no clue that cold shock could occur at water temperatures below 77 degrees. But medical professionals and law enforcement knew that the colder the temperature the higher the shock. This could cause cardiac responses leading to death.

Tyrone started to hyperventilate. At first he breathed very fast and deep, uncontrollably. He didn't know that generally a person could survive in 41 degrees for 15 to 20 minutes before the muscles get weak, and one loses coordination and strength, which happens because the blood moves away from the extremities and toward the center, or core, of the body.

He felt like he was in a drunken stupor, confused and even slurred his words when he tried to yell back at the stupid police. He heard a dog barking, but it wasn't Brutus. Bobbing icebergs littered the lake. The lake wasn't frozen but melting ice didn't raise the temperature much. The cops yelled that if he didn't come to them in ten minutes or so, he'd die. He didn't believe them. He could feel his legs tighten, unable to move. The coldness traveled up his torso and into his arms then shoulders. He couldn't move to swim toward shore.

Officer Kruse turned to McFeeters and said, "I've seen this before. Death can occur between three and 30 minutes after immersion, typically for those attempting to swim. It's not a pretty death."

The officers watched as Tyrone's hand slipped down the iceberg farther into the frigid water, now hearing the motor of the zodiac as it sped down the lake. The team, already donned in their thermal wetsuits, arrived at the chunk of ice that Tyrone still clung to, frozen. Two jumped in and signaled thumbs up, they had him.

Tyrone died in the lake that was created from the glacier where he killed his first victim. The sun peaked through the gray cloud bank turning the sky blue.

That afternoon Malloy contacted Jill first, then Tony, ending with Leon, and thanked each for their help. Next he called both Clint and Ericka's broken-hearted parents with the details. Then it would be Tyrone's next of kin.

Captain Malloy drove slowly down Trapper Lane avoiding potholes even though his two-year-old cherry red Ford F-350 could handle just about any road conditions. A dog crate and three bowls, each holding one pound of hamburger, were in the bed of his truck.

He stopped at the rundown shack where a barking German shepherd clearly was not happy with the intruder. Looking closer, the dog was a mix of some kind but Malloy couldn't tell what. Malloy left one food bowl in the crate, and carrying one bowl of meat in each hand he spotted a bucket of water and a nearly empty bag of dry dog food. Tyrone cared about his dog—one redeeming quality.

He spoke firmly yet in a calm clear voice "It's okay, boy, you're okay. Good boy." Repeating it over and over. The dog lover placed one bowl on the ground halfway between the dog and his truck. As he continued, talking evenly, he set the other bowl closer to the pooch who had settled down.

As the shepherd gobbled the food, Malloy walked into Tyrone's unlocked front door. His eyes circled the room until he found what he sought. A tattered brown wool blanket in a corner of the tiny kitchen. He picked it up and returned outside as the dog was finishing probably the most delicious meal he'd ever eaten.

Malloy unfastened the end of the 15-foot link chain keeping the blanket at his side. "Come on, boy," as he led him to the second feast. As the shepherd ate, Malloy placed the blanket in the bottom of the crate. He wondered if Tyrone had gotten him as a pup or maybe from a shelter. Finding no collar he thought, new life, new name.

The dog's personality shifted from protector to adaptable. The two walked to the back of the truck, and Malloy unchained the dog and said, "Up, Bandit," who promptly jumped up and stepped into the crate and third bowl of food. Closing the door, the man said, "Hey, Bandit, I hope you like your new name and family," and drove toward home wondering if their new family member would make a good police dog.

CHAPTER SIXTY-EIGHT

The following day Malloy held a press conference where details were given about both deaths and how the two were connected. It was reported in the *Juneau Empire*. Now checking the newspaper's website daily for possible updates, Anne read the vague article but thought best not to email Malloy for more details. Patience was not her strongest virtue.

CHAPTER SIXTY-NINE

Two evenings later Peter and Anne were sitting on their patio enjoying dinner, savoring fresh cherry tomatoes from their small garden, along with sliced lemon cucumbers. She took a bite of one of her favorite comfort foods, home-made mac and cheese with crusted cheddar that browned over a creamy pasta.

The couple discussed their workday. As Peter talked about his day he could tell Anne's mind was elsewhere. He avoided any mention of Juneau. Peter knew the two deaths were causing his wife some loss of sleep. He hoped to deflect her thoughts and a spur-of-the-moment thought came to him—upcoming explorations. She loved planning their journeys.

"What about South America?" he offered out of the blue and in no context of what they had been discussing between mac and cheese bites.

Confused she said, "What about it?"

"I've always wanted to explore the Galápagos Islands—you know, Blue-Footed Boobies and 100-year-old tortoises.

Penguins." He knew penguins would get her attention. "And then there's Peru and 10,000-foot Machu Picchu just south."

"Absolutely! Order some books for research, please," she happily replied.

Before bed Anne opened her email. There was a message from Malloy with the details she had been waiting for. When she read the last sentence about shots being fired and the zodiac rescue team not arriving in time, goosebumps appeared on her arms just like when watching a scary movie. And Ericka had been murdered by Tyrone. She reached up and touched her gold cross necklace that she happened to put on that morning. "Oh golly," she said out loud.

When she updated Lee, he just shook his head in silence. She crafted a two-line prologue then forwarded Malloy's email to her parents, brothers, Lee's sisters and Peggy. She stood at their open bedroom window and took a good, deep breath, then exhaled. It felt good. The moon was as bright white as the streetlight on their corner.

It couldn't have been eight minutes before Anne was in Slumberland. The glass of Prosecco might have helped.

She dreamed she and Peter were riding in a rickety jalopy in Peru taking several hairpin turns in steep mountainous country, heading downhill fast. The driver, trying to see through the dirt-encrusted windshield, made a hasty left turn onto a gravel lane near a building that was barely noticeable in the hazy light.

Anne's Alaska Cruise Facts

- Alaska spans four time zones.
- The state encompasses 656,425 square miles of which 571,951 square miles are land.
- Including islands, there are 33,904 miles of shoreline.
- The National Park Service oversees an estimated 54 million acres in Alaska.
- Inside Passage is the meandering, protected waterway that threads between the mainland and the coastal islands of southeast British Columbia and Alaska.
- The Iditarod commemorates the January 1925 lifesaving delivery of diphtheria serum to Nome by relay teams of mushers. The course alternates yearly between a southern and northern route. Depending on the route, it is a 1,100-to 1,200-mile race.
- State Motto is NOT North to Alaska but "North to the Future."
- Entered the Union on January 3, 1959, as the 49th state.
- Birds: Arctic Tern breeds in tidal flats, beaches, glacial moraines, rivers, lakes and marshes. It winters in Antarctica, bypassing the Lower 48 in its over 20,000 mile roundtrip migration.
- Bald Eagle: Found in coniferous forests, deciduous woodlands, rivers and streams, beaches and tidal flats, rock shores and reefs. Hints: When looking at a green forest and you see a white head and black body, it's a bald eagle. Especially in Juneau, look at the tops of light poles. And always watch directly above you!

- Glaciers are formed where, over years, more snow falls than melts. Alaska's glaciers fall roughly into five general categories: alpine, valley, piedmont, icefields and ice caps.
- Gold strikes and rushes began in 1848.
- Whales: Abundant, 15 species are found in Alaskan waters.
- State bird is NOT the mosquito but the Willow Ptarmigan, a small arctic grouse that lives among willows and open tundra.
- State fish is King salmon.
- State Gem is Jade.
- Land Mammal is the Moose.
- Marine Mammal is the Bowhead whale

Anne's Helpful Hints for Alaska
  Happy Preparing, Packing and then Pampering!!

- Make an attempt to **pack light**; the weather will vary. Don't take a heavy jacket. Layer clothing. Ladies: Try to get away with one pair of black shoes for dinner and for the formal nights, remember if you want, do the same outfit twice. The nights are not back-to-back and no one will notice or care. Men can rent a tux preventing from packing a suit. Dress has gotten more casual recently; sport coats and ties are fine, too.
- Take a **little purse or bag** to keep your room key unless you have clothing with pockets.
- Take a **cover-up** to wear from your room to the pool or beach. Big towels are provided pool-side.
- Take the **spa tour** when you get on board. This is

the only time they give tours. Say YES, if they ask for a volunteer!

- Reserve any **spa treatments** early in the cruise; they book up quickly especially for at-sea days.
- First afternoon on board, go to the Guest Relations desk and ask if you can get on a Bridge Tour list. You may not get a choice of when, but this is really interesting and it is *never* promoted.
- You don't have to buy any professional **photos**. They will appear the next day in the photo gallery.
- If you drink **soda**, you might consider a prepaid soda card. You can see anyone at a bar for that purchase. Usually if you drink more than 3 a day, this is a bargain. There is a charge for all pop. Same applies for alcoholic drinks.
- Buy a thermal or plastic **souvenir bottle** the first day and just fill it with iced tea, lemonade, water from the food court.
- If you like **wine** with dinner, buy a bottle and if you don't use it all, they store it and bring it out when you want it next. Watch for specials, like 3 and get a reduced price. Share with your tablemates; maybe a different person buys one bottle for everyone per night. They can bring you anything from the bar. Sodas at dinner will cost you but not if you have your soda card. Coffee, iced tea, hot tea are no charge.
- You cannot take an **iron on board**. It will be confiscated with your luggage and there is no guarantee when you will receive your luggage. Trust me on this, don't try to sneak it on; it happened on our Mexican Riviera cruise where a person in our group tried to bring on her portable iron. Her luggage didn't show up and we had to

find out what had happened. It was embarrassing for her; just follow their rules and use their laundry service if you need it. She got her iron back at the end of the cruise, which was another hassle.

- **Jewelry** or **valuables**, you will have a safe in your room. Warning: don't take anything that if it is lost or stolen you will be broken hearted for the rest of your life. You are in a relatively safe environment on board, but one never knows.
- **Room Safe**: when you get in your room, put your passport, credit card, all money and tip cash, in your safe. You will program it with probably 4 letters or numbers; it's easy and very convenient. You may wish to put your cell phone and camera in there, too.
- It is likely your **cell phone** will work but calling from Canada is a foreign country.
- Never ever, ever, ever (is this clear?) use your **stateroom phone** to call anyone *off* the ship. It will cost you at least $10 per minute. It's a phone for calling room to room, setting wake up calls, etc.
- **Announcements** will not be broadcast into your stateroom, in case you are trying to sleep. General announcements (not emergencies) are announced in the hallways and one of the stations on your television.
- Your **television** will have movie channels, shore excursion channel and you can even pull up your bill to see how you are doing on expenses. Maybe you won't want to do that.
- If you have any questions about your **room**, just ask your accommodating room attendant.
- Your staterooms will be somewhat dark at night;

leave the bathroom light on and close the door or bring a nightlight. It will get dusky briefly May-July then daylight again early a.m. Take some good old fashion clothes pins to secure the drapes/curtains in your room; the sunshine will come streaming through at all hours. Or just leave the curtains open and watch the scenery go by.

- There are **no clocks** in your room; bring one if you need it. Telephone is programmable for wake up calls. Always go by ship time; they'll tell you when to change your clocks and watches. Don't rely on your cell phone clock; it changes even when you don't want it to. People missed their Bridge Tour one morning because they used their cell phone clock which magically moved back one hour.

- **Hairdryer** in every bathroom. Efficient bathrooms with plenty of storage to unpack your toiletries. Bring your own shampoo; if they have some, it's not the finest quality.

- Plenty of **closest** and **drawers**; you will be amazed how they organize the space. Your luggage, opened flat, will slide conveniently under your bed.

- **Tipping policy:** Cruise lines provide an explanation and have made it very easy. You can also take cash and thank them at the end of the trip; just stick it away in your safe or charge it to your room. It's easier just to tack it on to your room account. They automatically do this on a daily basis.

- You'll want to **carry cash** and **credit card on shore days**. Fun shopping in all stops.

- Great art galleries and museums; sign up for a national park service walking tour in Skagway (for free).

- Best **fine jewelry** shopping in Juneau is at Monarch which used to be Celebrity Jewelry, which is directly across from the cruise dock. Celebrity was owned by Anne's good friend Vinni but he sold it to a friend and named it Monarch. Don't buy jewelry anywhere else; they have the very best prices and finest quality.
- Take a **small purse** or fanny pack on land. It's easier to keep both hands free for shopping, eating, hiking, etc.
- Try some yummy fresh seafood on shore.
- If you order **room service** for breakfast or need a snack at midnight, I always tip $2-3 per person.
- **Wash your hands a lot**; more than at home. There are at least 2,000 people on board, bringing on who-knows-what-kind-of germs from who-knows-where.
- Take **binoculars**, one per person; it's hard to share when you both want to look at wildlife.
- Take good **walking shoes**; lots of opportunities to hike or stroll on the ship or land.
- Take an extra **camera battery** and your charger. You will take a lot of photos on this trip; the scenery changes every minute it seems.
- Try something **different at dinner** that you wouldn't ordinarily eat at home; be bold. Be punctual for dinner. Do order room service and make sure to visit the alternative dining, both are good.
- Experience a **specialty restaurant** just one evening. Additional cost is worth it. Reservations required. Might I suggest not going on a formal night because dining room food is usually most unique on formal nights.

- Promise yourself to do something **new and exciting** like a zip line, helicopter to the top of a glacier or the fabulous historic train ride from Skagway.
- **Stay up late** – you're in the land of the midnight sun which means it will stay light very late (and early) and it's really awesome. Sit by a window or on your veranda and watch for whales at midnight plus the scenery is incredible.
- If you have a **veranda room**, watch the world go by from the privacy of your own space, soak up some quiet time. Enjoy it. But be sure to close the sliding door before you open the front door to the hallway; wind tunnel effect.

REMEMBER, IT'S YOUR VACATION. DO WHAT YOU WANT AND LET YOUR FAMILY & FRIENDS DO THE SAME. YOU DON'T ALWAYS HAVE TO DO EVERYTHING TOGETHER.

MaryAnne's Scrumptious Nanaimo Bars

First layer
    ½ cup unsalted butter
    2 oz. dark chocolate
    ¼ cup white sugar
    1 tsp. vanilla
Melt butter and chocolate the add other ingredients and heat thoroughly. Remove from heat then add 2 cups graham wafers and ½ cup finely chopped coconut.
    Mix well. Press in pan and chill well (a few hours).

. . .

Second layer

Cream ¼ cup butter and 2 cups powdered sugar then add:

2 T hot water

2 T custard powder (Bird's Custard from the UK)

2 T cognac or Irish anything (optional)

1 tsp. vanilla (or mint—can add a few drops of green coloring with mint)

Spread over chilled base.

Chill well (a few hours).

Third layer

Melt 2 oz. unsweetened chocolate with 2 T butter.

Spread over the top and chill very well for several hours.

To serve, let it set at room temperature before cutting.

Freeze or keep in a tin in fridge.

———

Gamberi all Fra Diavolo (Flambéed shrimp in hot & fiery tomato sauce) serves 4

20 shrimp

Fiery sauce

12 basil leaves

200 ml olive oil

1 kg fresh roma tomatoes

30 g finely chopped shallots

20 g chili flakes

20 ml tabasco sauce

100 ml balsamic vinegar

20 g butter

Garnish

10 halved cherry tomatoes

50 g broccoli florets

chervil picked off the stems to garnish

Shrimp marinade:

1. Clean and remove the shell from the shrimp except for the tail. De-vein the shrimp.

2. Marinade the shrimp in olive oil, salt, and chili flakes for at least two hours.

For the fiery tomato sauce:

1. Place a heavy pan on the stove and add in olive oil and shallots. Cook until tender.

2. Add the basil leaves with the chopped fresh tomatoes. Allow to cook and soften.

3. Add the dried red chili and the balsamic vinegar with the sugar and reduce util a light syrup.

4. Do not allow sauce to stick on to the bottom of the pan.

5. Blanch and refresh the broccoli. Reheat in boiling salted water then toss with butter, salt and pepper.

6. Dress the plate with the rice timbale and the broccoli.

7. Heat the sauce, adding in the cherry tomatoes, but do not stew.

8. Sauté the shrimp quickly with butter and flame with brandy. Add the tomato sauce to the shrimp and cook for one minute only.

9. Dress 5-6 shrimp on the plate and garnish with the picked chervils.

10. Garnish with the chervil leaves and sprinkle basil oil around the shrimp on the plate.

Bon appétit!

Made in the USA
Middletown, DE
29 July 2024